Faded Sweetheart

Natalie Ray Bennett

BLACK ROSE writing

© 2017 by Natalie Ray Bennett
All rights reserved. No part of this book may be reproduced, stored in a retrieval system or transmitted in any form or by any means without the prior written permission of the publishers, except by a reviewer who may quote brief passages in a review to be printed in a newspaper, magazine or journal.

The final approval for this literary material is granted by the author.

First printing

This is a work of fiction. Names, characters, businesses, places, events and incidents are either the products of the author's imagination or used in a fictitious manner. Any resemblance to actual persons, living or dead, or actual events is purely coincidental.

ISBN: 978-1-61296-812-4
PUBLISHED BY BLACK ROSE WRITING
www.blackrosewriting.com

Printed in the United States of America
Suggested retail price $20.95

Faded Sweetheart is printed in Traditional Arabic

I'd like to dedicate this book to Homer
who has been putting up with me for over 40 years.
You are my faded sweetheart always.

Faded Sweetheart

Natalie Ray Bennett

CHAPTER ONE

Inside the envelope was an old photograph of a young girl and a man in uniform. The hand-drawn sweethearts on the envelope had faded, as it remained in a drawer.

Julie plucked it out when she was helping her grandfather, who finally decided to buy new furniture. She hoped she could use it when she graduated and moved out.

"Grandpa, what's this?" she asked.

He smiled. "That's me and your grandma."

Before Julie could look at it again, it was in his pocket, and he was almost running to the bathroom. She decided men liked the bathroom. As usual, she had to put on her makeup and wash her hands in the kitchen. By the time he got out, she'd be on her way to school, which was probably his plan.

Rook worked at the garage in Corpus Christi, and his business had faithful customers. He worked there since he was sixteen.

Julie was a new customer who'd been driving north when her car broke down. "I'll stay and work to pay the bill."

"Denny's always needs help," Rook said. "You can stay in my spare room. I won't charge you anything. Let me drive you over there, then I'll show you the room."

"OK, I guess, but I insist on repaying you. I wanted an adventure, but this wasn't what I had in mind."

"People never plan on a breakdown. Is this your bag?" He heaved it into the back seat of the wrecker. He tried to be a gentleman, but, as a car mechanic, grease was in his blood. He swept all the trash off the front seat, so Julie could sit.

"Rook, clean the truck the next time you got a cutie in here," he muttered to himself.

CHAPTER TWO

"Hey, Rook, did you check the drop box?"

"I will, Sam," Rook replied. "Here's Mrs. Roscoe's envelope with a sweetheart. She forgot her name and address again."

"Do you remember when she forgot her car key?"

"Hey, she's a sweet old lady. What the…?"

Sam and the other mechanics looked up from their cars.

"She left her keys and a paycheck. She didn't have to do that!"

"Too bad, Boss."

"Sam, get to work."

"Will this morning ever end?" Rook complained. "Guys, I'm going to lunch."

He drove to Denny's, was escorted to a table, then the waitress asked, "Did you hear about Julie?"

"No. What's going on? Did her parents come after her?"

"No. It was an old boyfriend."

"Where is she?"

"An old lady took her to your shop."

"Was it Mrs. Roscoe?"

"All I know is that the guy, named Derrick, caused a riot.

Faded Sweetheart

They had to call the police, and the boss fired her."

"Sally, here's your tip." He grabbed his wallet. "I have to find her." He dropped a five-dollar bill and his napkin on the table.

She put the money in her pocket. Since she didn't take his order, did she had to report the tip? He was already out the door. Probably no one saw him.

Rook drove to Mrs. Roscoe's big yellow house on Maplewood, where he parked and tried to clean himself up, combing his hair and tucking in his shirt. When he knocked at the door, a maid answered, with Mrs. Roscoe right behind her.

"Rook, is my car finished?" Mrs. Roscoe asked.

"Almost. I'm looking for Julie. Is she here?"

Julie joined Mrs. Roscoe at the door. Except for hair color, they had the same features and height. Rook blinked.

"Julie, are you OK?" he asked. "You didn't need to turn in my key or pay me. I just...want you safe."

"I can keep her safe, Rook," Mrs. Roscoe said. "Her mom's coming for her soon. They live in Bishop, a small town, so it's no wonder she wanted to leave. You should never leave home. Home is where the heart is, eh? You know, Children, I need my nap." She turned back to Rook. "Go fix my car."

Mrs. Roscoe climbed upstairs to rest and drifted asleep quickly, haunted by flashbacks.

She remembered being seventeen years old and pregnant. She held onto the pillow, thinking it was her baby, and asked, "Aunt Mabel, do I have to give her away?"

"Honey, we need to leave her, get out of this town, and start over. You need a husband before you can have kids. You have your whole life for more."

She never became pregnant again. When her husband died, she kept everything that meant anything to him in pristine condition, like that old car in the shop. She lived very simply.

She pressed a tissue against her eyes and wept quietly, so

no one downstairs could hear her.

"I have to get back to the garage," Rook said.

"I've got things to do before Mom and Grandpa get here," Julie said. "I dread going back home, but spreading my wings didn't work out very well. Now that Derrick knows where I am, I'm scared. He's crazy."

"Is that why you left?"

"I'm looking for someone. I just don't know who."

Rook put his arm around her shoulder. Her hair smelled good. He wondered if she might be looking for him, then dismissed the thought. "I've got to go to work. Please call if you need anything. Do you have one of my cards?"

"Mrs. Roscoe probably has one."

• • • • •

Back at work, Rook went straight to Vicki, Mrs. Roscoe's car, hoping to get it finished before Julie left town.

Julie walked around the huge Roscoe home. She loved the grand piano with its beautiful, old wedding photos, with Mrs. Roscoe looking very serious.

In her newer society pictures, she looked like she finally found her comfort zone. She stood beside Mr. Roscoe, both in evening wear. Maybe she was just tipsy, but Julie doubted that. She never saw any liquor or glasses. Julie was glad the old lady became happier, because she seemed nice. She wondered where the pictures of the grandkids were.

• • • • •

Mrs. Roscoe woke. Her maid, Miss Lucy, came in, asking, "Mrs. Roscoe, where do you want your tea?"

"We can ask Julie what she wants, too. Did she get any rest?"

"She's been wandering around. She likes your pretty things."

Mrs. Roscoe blushed, and the heat felt good on her old,

wrinkled face, making it feel alive again.

"Let me help you down the stairs," Miss Lucy said.

Julie, hearing their footsteps, waited at the landing like a catcher at a baseball diamond, ready to assist. Julie said she wanted to eat in the sunroom. She smelled brewing tea and saw the white wicker chairs, sugar crystal-topped cookies, and soft, heart-shaped sandwiches that spoke of charming Southern comfort.

Mrs. Roscoe patted the chair. "Miss Lucy, come sit down."

Times had changed. They were almost like sisters.

Julie's family came up the driveway just before the Crown Victoria passed them on its way to the garage.

Rook got out. "I'm Rook. I fixed Julie's car. She needed a water pump. You never know when those will go out. How was your drive? Was there much construction on the way?"

Julie's mother thought he sounded a bit excited. "Thank you, Rook."

Rook offered his hand to the older man. They had a firm handshake.

"Thank you again, Young Man," he said.

Finally releasing his grip, Rook said, "It was my pleasure."

They walked together to the front door. Mrs. Roscoe waited, having heard the cars arrive. She smiled, and all smiled back.

After Julie entered the car with Grandpa, they drove off, and Rook stood at the door with Mrs. Roscoe, watching them go.

"Did anybody miss anything?" he asked.

"Honey, we all miss things," Mrs. Roscoe said. "It's best to just move on."

With the repaired car returned, Rook gave Mrs. Roscoe her car keys and headed back to the shop.

That night, she cried in her sleep again. She knew those people, but she wasn't sure anyone else did.

· · · · ·

When Julie was back at home, she asked Grandpa, "What happened to that picture in the envelope?"

"What picture?" He went to the bathroom.

· · · · ·

Rock went to Bishop to visit Julie. She wasn't back from community college yet, so he sat on the front porch with her grandpa. Rook came over every Friday, and the two men were becoming friends.

"I met my daughter by accident at the blood drive in Bishop," the old man said. "That was twenty-five years ago."

Rook looked up from his drink. "Really?" He held back a burp.

"The phlebotomist called us the AB team. That led to a father-daughter reunion."

Rook wondered about it, but he didn't ask.

"When Missy and her husband, Andrew, needed a place to stay, they came here. I helped raise Julie and her brothers. I never married, but I found my family."

"What about Julie's grandma?"

"We were two pawns when honor superseded love. Like this hard lemonade, our lives were sweet and bitter, cold but satisfying."

They finished their bottles.

Faded Sweetheart

CHAPTER THREE

The Rematch

Grandpa heard a car drive up. "Boys, get the door. See who it is, but be polite."

Billy chased Andy. "Oh, the doorknob got my shirt!"

Andy, seeing an older woman outside, almost bowed. "How do you do? May I help you?"

Grandpa pushed off the arms of his chair and stood, walking toward the door. "Back off, Boys." When he saw who was there, he jumped.

"Vivian?" He quickly corrected himself. "Mrs. Roscoe, what a pleasure. Please come in. You've had the pleasure of meeting the grandsons, Billy and Andy."

The older couple looked at the boys, who smiled as if frozen in place.

"Gentlemen," Grandpa said, "please show Mrs. Roscoe to the parlor. I'll be right back."

"Grandpa, where's the parlor?"

14

"It's the living room, Andrew. Take her to the sofa."
"OK."

Both boys took her hands and led her to the loveseat. As she bent over to move the newspaper off the seat, she worried the boys might push her down, too. When she sat, the boys sat beside her.

"Do you want me to read the funnies?" asked Billy. She thumbed through the paper, looking for a good one.

"Billy likes Beetle Bailey the best," Andy said.

"OK. Let's see where that is." She started reading. When she finished, Andy pointed to another one. Both boys enjoyed having her read to them. Andy was old enough to read, but he still liked hearing someone read to him.

Grandpa came out of the bathroom with his hair combed and a photo in his pocket. "What's going on?"

"We're reading the paper."

"I'm sure Mrs. Roscoe didn't come all the way from Corpus Christi to read to you boys. Why don't you go play?"

The boys looked at her as if she might want to join them.

"Thank you for entertaining our guest," Grandpa said. "You may leave."

Julie burst in through the door, having recognized the car outside. "Mrs. Roscoe! How nice to see you."

"It's wonderful to see you again, too."

Julie walked up to her and hugged her; then she hugged and kissed Grandpa. "Can I get you something to drink?"

"Please get some iced tea, Julie," Grandpa said, "and take your brothers away."

"Yes, Sir." The youngsters retreated to the kitchen, and a moment later, Julie returned with beverages.

The boys pulled their chairs closer to the kitchen door to listen as they peeled potatoes, but all they heard was mumbling.

Julie returned and said, "Boys, go outside that way!"

They shot out the back door.

Julie filled the biggest pot with peeled potatoes, then put the extras into the biggest bowl that would fit in the fridge.

They had enough peeled potatoes for French fries for a week.

After a while, Julie thought she heard snoring. "Oh, Grandpa, you didn't." She quietly opened the door and saw the two old people holding hands on the love seat, sleeping.

The phone rang, and she hurried to answer before it woke them.

"Miss Lucy?" Julie asked. "Yes, she's here. She's having a fine conversation with Grandpa. I'm fixing dinner. If she's tired, she can certainly stay overnight in the guest room. Right now, they're taking a nap." She wished she hadn't said that. "They're dozing on the loveseat."

"OK," Miss Lucy said. "I just wanted to make sure she was all right. Thank you."

When Rook knocked at the door, Julie rushed to answer as quietly as she could.

"Is she OK?" Rook asked.

"Shhh!" She stole a kiss with him. "Look and see."

He poked his head inside and saw the sleeping pair. "Interesting."

"Why are you here on a Wednesday?"

"Mrs. Roscoe's maid called the shop for your number."

"She just called here."

They sat on the porch swing, holding hands as usual.

Julie looked at him. "What's going on with them?"

"When she dropped off the car, some of the guys sang, 'Here comes the bride.' Then she got in her car and came here. I don't know what it was about."

"Maybe you can ask her at dinner. Do you want to stay?"

"I want to spend the rest of my life with you. What do you think?" He hugged her.

"I need to check dinner. Come with me." They slipped into the kitchen. A few minutes later, they didn't hear the old couple leave the house.

"Vivian," Grandpa asked, leaning over her car window, "why are you leaving?"

"Come along. I need to tell you something."

William got into the passenger seat, and Vivian drove off.

Julie's mom arrived and thought she saw a yellow Crown Victoria, but she wasn't a car person, so she wasn't sure.

She walked into the house and saw Rook. "Is it Friday already?"

"Mom, we have a guest in the house with Grandpa," Julie said.

"I don't see a guest or Grandpa."

"Where'd they go?" Julie went to the front door. "The car's gone."

Rook took his future mother-in-law's arm. "It's your mother."

Julie looked at him. "How did you know she's my grandmother?"

"Your grandpa told me way back when we waited for you to come home from school. He said we were two pawns when honor superseded love."

"What does that mean?"

"It means," her mother said, "that when he left her to join the paratroopers, he left her with me. Nice girls don't have babies out of wedlock, and her aunt insisted she give me away. It broke her heart. My adopted parents gave me her letter when I was older I threw it away, but I remember every word. Seeing Grandpa watch his grandchildren grow up probably made her feel really bad."

"Will you be OK, Mom?" Julie hugged her tightly.

"God has a plan. He was there when Aunt Mabel put me in a stranger's arms. For my mom, I'll bet she felt she'd been through hell all her life."

"She looked happy in her pictures, but they looked hollow, like magazines. That bugged me when I was at her house, even though she felt so familiar."

• • • • •

In the car, Mrs. Roscoe looked at her first love. "When we napped just now, I dreamed your daughter burst into tears and knelt between us, crying and hugged us both. She said,

'Mama, I'm so glad to have you home. Please don't leave again. Please stay with us.'"

Grandpa didn't know what to say.

"Missy said, 'I've been strong all my life. Now I want to be less strong. I want the comfort of my family, people who love me, and grandparents for my children. Let me enjoy you. Let's spend the rest of our lives together.'"

"What?"

"She kept saying, 'I forgive you. I know times were different back then. I had a good childhood, but you're my mother, and I can feel it. Can't you?'

"William, I knew her the day she stepped into my house. I don't know how, but I knew who she was. When you came to get her, seeing you again made me ache so hard. I was lovesick for days. That's foolish for a woman my age. I was always strong and supportive for my family and friends."

"My dear Vivian, times have changed. We should finish our lives together. I know this is sudden, but we aren't young like Julie and Rook. I know you need to take in your family slowly. Let's call Missy and see if she wants to meet us for dinner. We'll start one person at a time. We could eat somewhere in Corpus Christi, so you can go home afterward and sleep in your own bed."

"That sounds good, but could you drive? I don't do well after dark."

"No problem. Pull over."

She did, and he got behind the wheel. Driving back to Corpus Christi, they talked. It was a short drive, but they forgot to call Missy. They didn't remember until eight o'clock.

"Missy, I'm on a date," Grandpa said. "We were going to invite you, but we got to talking, so it's too late."

"Yes, Dad it is. Where are you? Who are you with?" She could guess who, but she wondered where they were.

"I'm with...your mother. I drove her home. I thought her meeting the whole family all at once might be too much. I'll catch a bus back tomorrow."

"Nonsense. I'll come get you. Are you happy?"

"It's like the day I found you."

A tear rolled down her cheek. She remembered that day, and now she had her mom back. She couldn't wait to meet her. She hoped they would learn to love each other. "Be safe, Dad. Give my mother a hug for me. I can't wait for tomorrow."

After Missy hung up, Julie asked, "Mom, what's going on?"

"Grandpa ran off with Mrs. Roscoe for a date. He called her my mother." When she burst into tears, Julie and Rook comforted her.

"I'm not sad, Guys," Missy explained. "I'm really happy. Grandpa finally found his true love, and I have a mother. I'm sure they left, because meeting all of us together would have overwhelmed her."

'She seemed OK when we met her."

"Boys, it's bedtime," Missy said. "Rook, since Grandpa is on a date, we have a guest room. If you go to bed soon, you can still get to work on time tomorrow."

"Thank you, Mrs. Queen. It's been a long day. Julie, let me do the dishes. You and your mom can talk."

"Let's all do them," Missy said. "You know Mrs. Roscoe more than I do. Please tell me about my mother."

"I don't know that much about her, just that she's real nice."

"She has a maid called Miss Lucy, but they've become like best friends. I wonder if Miss Lucy told her to come?"

• • • • •

After dinner, Grandpa took Vivian to her home.

"William, please come in. We can find you a place to sleep."

He parked the car, and they walked inside. When Miss Lucy saw him, she stepped back in surprise.

"Mrs. Roscoe, I'm so happy to see you and this fine

Faded Sweetheart

gentleman," Miss Lucy said.

"Lucy, this is William."

Miss Lucy blushed and shook her head. "I'm very happy to meet you." She stepped forward to hug him but stopped.

He reached for her and hugged, and Vivian joined them.

"William, when will someone pick you up?" Vivian asked.

"Tomorrow, after Missy is off work."

She held up the photograph from his pocket. "Miss Lucy, look at this. He saved it all these years."

Miss Lucy looked very happy. Vivian had a broad smile, and Miss Lucy matched it, humming softly.

Finally, they went to bed in separate rooms. For the first time, Vivian didn't cry in her sleep.

• • • • •

At 8:30 the following morning, the smell of bacon and coffee filled the house. Though it was early, Miss Lucy knew Mrs. Roscoe always got up early.

She kept the food warm, but when no one came down in thirty minutes, she went upstairs and found Mrs. Roscoe and William dressed and talking.

"Can you talk over breakfast?" she asked. "I've been keeping it warm."

"Oh, Miss Lucy," Vivian said. "Let's go down there, William."

The sunroom was as warm as their breakfast. Eating interrupted their conversation, but the food was delicious.

"Miss Lucy, that was sensational." William insisted on cleaning the kitchen for her. Since she had an errand to run that day, she left, saying she'd be away until late.

After a quick clean-up, Vivian asked, "Would you like to sit in the parlor?"

They sat, regarding each other.

"This is a great house and a great room," he said, "but can we go outside?"

They went to the balcony porch, where Miss Lucy found them that morning.

"Why do you prefer this?" she asked.

"It's less fancy. You can look out at the trees and nature, all peaceful in God's plan."

"My husband never felt that way. I always liked being here, but I hated it when the weather turned cold."

"So you aren't fancy?"

"Not really."

"If you were to accept my proposal of marriage, could we move to a simpler house in Bishop? We could return here whenever you felt lonely for it."

"The only thing I would miss is Miss Lucy."

"Vivian, you're wonderful."

• • • • •

Missy knocked on the door a long time. She sent her dad a text, but he didn't answer. She finally walked around the house and saw her parents sitting on the porch.

"Dad, I'm here!" she called.

He looked down at her. "Missy, come in through the back door. Is it open, Vivian?"

"I believe so. Missy, just take the back steps to find us."

When Missy arrived, William pulled an extra chair from the bedroom to the porch. "Have a seat, Missy, and meet your mother."

She sat beside the older woman and took her hand. Vivian squeezed it, and they looked at each other. Suddenly, Missy lunged forward and embraced her. They remained like that for a few minutes before separating and hugging again.

"Mom, it's beautiful out here. I love the trees."

"Your father likes it, too. I always found it to be my getaway place, my sanctuary."

"How was your date last night?"

"It's still ongoing."

"Should I be here?"

Faded Sweetheart

"We've been waiting for you. We have a lot to talk about. Can I call you Daughter?"

"That would be wonderful."

A car drove up and parked. It was Miss Lucy returning from her appointment.

"Let's go downstairs," Vivian said. "I want to show you some things I saved for many years."

They went downstairs to the basement, which was filled with boxes, where Vivian found a box labeled *1963*, filled with newspaper clippings and pictures of her and her soldier boyfriend, standing in the same location as the one Grandpa carried with him.

Deeper inside were baby clothes that were never worn and some hospital papers sealed in an envelope.

"There was a picture of you in here," Vivian said. "I hope it's still OK. I never let myself look at it. I felt I was being punished.

"Miss Lucy caught me looking for this box the day you came to get Julie, William. That's when I told her my story. I'd known her for forty years, but she never knew. We cried together for a long time. She told me to live again, to find my true love and you. She said I should go for the gusto. That's why I drove down to see you. I wanted to ask you a question."

"What?" Missy asked.

"I forget now, but it's been answered."

They hugged again in the dusty room. Finally, they rose from their knees and walked upstairs arm-in-arm.

"We need to head home before it's too dark," William said. "Do you want to come with us?"

"Should I, Miss Lucy?"

"Mrs. Roscoe, you should follow your heart. Let me help you pack a few things."

Vivian looked at her fine living room with its chandeliers and grand piano. She noted the photographs of herself with her husband at social gatherings and the fine Persian rug under her feet.

"Would you like this house?" she asked Miss Lucy. "Your children could come and live with you."

"Vivian, are you sure?"

"Absolutely. I'll need to get some things later, but I'll have the lawyers make the arrangements."

They hugged, then Missy helped her mother out the door. They looked at the yellow car.

"William, give these keys to Lucy," Vivian said.

Getting into Missy's car, they drove home.

• • • • •

The following day, William and Vivian began searching for their dream home.

"I have a few rentals," William said. "Do you want me to show them to you?"

"Sure." She sat in his old Ranger with his assistance. "How old is this truck?"

"It still works. Should we buy a newer car?"

"Vicky was even older than this. Rook loved that car, because it didn't have any computers."

"This one doesn't have much, but I like how it feels. Is it too difficult for you to get in?" Like Julie, Vivian was a petite woman. "Have you noticed how you and Julie resemble each other?"

"I'm sixty-two. How can you compare this old lady to that young thing?"

"Like the kids say, been there. Watching my Julie grow into a young lady, I missed you even more."

"But it's been years!"

He took her hand. "Long years. I'm glad we're back together. Here's one of my houses that just was vacated. The Joneses were transferred to North Dakota."

"Well, Mr. Real Estate, sell me on it."

He parked and got out to open the door for her. Taking her hand, he assisted her from the truck and led her down the sidewalk.

"This place has two bedrooms, two baths, and is on a single level. It needs some work, which I plan to start soon. The renters did a wonderful job in the backyard. Let's see if I can find the key." He looked at a large key ring on a retracting cord on his belt. "There it is." Opening the door, he let her inside.

She gasped.

"You don't like the carpet?" he asked.

"It might need to be cleaned. Did they have cats?"

"I can have my crew tear it out and clean off the smell. Hold your nose, and let's keep going."

She liked how the house flowed, and the rooms were big enough.

"I like the kitchen. Oh, look outside!" She struggled with the back door.

"Let me." He opened the door onto a deck surrounded by rows of flowers and gardens.

"I could get lost out here." She smiled.

"Madam, this is only the first house. Don't you want to see more?"

"Well, Sir, I usually know what I like, but you can lead the way."

They got back in the truck and drove around town for three hours.

"Would you like lunch?" he asked.

"Sure. What did you have in mind?"

"Chicken?"

"Yum."

He took her to a local café, where they sat at a table.

"I like the red tablecloths," she said.

"I thought you would."

They saw orders of fried chicken delivered to other diners.

"That looks good," William said. "Let's hope they don't run out."

"If they do, I'll make some at home."

"You cook?"

"Of course. I used to cook for Miss Lucy."

"When did you cook for your maid?"

"She's been my maid for many years, but she's been a friend for life. I made meals for her and her family when she had her babies. She shared them with me. My husband didn't like it. I called it my volunteer work. He didn't ask what I was doing. Lucy taught me a few things, and we had good times."

"It sounds almost like you were in prison."

"It felt that way at times. I always hoped *Beauty and the Beast* would come true, but it didn't. I was faithful and caring, but my true love was in Bishop, buying houses."

They held hands until the waitress came to take their orders, which they placed quickly, wanting to continue their conversation.

"I hope they hurry," William said. "It smells good."

"Should we bring some home for the boys? Lucy's kids always liked chicken."

"You bought or made chicken?"

"Both. Will Andy and Bill want some?"

"They're bottomless pits who eat anything. Maybe we can drive to McDonald's."

• • • • •

They returned home just before the school bus dropped off the boys. Vivian opened the door to greet her grandchildren. She had several years to catch up. She wanted to kiss them hello, but she held back until after they dumped their book bags on the foyer floor and hopped beside her on the sofa.

"Hi, Grandma," Andy said.

Bill gave her a hug and kiss.

"Are you two hungry?"

"Did you make us cookies?" Billy asked.

"No. We bought happy meals for you. Maybe we'll have cookies tomorrow."

"You have to wait and see, Boys," William said, returning from the bathroom. "Your grandmother might be busy with

Faded Sweetheart

me tomorrow."

As she guided the boys to the table, Vivian asked, "What are we doing tomorrow?"

"I want to prepare that house, so we can move in. We also need to get married. We'll have to choose wedding rings, carpet, and furniture."

She shook her head. "I might need to borrow some fries. He's making me tired."

"Here, Grandma." Billy dunked a fry in catsup and put it into her mouth.

"Thank you, Sweetheart. That tasted wonderful."

"Billy, if Grandma wants a French fry, she can get it herself," William said. "She's not used to being hand fed."

"I'm not used to many things, but I can learn."

"Grandma, if you want to learn, I can teach you better," Andy said. "I'm older and smarter."

"I can teach you, too," Billy said.

"Boys, we must work together. Right now, you two need to eat, then let's check your homework. If you finish now, you can play later."

"OK. Can you help me with my spelling words?"

"I have math," Andy said.

"I'm good at math, Andrew, but we need to put Grandpa to work, too, so he can help you today. Maybe we can trade tomorrow."

"OK, Grandma." He finished his snack in a few minutes.

When Vivian started to collect Andrew's trash, William gave him a look, and he did it himself.

"I can get that, Grandma," he said. "Thanks."

She hadn't seen William's look and was impressed. "You're very welcome. If we get homework done quickly, maybe you can play outside before it gets dark."

Billy had to learn twenty new words. Vivian drilled him and had him take written tests. She had a surprise waiting. On his final test, every correct word earned him an M&M. He got twenty, plus two more for being neat.

Andrew, seeing his brother getting treats, looked

dismayed. When Billy was allowed to go outside, Grandma volunteered to take over Grandpa's job.

She handed him the rest of the M&Ms. "This should help with math today."

It did, and he got to go outside, too.

Grandpa looked at her. "Where'd you learn to do that?"

"I helped with Lucy's kids. They all got scholarships."

"Hmmm. You did well. Missy and Andrew will be late tonight. Maybe we should have brought more chicken."

"Nonsense. The boys had a big snack. We could probably just have a big salad for dinner. When the others get home, they can have salad, too."

William wondered if the boys would be willing to eat salad, but they were. After watching TV awhile, they prepared for bed.

Vivian and William had a long day. Missy caught them asleep on the couch again. She and her husband looked tired and tried to be quiet, but Vivian woke.

"Good grief, William," she said. "We fell asleep again! I made salad for dinner. Let me make something for you two."

"It was really good," Julie said. "Even the boys ate it." She was doing homework on the dining table. She usually did that in her room, but her project required her to spread out her pages.

• • • • •

Vivian's 8:30 wakeup time changed when she moved to Bishop. She got up at 7:00 so she could see the kids before they went to work and school. Mornings were a bit crazy in the house, but she helped a lot. Missy loved having her mother hand her a cup of coffee. When Vivian and William finally moved into their new home, Missy's coffee would be instant again.

Once the family was on its way, Vivian returned to bed. William usually slept until 9:00, so she had an extra hour to snooze. She slept in William's room. Grandpa shared a bunk bed with Billy.

William got up early that morning, surprised to find Grandma so sleepy. "Did you get up with the kids this morning?"

"Yes."

"Do you like it?"

"Yes."

"Well, we've got things to do today. What would you like to do first?"

"Let's shop first, then eat."

"OK. What kind of ring do you want?"

"Just something simple."

"Where should we get married?"

"I thought the backyard would be nice."

"Really?"

"Yes. Are there a lot of people to invite?"

"Just Lucy and her kids if they can come."

"We could invite everyone in Bishop, but let's just keep it to our kids and a few neighbors."

"That sounds great. We need to get a marriage license and find a preacher. I know one in Corpus Christi."

They had a small ceremony in Bishop before moving to their new home. Their lives were finally perfect.

Julie had only one semester left in junior college and two years of internship to get her nursing degree. She had good grades, and Corpus Christi had a couple of teaching hospitals. Any hospital would take her. After Rook married her, they could live in his house as man and wife.

CHAPTER FOUR
Baby for Grandma

Between her father's wedding and that of her daughter, Missy realized something was going on with her. She wasn't sure what was wrong. She was too young for menopause, but her mother told her she went through the change early.

When she saw a doctor and received the test results, her head spun. Andrew was delighted, but he worried that with Julie away, the boys wouldn't be much help with a baby. Grandpa was living with his new wife. Maybe she could help. It would be the first baby she could help raise.

Missy's pregnancy was fine until her second trimester. She was a high risk due to her age, and her doctor thought she might be developing preeclampsia.

At six months, she was told to stop working and stay off her feet. Vivian went to Missy's house every day to check her. William kept a grocery list, so they could prepare dinner for Missy's family when everyone came home from school and work.

Vivian took Missy to her doctor appointments when Andrew was working.

At the most recent visit, Dr. Spence told Missy, "You need to go to the hospital. The baby might be in trouble, and we need to verify it. We might have to take her out early."

"We'll call her Emily."

"I can't want to meet her, but I hope we can stall awhile. We'll do our best."

"Thank you, Doctor." Vivian patted Missy's hand.

When Emily arrived the same day, almost three months early, she was barely three pounds. Since there was no NICU in Bishop, she was taken to Corpus Christi. Missy remained in post-op and asked Vivian to watch over Emily until she was released from the hospital in four to five days, depending on her condition.

When the helicopter landed in Corpus Christi, the baby was rushed to NICU. Vivian did her best to keep pace with the nurses. Once they reached the correct floor, a nurse directed her to the lobby.

"I need to stay with my baby," she said. "My daughter put me in charge."

"Mrs...? We'll get you as soon as we take care of your granddaughter."

"Her name's Emily."

"Yes, Ma'am. Emily will be ready for you in about ten minutes. We need you to check her in." Turning to another person, the nurse said, "Kelly, can you help her?" The two nurses rushed off with the baby and went through an electric door.

Kelly smiled and gently took Vivian's arm. They sat at a table. "We have a little paperwork, and I'll need a photo ID so you can come in here. This will last until Emily is discharged. We have very strict visitation rules, but you'll have none except emergencies. When her parents arrive, they'll be given the same privileges. Only two people can visit her simultaneously, so you might need to take turns."

They barely finished the paperwork when a nurse walked

up. "Emily is settled now. Would you like to take your post?"

Vivian wished for a cup of coffee first, but she was on duty. Her granddaughter needed her. Getting up from the chair, she walked proudly through the door and down the bright hall to another room. The NICU had private rooms with a couch so the parents could rest.

The nurse offered Vivian the recliner beside the bed. Emily lay in a large plastic bubble called a giraffe and had a taped nasal canula, which meant she was breathing better than expected. She counted seven different lines coming off the baby and asked what each one was for. Missy would want to know.

"Can I use my cell phone and camera in here?" she asked.

"We'd prefer the cell phone be kept off," Kasey said. "If you have camera without flash, that's OK. We have a phone in the room you can use, and, if you have a tablet or laptop, you can use that."

Vivian thought fast. "I can call Miss Lucy to bring me one. Maybe Julie has one. May I use the phone?"

"Certainly. It's right here. Dial 99 to get an outside line."

Unlike the modern generation, Vivian knew Lucy's number by heart. "Hello, Lucy. I'm at the hospital with my new grandbaby. Can you do me a favor?"

"Absolutely, Mrs. Roscoe. I mean, Mrs. Morgan."

"I need a tablet or a laptop so I can reach Missy while I'm in NICU with Emily. She came a little early, and they didn't have this kind of facility in Bishop. Do any of your kids have one they aren't using, or could you buy one for me? I'll pay you back."

"I'll get you one. I'll be there in twenty minutes."

"You're a wonderful friend. Thank you."

They hung up.

Vivian called the Bishop hospital to tell Missy they were settled in. She tried to recall all the tubes and their purposes. She described the baby's hands and mouth, as well as her eyelashes.

"Missy, I remember your eyelashes when you were born."

Missy said, "Oh, Mama!"

"The staff is really nice. There are visitation rules, but you will be exempt," Vivian continued

Missy was very happy to receive the call, but Vivian heard her yawning and suggested Missy get some rest.

"I forgot to add that Miss Lucy is bringing me a laptop, so I can type down what's going on and send you pictures. Have William bring yours to the hospital if you don't already have it."

"OK." She yawned again. "Thanks, Mom. Take care of our baby. I'm going back to bed. Julie and Rook will be there soon."

When the nurse came in again, Vivian sat in the chair. "Grandma, would you like to hold the baby? We like them to be skin-to-skin, so perhaps we could tuck her into your sweater. It's called a kangaroo. It helps them develop. I can help you with it."

Vivian unfastened her sweater, she had a sleeveless silky shell underneath. They placed the baby over her chest, with the head under her chin. The nurse helped button up the sweater. Vivian sat in the recliner with her feet up and this bundle of life against her.

"Let me tuck pillows around you, so you won't get worn out. We'll check you every so often. If you want to be rescued sooner, here's the call button."

"Thank you. Should I talk to her?"

"Of course, but keep your voice gentle."

"OK." She looked at her shirt, as the nurse left. "Oh, my precious Emily. You have a lot of hair. Did you know that? You feel so wonderful. Let me shut up, so you can rest."

She hummed softly, remembering a song Miss Lucy sang to her babies, which Vivian learned. She was singing the song to her grandchild!

• • • • •

An hour later, Rook and Julie came to the front desk and asked to see the baby. The nurse checked the list and let them in, even though the limit was only two at a time. They walked to the room and saw Grandma sitting beside an empty crib.

"Where's the baby?" Julie asked.

"I'm so glad to see you two. She's in here. It's called a kangaroo."

Julie took pictures of her mom before Vivian could stop her.

"Julie, the nurse said not to use cell phones in here. Call your mom on the room phone and talk to her before she can call you back. Cell phone signals can mess up the telemetry of the medical gadgets."

"OK." She should have remembered that, since she was a student nurse. Once her mom answered, she said, "Hi, Mom. We now have a kangaroo."

"I saw that. They look natural, don't they? Look at the monitor. What does it say, Miss Nurse?"

Julie studied the split monitor. Emily's side of the screen was the largest, but there were two others the nurse was watching over simultaneously. "Looks like her readings are perfect, but the other babies aren't doing so well. Emily has a good keeper."

"I sent the best for her. Finish your visit and talk to me later when you're home."

"OK, Mom."

The nurse came in and saw the newcomers. "My name's Alice. I'm Emily's nurse, and you are…?"

"I'm Julie, her big sister. This is my husband, Rook. We live here in Corpus Christi. I'm a student nurse at the university."

"Your grandma is doing a wonderful job of keeping Emily's heart rate steady. She was the worst one on the board earlier. Since you're here, and Grandma has been doing this for almost two hours, we need to give her a rest. You'll be able to see her better, too.

"Grandma, let's get your little baby up. You can stand up, stretch, get some coffee, or lie on the sofa."

"OK. It's been wonderful holding her."

"You'll be back on duty soon enough. This is just a break."

She placed Emily in the bed. "Do you want to feed her, Julie?"

"Certainly."

"Wash your hands and have a seat. Since you're a nurse, you know how, don't you?"

"I do. I also have two little brothers."

"This is a little different, because she's a preemie."

"I understand."

They fed the baby, then Alice suggested Rook take Grandma to the cafeteria for something to eat. She'd been in the room most of the day. Food wasn't allowed in the NICU rooms, so Vivian was hungrier than she realized. She didn't feel bad about leaving, as long as there was backup. The baby had a nurse, of course, but Vivian thought family was best—a thought she never had before.

The short time they were away, the sisters didn't get along as well. Julie was anxious to feed Emily, but she didn't want it. She wouldn't latch onto the nipple, and milk seeped out the sides.

Alice came in and suggested a different nipple, maybe a Dr. Brown. "You did a good job. Emily's the problem, but she'll get better. Maybe she needs breast milk from her mother. With her IV, she's getting calories."

Alice put Emily back into bed, changed her diaper, examined all the electrodes and lines, and replaced the hood.

Emily fussed a bit before accepting the pacifier.

"That'll teach her to suck," Alice explained.

On the monitor, Emily's heart rate decreased.

"Grandma already has her spoiled," Alice said. "Was she like that for all of you?"

It was a long story, so Julie just said, "She's the best grandma."

When Rook and Grandma returned to NICU, only Rook came into the room.

"Where's Grandma?" Julie asked.

"She went to see Mother Nature. She still had some coffee left, too. How's the little sister?"

"Just like her brothers. There'll be problems."

"That's how siblings are. I didn't think it started this soon."

"She wouldn't take the bottle. Alice said that was normal. She'll get better. They'll try a different nipple."

Rook looked at Julie, confused.

"No, Silly Boy! They have different kinds at the stores. You never looked in the baby department?"

"Do they have baby car parts?"

"No. Well, there are car seats, but...."

"Well, then, what do you think?"

"Oh, Rook!" She hugged and kissed him.

"I can't wait until we start some of these."

"We have plenty of time."

They admired Emily until Grandma returned.

"I feel refreshed. How about you?" She carried a box.

"What's that, Mrs. Roscoe?" Rook asked, using her old name out of habit.

She ignored his mistake. "Miss Lucy's outside. She bought me a laptop so I can talk to your mom with day-to-day reports. Show me how this thing works."

"Is she still out there, Grandma?" Lucy asked.

"Yes."

"Well, bring her in."

"They said Emily can have only two visitors at a time."

"Let me go. Then she can come in."

Julie left, and Miss Lucy hurried in.

"I can't wait to see that baby. I love babies!" Once she saw Emily in her bassinet, Miss Lucy cried.

"Why are you crying?" Rook asked.

"As you get older, you realize how precious life is. For so long, Vivian had only me as her family. Now she's got the

Faded Sweetheart

man she loves, her daughter, all these kids, and you. It's your fault for taking in a girl with a broke-down car. You started this, and we're all grateful."

She hugged him fiercely, while Vivian and Lucy watched arm-in-arm through the glass.

"She's so precious," Vivian said. "How's her mother?"

"Andrew says she'll be fine. She has a few days before she can leave the hospital. The plan is for them to stay at Rook and Julie's house until the baby is discharged."

"They could stay at your house, too."

"Miss Lucy, that's *your* house. We considered asking you, but their house is closer to the hospital. There's no telling how much help Missy will allow. William and I might take up your offer for a few days, but the boys have to stay with Rook and Julie, because they're rough. If school is in session, someone will have to stay in Bishop. We'll wait and see."

"I'm always there for you."

"You always have been."

After Rook got the computer working, he took the first picture of Vivian and Lucy behind the baby. He sent it to Julie in the waiting room, Missy, and Grandpa, who was at home with the boys until Andrew came home from work. He also added the photo to the desktop.

"I've got the computer working," Rook said. "Do you need help with it?"

"I should be able to figure it out. If I can't, I'll call you. Type your numbers on it somewhere, so I can dial them with this phone."

"I already did. I'll leave, so Julie can come in and say good-bye. She's got homework tonight."

"No, Rook. Let me leave. I just came to see the baby and drop that off. I've got to start dinner for the kids. Call me later when you aren't busy. Maybe you can visit me when you're off duty." She laughed.

"Ha ha yourself. Love you, Miss Lucy."

The older women hugged good-bye.

Julie, returning in a moment, looked very excited. She

grabbed the laptop and started Skyping Mom and Grandpa. She walked around the room and pointed the screen at the baby. "Isn't she precious? Mom, she smells so good! Do all babies smell that way?"

"Only the girls," Grandpa said.

"Grandpa, boys smell good, too," Andrew said, who was with his wife at the hospital.

They talked until the nurse returned. "Emily needs some quiet now. How many people are we talking to?"

"Ten, including Emily."

"Tell them good-bye for now. She feels the love. Look at the monitor."

Julie turned the laptop toward the monitor and covered her mouth. "Oh. I had no idea. I forgot. Mom, I'll call you later."

"Just a minute. Alice, is my baby all right?"

Alice took the laptop to the hall and set it on a table. "Mrs. Queen, your Emily is doing wonderful, considering."

"Considering what?"

"Her premature condition. She's breathing on her own. When your mother held her, her heart rate was wonderful. She wouldn't take the bottle from Julie, but that's perfectly normal. Maybe she'll like breast milk better, or we can try a different nipple. She's on IV, anyway, so she won't go hungry. How do you feel? We heard it was rough."

"I'm getting better. I might get to go home at the end of the week. I'll be there then. I'm collecting milk, but it's not much right now."

"See if someone can bring it here. Your nurse can help you label it so we can feed her. Your mother is wonderful and devoted. She's making a world of difference."

"That's my wife!" William said.

"Yes, Mom's wonderful," Missy said. "We're lucky to have her."

"Missy, get better so you can be together again," Alice said. "I have to go. It was nice meeting you."

Handing the laptop to Julie, she asked those present to say

Faded Sweetheart

good-bye, so the baby could rest. Julie and Grandma sat on the bench to say good-bye. Julie had homework to do, and the baby needed quiet, as did Grandma. It would be a long night for her.

The others left, and Grandma remained at the hospital. She was on duty, but the baby was resting well. Emily was captivating, but Vivian needed her feet up and a glass of water. Luckily, water was allowed in NICU.

• • • • •

They created a schedule over the following days. Miss Lucy came by from 11:00 to 1:00 to give Vivian a break, take a bath, and eat lunch. Rook and Julie were there from 3:00 to 5:00 to give Vivian a dinner break. There was no set time for Andrew, William, and Andy, but two breaks were all Vivian needed.

When Missy was discharged from the hospital, she wanted to see Emily that day, but Andrew suggested she have one good night's sleep before taking over. She wasn't happy, but she agreed.

• • • • •

The next day, Missy packed and was ready after the boys left for school at 7:30. The fifteen-minute time for preparations seemed too long to Missy, who was seeping milk. She and Andrew faced a drive of one hour and forty-five minutes, but rush-hour traffic made it seem longer.

"We should've left at five o'clock," Missy said. "Grandpa would've taken care of the kids."

Andrew shook his head. "Try to rest. We'll get there as soon as possible. The doctor said you need to take care of yourself, too."

"I know, but I miss the baby so much. It's been a week!"

"I know. She's awfully cute. She'll be happy to see you, too. I'll bet Vivian will miss her, but she needs rest."

"Isn't it wonderful we found my mother? It's like we always had her."

"What should we give her for doing this?"

"She has what she really wants—a family."

Finally, Missy fell asleep on the way to see her fourth child and her mother.

The car stopped.

"Missy, we're here."

She opened her eyes sleepily. "This is McDonald's. Why are we here?"

"I thought you could use a snack before you went up. Tell me what you want, and we'll use the drive thru."

"OK." She gave him her order. "If it takes too long, I'll have whatever they have ready. We can also try the hospital coffee shop."

Andrew had been at the coffee shops in both hospitals, and neither was much good. "No, Honey. You must be starving to want to go to the coffee shop."

They got their food, and Missy ate hers on the way. He planned to take his food upstairs and eat in the lobby, but he was so hungry, he ate his Egg McMuffin in two bites with gulps of coffee.

"You should eat slower," she said.

"Yes, Dear, but guess what? We're here."

"Do you want to drop me off at the door?"

"Only, if you wait for me. I know where to go."

"In that case, I will, but hurry." She got out and sat on a bench, which was painful after her surgery.

Andrew, parking in the first available space, left their bags in the car except for items needed for breast milk and rushed to meet Missy at the door. He helped her stand; they went inside to see Emily and Grandma. It was only 9:15. Despite traffic, they made excellent time.

• • • • •

Faded Sweetheart

Alice was returning from her break when she saw the couple. She recognized Andrew, and she remembered Missy's face from the laptop.

"Emily's parents," she said. "I'm glad to see you. I can let you in." She buzzed open the door.

"Honey, she's this way." Andrew almost had to hold Missy back.

When they entered the room, the crib was empty.

"Where's my baby?" Missy asked loudly.

"Hush, Missy. Emily's here. She likes the kangaroo. It's almost a morning ritual."

"Missy, your mother has almost spoiled the baby. Everyone needs to wash his hands before touching the baby. Missy, let me give Grandma a rest, then you can take over."

Vivian got off the chair, and Missy sat down. Finally, mother and baby were together. Emily smiled when she saw her mother.

"Once you get settled, maybe you'll want to try nursing her," Alice said.

Missy's face glowed. "Mom, thanks so much for taking such good care of my baby!"

"My beautiful Missy, you don't know how happy I am that you chose me."

Missy took her mother's hand in her free hand and kissed it. "I love you so much."

"I love you, too." Vivian reached for her purse.

"Where are you going?"

"We've got a system. Miss Lucy comes each day from eleven to one, so I can get some food and take a shower. Today, Miss Lucy and I will shop for the baby. I felt that you might need to stay in Corpus Christi for a while after Emily is discharged, for follow-ups and other things. We need to buy a few items for Julie and Rook's house. I'll be back soon. You can rest in that bed. I won't leave unless you say it's OK, but I felt you and Andrew could cover for me. Is that all right?"

"OK."

"Andrew, you might want to give Missy some of those

pillows to support her arms, so she won't get too tired. They have water outside if you're thirsty. Love you." Kissing her daughter and son-in-law, she walked off.

Outside NICU, Vivian dialed her phone. "Miss Lucy, are you and Vicki downstairs?"

"Yes, Ma'am. We're ready to shop!"

• • • • •

Like two teenagers going to the mall, Miss Lucy and Vivian couldn't wait. First, they wanted a snack, and Denny's was on the way. To their surprise, Rook walked in behind them.

"Rook, why aren't you at work?" Vivian asked.

"I'm hungry."

"Didn't Julie make breakfast for you?"

"She had an early assignment, and I prefer this cooking to mine. What are you doing here?"

"We're getting a snack before we go shopping for the baby."

"I thought Missy had a houseful of stuff already."

"This is for *your* house."

"Why do we need baby stuff? Julie and I have been very careful."

"It's for Emily, in case you have house guests after she's discharged. Sometimes, the doctors want to see the babies a few times after they go home. I thought they might end up living with you for a few weeks, or maybe not."

"My wife's been buying stuff for Emily, too. Maybe you should stop by and see what we have first. It's all in the guest room. The key is under the mat."

A waitress came to their table and took their order. Once their food arrived, they ate quickly. Rook had to get to work, and the ladies were on a mission.

They went to Rook's house and checked the baby supplies. All they saw were a few outfits, plus a sink full of dirty dishes and floors that needed sweeping.

Vivian looked at Lucy. "Once we're finished shopping,

Faded Sweetheart

we'll fix this. I know with the baby, school, and work, they haven't had time."

"I like a good clean house as much as the next person."

They looked at each other.

"Let's call Merry Maids," they said simultaneously.

"Yes. They can come by while we're unloading and setting up the nursery," Vivian said.

"Great idea."

"We always had great ideas."

"Let me call the hospital first to see if they need me. Otherwise, it'll be a long day of shopping for us."

"I'll call the service. They can meet us here at three."

"That sounds about right. Maybe we can make dinner for them, too."

"Let's try Sears and Wal-Mart. Maybe we can visit Buy Buy Baby."

"That might be a one-time stop. Let's try that one first."

• • • • •

They went to the store, got a cart, and needed help with several items. They got a super playpen, bedding, cloth and paper diapers, and a baby swing. Lucy spotted a combination car-seat stroller. They had to ask for help out with all their stuff. The Cadillac had lots of room!

They returned to the house at 2:30, and the Merry Maid team was waiting. They let them in to start on the kitchen and bathrooms, while Vivian and Miss Lucy took their purchases to the guest room. It was pretty clean, but Vivian borrowed a vacuum cleaner from the service women and gave the room a quick cleaning. They opened boxes and began trying to assemble things. Luckily for them, Rook came home from work.

"What's going on?" He didn't see the Merry Maids car pull out just as he arrived.

"We're so glad you're here. We need help assembling this stuff." Vivian walked him into the room, and he almost tripped over the boxes.

"What *is* all this stuff?"

"This is the playpen. We can't get it to stay up, though."

He bent over the bed and read the directions on the base. "You need to pop it first." He did, and the bed was ready. The playpen adjusts for younger babies, so he quickly added that. Vivian handed him a mattress cover, which fit perfectly.

"I hope this doesn't get Julie in the mood. She needs to finish school. She's so close to graduating."

"We hope she will, too. Should we take all of this to Miss Lucy's house?"

"No," Rook said. "If her mom has to stay, Julie will want her here."

"When Emily hollers all night long, Julie's desire will diminish."

"Do you think so?"

"No. Let's take it one day at a time. We also have this easy-to-assemble stroller, but we haven't been able to build it."

He had it operational quickly, making the older women wonder if it was an age thing.

They walked into the kitchen, followed by Rook.

"How'd you get all that shopping done and clean the house, too?" he asked.

As they put diapers into the washer, Vivian and Miss Lucy checked the condition of the house.

"We did a good job, didn't we?" Lucy asked.

From the corner of one eye, Vivian spotted a Merry Maids card and casually covered it with her hand. With the other, she removed pasta from the counter.

"We plan to make dinner, but you got home too fast."

"If it's OK with you two, I planned to clean up, pick up Julie at school, and go to the hospital."

"That would be perfect. We can start dinner, then Miss Lucy can take me back to the hospital, and your mother-in-law can come back to eat and rest."

"OK." He walked into the bathroom and called, "How'd

you find time to clean in here, too?"
"We're that good!" Vivian replied.
The two laughing women began heating water for pasta.
"Meat balls or sauce?" Miss Lucy asked.
"Who should we call?"
"Miss Vivian, we don't call for takeout!"
"Of course we don't."
"What are you two talking about?" Rook asked.
"Nothing. We were just being silly."
"A week at NICU made me a different woman."
"You've been that way since William."
"I guess."
A few minutes later, Rook said, "Good-bye, Ladies. I'm leaving."
They hugged him good-bye.
"Bring back the family for dinner," Vivian told him. "I'll be there for Emily."
He left, and they made dinner. They took the diapers from the dryer and folded them, placing them in a drawer.
"Do you know what we forgot?" Vivian asked.
"What?"
"Pins and plastic pants."
"Oh, yeah. We'll need those."
"Maybe some bottles and baby washcloths and a towel."
"Yeah, but we need to watch it."
"Of course we will."
"That's right. We *always* watch it."
They laughed, enjoying the great day. They had fun buying for the baby and cleaning up the house. The Merry Maids did a great job, and so did the grandmas.
Vivian called William. "How are you doing? Got the boys?"
"I made dinner. Is it too late to come up? You could spend the weekend here."
"We'll pack and be there soon."
"I told Missy I'd take the night shift, but maybe you could be with me for part of it."

"Sounds good. We'll be there. Boys, we're going to see Mama! Here. Talk to Grandma."

"Hi, Grandma," Billy said. "I'm hungry."

"I miss you, Grandma," Andy said, taking over the phone. "We haven't had any cookies since you left."

"I thought I left plenty in the freezer."

"Grandpa?" Andy asked. "Did you forget to look in the freezer for cookies?"

"That was my breakfast, Son," William replied. "I had to eat something."

"Andrew," Vivian said, "put your grandfather on the phone."

"Tell Grandma I'm busy packing," he said hurriedly. "I'll talk to her later."

She heard the men laughing, and Vivian and Miss Lucy laughed, too.

"Andrew, tell your grandpa he's in trouble if he ate all my boys' cookies!" Vivian said.

"I thought I was your boy," her husband said.

"You're my number-one boy, and I really miss you. Please be careful. Come back to me."

"That's so sweet," Miss Lucy said.

"Hush. I'm trying to be strict."

"When did that start?"

"'Bye, Honey. See you soon." Vivian hung up. "Lucy, let's go."

"Where?"

"Wal-Mart. We have to buy the things we forgot and get some cookie dough."

"What a grandma."

"Taught by the best."

• • • • •

After they made a quick trip to the store and back, the cookies were soon in the oven. When the family arrived, Miss Lucy took Vivian to the hospital.

"Thanks for a great day," Vivian said.

"I had a great day, too."

Vivian took the elevator up to NICU. "Missy? I'm here. Andrew, take this tired mama home. Dinner's waiting for you at Julie and Rook's. We bought a few things for Emily for after she's discharged. The doctor said she might need to stay in town for a few weeks. Lucy helped."

"OK, Grandma," Missy said. "I don't want to go, but I'm tired. Will you be OK with her tonight?"

"I had the whole day without her. I missed her. She and I will be fine. You two go home. Grandpa and the boys will be there soon."

Missy and Andrew left, and Vivian took over. Emily was fussy. The nurse explained she probably wanted a bottle and Grandma.

Emily wasn't the best bottle baby, but she finished one before resting against Grandma's chest. It would be a long night. When Grandpa arrived later, he was surprised to see the two of them.

"William," Alice said. "How are you tonight?"

"Same as usual. Thanks. Are you ever off, or maybe they haven't finished your mansion yet?"

"Did you think they pay me?" She laughed. "No. I switched shifts today. Vivian, I heard you were off today, too." She walked into the room where Grandma sat with the baby.

"Yes," Vivian replied. "How'd you know?"

"The day nurse said the rookies had a rough time. Emily gave them a run for their money."

Looking down, Vivian said, "Emily, shame on you for giving Mama a hard time."

"It was good for her to know what you've been through."

"I've had a wonderful time with the baby."

"Let's keep that to ourselves. They don't need to know. When Emily is accustomed to her parents, she'll be the good girl you've known."

"Mum's the word."

William chuckled. "Missy had a hard time, but you've mastered this? Have I told you recently you're a wonderful woman?"

"No. Tell me again."

"She's beautiful."

"Just like Missy when she was born. I had to fight my aunt to hold her. For years, I hated my aunt for doing what she did."

"That was a long time ago, but look at us now. You're the baby's favorite, and we're together."

Alice, overhearing, wondered what they were talking about, but who could she ask? It would have to remain a mystery.

It was time for Emily to go to bed, so Alice took her from Grandma and suggested the grandparents go down for coffee while she did her nurse work.

William and Vivian went to the cafeteria for coffee and a snack.

"These aren't as good as the ones at the house," William said.

"Thanks, but those were for the boys. Did you really eat all of them?"

"No. Some are still in the freezer."

When they returned to NICU, they found the family. Andrew was walking back to the lobby to get Billy. Andy thought his little sister was noisy.

"You left your post?" Andrew asked them.

"Just for coffee," William said. "Is she OK?"

"Sure. We passed you in the elevator, but you weren't paying attention. You make a cute couple."

"Thanks. Did Missy get any rest?"

"Not much. If we can get her home, she'll pass out later. She loved all the baby stuff."

After Billy saw his sister, he came out alone. "Mama wanted to be alone for a few minutes."

"Did she say she wanted to nurse?"

"Yeah. What's that?"

"I'll tell you later," Andy said.

Andrew looked at William, both of them wishing they could hear that conversation.

Missy called Vivian from the room. "Are you ready to resume your duty, or should I stay here? I can. I'm her mother."

"Missy, you need your rest," Vivian said. "Please let me watch her for you tonight."

"In that case, come in, so I can show you something."

Vivian had the nurse buzz open the door, and she and William entered the room.

"I fixed your desktop," Missy said. "I added a couple of kangaroo shots. Look what happens when I change them to black and white."

She clicked a button, and the two women holding Emily looked almost identical. "I asked Alice, and she agreed. We look very similar."

"Hmmm. Maybe she needs new glasses. You look much younger, than me. Maybe it's because we're all in love."

"Doesn't matter, Mom. I love you and Grandpa so much for all you do for the kids and me and Andrew." She hugged her mother. "I'll be here first thing in the morning to take over, OK?"

"Just be sure to eat breakfast first. They have rules."

"OK. The baby stuff was very cute. Miss Lucy and you must've had a great time.'

"Who doesn't like to shop?"

Missy looked at Emily in her bed, then she hugged her dad and walked backward from the room until she was in the hall. Turning to Andrew, she said, "We need to hurry home, so we can be here first thing in the morning."

"Yes, Dear." He put his arm around her, corralled the boys, and asked, "Can you two behave yourselves for a few hours tomorrow, while I take you mama back to the hospital?"

"Sure. We can sleep," Andy replied.

"OK. Grandpa will probably be there. He won't spend the entire night here."

• • • • •

William spent the night at the hospital, taking turns sleeping with Vivian, as they cared for Emily. She was becoming accustomed to being spoiled. Little sisters and brothers quickly learned that nighttime was the best time for a captive audience, because the older kids were asleep.

• • • •

Missy arrived at 9:30 the following morning. She wanted to come sooner, but everyone was moving slowly.

"Did you get any breakfast?" Vivian asked.

"We could get a doughnut or something." That was a joke, because Missy ate only health food.

The two women went to the cafeteria, while William stayed with the baby. As they left, he said, "You do know they have licensed nursing staff to watch over the children."

The women stared at him as if he said there were strip teasers for the babies.

"What did that mean?" Missy asked.

"Honey, your dad's out of baby night-duty practice."

"Despite what he might say, he never did that. I always had the nights. He did the middle of the day while I did laundry or made dinner."

"Oh. He painted a different picture."

"Like I left for a twenty-one-day cruise after giving birth?"

"As a matter of fact...."

After their coffee, Vivian went back to NICU alone.

Missy visited the restroom. Vivian brought William breakfast and set it on the table in the NICU waiting area before calling, "William? Come and get it."

"Here at the hospital?"

That made her pause in thought. "I brought you food. There's nothing else except maybe a kiss."

"How disappointing." He walked out and saw her at the table.

"I hope you like this. Let me check Emily."

"She's not doing much, just sleeping and sucking her thumb. She's reading page two of the *Wall Street Journal*."

"How did that get started?"

"She ate the sports page."

"Is that considered solid food?"

"No, that's just a bad baby, like her brothers. We'll have to keep the news away from her."

"Very funny!" She bent over and kissed him. "I'll see you in the ward."

"Maybe we can get her to bed, and we can smooch," he whispered.

"William, hush!"

Other young couples watching them snickered, as he watched her walk away.

Vivian found Emily sleeping and sucking her thumb, so Vivian sat in the recliner. Like most children when their grandmothers finally got comfortable, Emily woke up. Vivian got up to pat the baby's bottom, and she hushed for a while, then she wailed like an injured bird.

Rose, the night nurse, walked in. "Did you pinch her?"

"No. She saw me sitting down."

"Yeah, she can do that even with her eyes closed."

"Maybe she'll be a teacher like her mother. They need eyes behind their heads. Seeing with your eyes closed is the first stage."

Looking at each other, they smiled, and Emily fell asleep again.

"We'll change her diaper soon," Rose said. "If you do it first, leave it here so we can weigh it. Her next bottle should arrive in an hour. If she wants it sooner, she can tell us."

William walked in and sat in the chair.

"I was sitting there," Vivian complained.

"Come on. I have a space right here." He patted his lap.

• • • • •

As Emily improved, Missy planned to stay at Julie's house until the discharge day.

"Let's leave the new parents alone to enjoy Emily while those patient young men get a reward," Vivian said. "Have you ever taken them anywhere?"

"To school. Does that count?"

"William."

"Yes."

"Since Missy is discharged and feeling better, we need to plan a trip, just the two of us and the boys."

"Do the boys have names?"

"Andy and Billy. What were you thinking? Oh, my. For an old man, you have lots of young ideas, don't you?"

"I try."

"Yes, you do. Anyway, they'll be out of school, and we could take them to Six Flags or a baseball game. Where should we take them?"

"Reform school?"

"Will?"

"Just kidding. Have you discussed this with Missy and Andrew?"

"Kind of, but I wanted to ask you first."

"Why, thank you. Let's start packing the RV."

"You own an RV?"

"Yes. It's in storage. I'll show you tomorrow once we're off duty. I need to go home now and rest. Will you be OK alone?"

"Actually, Missy will be here today!"

• • • • •

Vivian returned at dinnertime to relieve Missy, who looked tired.

"How'd you two get along today?" Vivian asked.

"Like salt and pepper."

"That sounds good. We were thinking about leaving you three for a few days."

"Which three do you mean?"

"We might take the boys on a vacation, so you can just be here with Emily. Would that be OK?"

"My dad wants to take the boys somewhere? You must've really softened him up."

"That's my job, and I'm awfully good at it. Would that be all right with you and Andrew?"

"Absolutely. With you, I know they'll eat more than candy and chips, and they'll have a bedtime. We also won't get a call from the police."

"You got a call from the police?"

"It was a long time ago, when Billy got left behind at the Quick Trip. He was pretty little, and it took him a few days before he mastered his name and phone number."

"Are you kidding me?"

"Yes. You should've seen your expression. It's the same look Andrew said I had when we got the call. It was one of Dad's friends on the police force. Dad suggested it as a practical joke. They were actually sitting in the driveway when they called. Has he always been so funny?"

"That must've developed later. When I first met him, he was fine and sensitive. He wasn't stern, but he didn't make jokes all the time. We were so in love, but he signed up with the military. I think he was afraid he might die. That's why we had sex, because he thought he'd never see me again.

"It's kind of embarrassing to admit that, but it's true. I thought it was like Romeo and Juliette, two young lovers torn apart and dying. I tried writing him, but I didn't know what address to use, nor did he know mine. I have a lunch sack at home full of my letters to him. I assumed I'd give them to him when he returned.

"Then I found out I was having you, and I wrote you a journal, since my aunt wouldn't let me keep you. That's in the box, too. Then my life went in another direction. I was still breathing, but I was totally unemotional. When I saw people with babies, I was polite but moved on.

"Every month, it was a relief when my period came, because I feared I wouldn't love any baby I had. What kind of mother was I? I let my aunt give my first one away. Mr. Roscoe was a dear man who loved me more than I loved him. He never understood me, but he never asked, and he never got deeply into my thoughts or his emotions. He might have, if I was willing to let him, but I was too bitter after losing you and the love of my life.

"When there were parades, I went to look for William's face, but they didn't celebrate men returning from that war. I figured life dealt my cards, and I was a loser.

"Lucy was my salvation. She let me share her children. Mr. Roscoe didn't know, but when Lucy had days off, I was at her house, tending the kids and cooking. She was a wonderful sister to me. She didn't know my past, because I never dropped my guard until the day you came to pick up Julie.

"Somehow, I felt she was mine, though I didn't know her background. Then, when I saw you and your dad, I wondered how two people could so resemble the ones I knew in the past. Why did he come with you that day?"

"He said he was there to protect us. He certainly wasn't happy we allowed Julie to have an adventure without us. I sensed urgency in her. I didn't know what it was, but it seemed monumental, and that turned out to be an understatement.

"Prior to that, she was a pain in the you-know-where. She carried on constantly about being a baby, saying we had no faith in her. The stupid girl didn't even know to come in out of the rain. She said we'd let the boys go once they were eighteen. She began talking about joining the Marines, because they'd take an eighteen-year-old.

"That did it. We didn't want her in the Marines, so we thought a short trip would be better than forever, maybe even death. She had a restless spirit. I had one, too. I really frustrated my adoptive mother. She pretty much kicked me out. Most of my siblings couldn't wait to leave."

"Was your childhood good?"

"Yeah. I never wanted for anything. She had lots of foster kids, so there was always someone to play with. I liked school, because my teacher really liked me. She gave me plenty of praise. Mrs. Ryan, my second-grade teacher, taught me to read, and that opened a new world.

That's why I became a teacher. My second choice would've been as a nomad looking for something or someone. When I heard Julie talking like that, I knew she was searching for something, too. I'm grateful she found you for all of us. She didn't even know you were missing.

Dad never talked about it much, except when he remarked how similar we were. He never married, though many women threw themselves at him. He always said no. When we met at the blood bank, he looked at me oddly. The next time, he asked my mother's name. I didn't know what his problem was.

When the nurse announced we had the same blood type, he asked if my mother gave blood, thinking she had the same blood type, too. Irritated, I blurted out my birthday and that I didn't know my mother. He told he probably did, then he added he was my father."

Vivian listened.

"I was floored. We asked the blood bank woman how to get a genetic test, and she said they could do it for us.

We got the results a couple weeks later. My adoptive

mother opened my mail and was furious at the news. She told me to pack my bags and go live with my father. I was no longer her child. I think now she was going through menopause. I certainly didn't expect her to say anything like that.

Since I had nowhere to go, I called my dad. He was a gentleman and didn't let me move in with him. Instead, he found me a furnished apartment in a safe neighborhood. He also bought me a car and gave me money each week for groceries and necessities.

When I said I planned on going to college, he got me enrolled, claiming he wanted to make up for lost time. By the time Andrew and I were ready to marry, he was a natural at being a dad to me. He took us into his home when we were in college, and we graduated and eventually had three kids. Now we've got a complete set, because you're back.

I think he started acting chipper when I had my first apartment disaster. A water line broke, and he rescued me. He just came from church and joked that he was being baptized again. He was determined to repair it himself, but the plumbing was so old, no modern fitting would work. He managed to turn off the water and called a plumber the following day. He certainly knew a lot of people. Every body came to him like a bee to honey. He is generous but gives friendship and help."

"He's pretty wonderful." Vivian answered.

They both nodded.

• • • • •

As days passed, baby duty at the hospital became second nature to everyone.

"Just put a *Do Not Disturb* sign on your belly," William told Vivian.

"Why didn't I think of that?"

"It's recycled. I used it for all my grandkids."

"Did it work?"

"Only for adults. Kids can't read yet."

"Makes sense, but it's time to go. Good night, My Prince. Get some rest."

After he left, Vivian went to the vacant chair for her watch. She dozed off quickly, and the nurses worked quietly to let her sleep, but Emily had different ideas.

She had a three o'clock feeding, and the nurse took her to the end of the room to feed her on the cot. Though Grandma heard them, she just closed her eyes and slept.

Missy came early the following day, as usual, saying she ate a big breakfast and was ready to spend the day with Emily, who was bigger and stronger than ever. If there were no setbacks, Emily would be discharged soon.

Vivian went outside to look for William's car. He usually circled the lot until he saw the top of her head, because she was so short.

CHAPTER FIVE
The RV Vacation

William took Vivian to the Safe Place, which housed people's storage items like boats and RVs. In lot 27, he got out and searched for the key. As he opened the door, he asked, "Did you want to check it out?"

They went inside the RV.

"It's a little musty, but that can be cleaned out." She checked cabinets and drawers to see if they needed to pack anything.

"What do you think?" he asked. "Should we check out someone else's stuff?"

"No, we just need to freshen this up."

"I have men to do that. Do you want them to pack the cupboards, too?"

"They'd do that?"

"Yes. That's a special feature here at Safe Place. If a family needs to get out, we can detail the machine so they can travel safely and in style."

"Will they make sure it runs well, too?"

"Of course. Let me call them. They can bring it by the house tomorrow."

"OK. Then we can pack the boys' things, too."

Despite allowing professionals to clean the RV, it was a lot of work to pack, clean the fridge at home, finish laundry, bring all their medications, find pillows, shoes, coolers, and favorite pots and pans for the trip.

"Thank God we don't have a dog," Vivian said.

"Do you want a dog?" He pretended he was calling someone.

"No, thank you!"

"How about a couple cats, or a set of guinea pigs? We could get a six-foot snake and a small elephant."

"No. Feeding the boys will be just as challenging."

"Did you pack cookies?"

"You're so cute. Let's get the boys from their baseball camp."

They brought the boys home, cleaned them up, told them to bring a few items to the RV, and announced they were leaving in the morning.

• • • • •

The RV man brought over the vehicle by six o'clock and helped them carry everything inside and pack it in storage places Vivian hadn't discovered.

"It's a good thing I'm watching," she said. "I'd never know how to find some of those places. It sure smells better than before, too."

She noticed when William paid the man he gave him a box of the food they couldn't bring along that would go bad before they returned. Bill later told her the man had a lot of kids who could use the food.

The RV rule was to remain seated while they were in motion. There was no jumping up and down, no running, and no fighting. The boys could do all of those when they stopped, though they might be left behind at the gas station.

"Just remember your phone number," Bill told them.

Six Flags was fun. The boys needed the trip, and their grandparents rested on benches while the kids enjoyed themselves. They reached Dallas late at night.

"Let's go to a hotel and then use the RV again when we're ready to leave," Bill suggested.

Once they were shown to rooms, he asked Billy, "What do you think of this one?"

"That is great, but where will you and Grandma be?"

"It's a two-room suite. You guys go over there." He pointed to the right. "We'll be in the left one." He turned to Vivian. "Is that OK with you?"

"I wanted the bunk bed," she said.

Andy looked up at her. "They don't have bunk beds, Grandma. I was hoping for one, too."

Vivian looked at William, grateful she was right about the beds. She heard some places were accommodating families, but she didn't want a bunk bed. "Let's explore our suite, OK?"

Andy saw a sign near the phone. "Wow. We have room service. What do you want? What do they have?"

"Put down the phone, Son. We don't need room service yet."

"What's it for?"

"If we wanted, they could bring us lunch. If we need an iron or an extra pillow or anything you forgot, you could ask them."

Looking out the window, Billy asked, "Grandma, Grandpa, can I jump out the window? We've got a pool!"

"Absolutely not!" both replied.

"Move away from there and sit down," Vivian said, pointing to the sofa. "Here. Let's look in the kitchen." She took his hand and walked him into the kitchen, but Andy beat them to it, checking the fridge and the cabinets.

"Grandma!" he called.

She was right behind him. "Hush, Baby. Use your indoor voice. We're in a hotel. The neighbors can hear us."

"There's nothing in here," he whispered.

Billy reexamined the cabinets. "Maybe room service can bring us plates, forks, and a pan."

Grandpa sat in a chair in the living room, but he overheard. "Leave the phone alone! We don't need that stuff yet."

Billy ran into the room. "Grandma said we shouldn't yell. People could hear us."

"I guess she must be right, because you heard me."

"Yes, Grandpa." Andy came in next. "Can I sit beside you?" He climbed onto Bill's lap.

Bill, adjusting his jeans, looked around the room. Vivian noticed. She found the ice chest and took out bottles of soda. "Andy, why don't you sit by me instead of on Grandpa? His legs are tired from driving all day."

She passed out the bottles and added chips. Handing her husband the remote, she said, "Let's rest awhile before dinner."

"Boys, we have a kitchen," Bill said, "but Grandma's on vacation, too, so we don't want her cooking for us all the time."

"I love to cook for you guys," she added, "but I didn't see a dishwasher."

"I don't do dishes very good," Andy said. "I guess we have to eat out."

"Practice makes perfect," Billy said.

"Boy, you're doing a lot of talking instead of watching TV," Bill said.

"Why don't you two look at your bedroom and see if you have a TV you can share in there," Vivian added loudly.

Andy looked at her. "Indoor voices, Grandma."

She eyed him. "Take off your shoes before you get on the bed, and no jumping."

He looked at her. "OK."

The boys remained in their room until dinnertime. Vivian

was good at being a grandma.

"You're a pretty good dictator," William said.

"Thanks. I learned from the best." She smiled.

The hotel offered washing machine services, but they didn't need that as long as they could have fresh towels. The older folks got to lie in bed and watch TV, while the younger ones slept. Vivian called Missy to check the family and was glad everyone was OK.

• • • • •

The next day, they drove their little Honda around Dallas to see the Rangers and the zoo. Vivian saw World Market and Ikea. They ate some good food and decided to return to the RV.

They had a great week and a half. They got back to Corpus Christi to see how the family was doing. Emily passed her car seat check and was going home the following day. Since Julie and Rook's house was full, the boys slept in the RV that night.

In the morning, William said it was their turn to sleep in the RV, because the baby was so loud.

"No," Vivian said. "We can go home now."

"We can, can't we?"

They drove home and enjoyed their time for a few weeks.

• • • • •

After three months, the entire family reunited at the home in Bishop. They were a real family, as if Grandma had always been with them. When Missy returned to work, Vivian and William furnished the guest room with a crib and diapers. After-school snacks for the boys were in the pantry. Vivian's life was full. She went to bed exhausted each night, but she was happy to have the man she loved at her side.

CHAPTER SIX
Tragedy

Missy and Andrew taught at Bishop High School. One day, a lunatic broke into the building with two rifles and a handgun. He shot everyone he could, including the lovely couple. After the police arrived and subdued him, they counted a total of twenty injured and four dead, including the gunman.

The autopsy showed Andrew bled out, as he tried to pull his wife to safety. He didn't know she died instantly.

• • • •

Vivian just set down Emily for a nap when she turned on the news, hoping to see the *Pioneer Woman* food show, only to have local programming interrupted.

The doorbell rang. Answering, she saw Captain Depew, William's friend from the police department. Holding his hat in his hand and looking weak, like he'd been up all night, he came inside and quickly turned off the TV to talk to her.

"Where's Bill?" he asked.

"He ran out to buy more diapers. Do you need him?"

"I've got something to tell both of you. Do you have coffee? It's been a long day."

"Sure. Let me get some." Vivian walked into the kitchen just as Julie called, sounding hysterical.

"There was a shooting at the high school. Four people died and twenty were injured. Are Mom and Dad OK? I tried calling them, but they don't answer."

Vivian dropped the receiver, as she collapsed to the floor. Captain Depew rushed in and spoke into the receiver.

"Is this Julie?" he asked.

"Yes. Who's this?"

"It's me, Coach Depew." He also coached the boys' soccer team. "I have terrible news. Your folks aren't injured. They're gone. I'm so sorry. I need to help your grandma up. She must've figured out why I came here when you called. Let me call you back."

Sobbing uncontrollably, Julie hung up. Luckily, Rook was with her, and they mourned together.

William returned, bringing both boys, wanting to keep them safe. He saw his friend kneeling over Vivian in the kitchen.

"Honey, are you OK?" he asked.

She nodded slowly. "I think something terrible happened to Missy and Andrew. Captain Depew came, but he turned off the TV before I could see anything."

"I heard a news report in the truck. I went to get the boys before I ran my errands. Depew, what do you know?"

"Julie just called. Bill and Vivian, I have terrible news. They're gone."

"To the hospital? Which one?"

"They're in the morgue. They died quickly, in each other's arms. I'm so sorry. We got to the school in less than three minutes after we got the call. That madman ran through the halls. Andrew and Missy were in the hall. Andrew tried to

Faded Sweetheart

tackle the man, but you can't tackle someone with a gun. He knocked Andrew down and shot him in the gut, then he shot her in the head.

"Andrew tried to drag her to safety not knowing she was already gone. That made him bleed out, though he got hold of one of the guns and shot the gunman. Andrew was a hero. He saved the lives of everyone at the school."

The boys walked in, their eyes vacant.

"My mom and dad are dead?" Andy asked.

"That can't be right," Billy said. "You need to check again. Give them a transfusion and use those spark things."

Vivian sat up on the floor with the boys on either side of her, all of them crying.

"Boys, let's help Grandma off the floor," William said. "Depew, thanks for coming by. We've got a lot to do now. We appreciate all...." He offered his hand for a handshake, then he grabbed his friend and started crying.

The two men held each other and wept. They'd been friends for decades. Depew came to Missy's wedding.

They heard crying from the nursery, and Vivian staggered to Emily and carried her into the living room. Andy and Billy sat beside her. Emily would never remember her parents or find them later in life.

• • • • •

Julie and Rook were packing frantically when Lucy stopped by.

"I just heard the news," Lucy said. "I'm so sorry. Let me come with you, so I can help for a while." She carried a small packed bag.

Julie hugged her fiercely. Once again Lucy was there to rescue them. "Sure. We're almost ready to leave."

They got into the car and drove off. Julie called her mom's number and stopped. "I guess I need to delete this one."

The others were silent. Rook drove carefully, protecting his precious cargo. He didn't want any more tragedies.

• • • • •

When they arrived, William and Vivian's little house was full. The boys, exhausted from their sorrow, slept on the couch. Vivian was in the kitchen. Neighbors brought food and offered help. TV people wanted interviews, but Bill refused.

The baby was in her swing in the kitchen, filled with giggles and smiles.

"I look at you," Vivian said, "and you remind me so much of your mother." She tried not to cry. She had to be strong. There would be time to be weak later.

When there was another knock on the door, Bill felt aggravated. "Yes?" he demanded, opening the door. "Oh. Julie, Rook, and Lucy, we're glad you're here."

Julie hugged him. Rook, stepping inside, saw the boys sleeping and placed a throw over their legs in the center of the couch. Their heads were at either end.

Lucy went into the kitchen to find her friend. Holding each other, they cried, then Lucy went to the sink, washed her hands, and asked, "Have you had dinner yet?"

"No. We aren't hungry, though there's plenty of food. Help yourself if you want."

"Nonsense. We need to eat. We have a lot of work ahead. Let me set the table. Where are the dishes?"

Vivian pointed to a cabinet, and Lucy quickly set out a meal. The boys got up, hoping it was just a bad dream. At least they were in a loving family. They admitted they were hungry.

When people are in mourning, even if they think they are hungry, the hunger vanishes after a few bites. Lucy knew that and started baking cookies. The six people at the table combined ate only one serving, but she expected that. She brought out a pie a neighbor brought and found ice cream to go with it, serving it in the smallest dishes she could find, so the family wouldn't notice how little they ate. When most of them finished their dessert, she knew her idea worked.

All their cell phones were being charged, because they rang constantly. All their friends, including Missy's adoptive mother's kids, tried to call. Andrew's parents were dead, but he had many aunts and uncles, siblings, and cousins. Some even called Missy and Andrew's phones, because they didn't know the house number.

Lucy tried to address as many calls as possible. Taking notes, she requested a return call whenever possible.

After nine o'clock that evening, all the phones but the land line were turned off. Everyone needed rest. Vivian wondered how to accommodate all the kids. The boys seemed OK on the couch. The baby's bedroom had a crib and a small bed, with a full bed in the guest room.

Lucy stepped in. "I'll sleep in Emily's room. Rook and Julie can take the guest room. If I have a bad night tonight, they can watch the baby tomorrow."

The others were too exhausted to fight. Emily had a bad night, waking Lucy several times for feeding or diaper changes. The old woman wondered if she was always like that and finally decided to sleep in the recliner in the living room with the baby in her lap and a bottle and diaper nearby, which worked.

• • • • •

In the morning, Julie took the baby off the sleeping woman and brought her to the room she shared with Rook. She studied the little girl, wondering who would raise her.

Would Grandma and Grandpa be able to, or would Julie have to quit school to care for her sister and brothers? She looked at Rook, who fell asleep with his arm around the baby's stomach. He would be a good father, but did it have to be so soon?

• • • • •

Vivian woke and went looking for the baby. She found her sleeping with her sister. Lucy woke up, too, and helped Vivian in the kitchen, making coffee and talking. William soon joined them.

"We need paper to make a list," he said.

"List things in priorities. What do we need to do first?" Vivian asked.

"I guess that would be the funerals," Lucy said sadly.

"Hmph." He took a deep breath. "You're probably right. I'll call Stan and see if he can come by."

"Who's Stan?" Lucy asked, trying to help Vivian.

"He's the funeral director," Vivian answered, having met Stan when she and William bought their plots. "Can he use our plots for them?"

"I'll call now." William dialed the number from memory, because he and Stan played golf occasionally.

Stan agreed to stop by in an hour.

• • • • •

When Stan arrived, the adults gathered around the dining room table to make the arrangements. The boys, baby, and Lucy were in the backyard. Emily was in her stroller, and her brothers drove her around until they started playing basketball. Lucy took the baby inside, so they wouldn't accidentally hit her. The adults might need coffee, too.

Hearing the door open, everyone turned, as thirteen pounds of joy came into the house. Stan hadn't seen Emily in weeks. The younger people took turns holding her.

Plans were sketched out. Julie looked through the pictures on her phone for a good one to submit to the newspaper. After scanning through them all, she didn't find anything that good.

When Julie became upset, Vivian got out her phone and showed her an album. "How about this one?"

"Grandma, that's perfect. I like that one."

Stan suggested the funeral be held at the high-school gym,

Faded Sweetheart

because it had enough space. "I can get it done tastefully. Missy and Andrew had a lot of friends and family. Your church has a big reception room. The family can meet there for a meal afterward. I'll make the calls. Julie and Lucy, if you have family phone numbers, you can send an announcement to the family phones."

"That sounds easy," Julie said.

"That's what I'm here for."

"Thanks, Stan," William said. "We'll use our plots for the kids."

"Absolutely."

Once everything was settled, Stan left.

"It's time for a nap," Vivian said. "Then we can go to the kids' house. Maybe we'll sleep better there, and we can pick up some toys for the boys."

"I'd like to get some of the boys' things, but we should stay here. The other stuff comes later on the list."

"I agree. Maybe we should have Depew drive by, so we don't get robbed."

"We have good neighbors. They'll watch out for us, too."

While the family was inside, making their decision, the boys decided to go home. They weren't thinking clearly. Maybe they forgot their parents were dead.

When they got home, they found the key and went inside. It was quiet in the house, and it smelled funny, because no one had been home in a while. They ran into the kitchen and saw dishes in the sink. Andy remembered the cereal bowl he left with milk thickening inside. Mama always told him to drain it, but he didn't.

Billy saw his socks on the floor. That looked bad, because Mom always asked him to put his dirty clothes in the laundry.

"Darn, Billy. Don't you remember what Mom said about dirty socks?" Andy asked.

"Look at these cars," Billy said, pointing at the floor. "Someone could get hurt if he stepped on them, Andrew."

They accused each other of several things, then they started fighting, but it wasn't like a normal fight. They were crying, and they hit each other harder.

Mrs. Jones walked by and heard the kids making noise in the house. She opened the door and asked, "Boys, what are you doing in here? Why are you fighting?"

They stopped, staring at the floor.

"We live here," Andy said, sniffling.

"We used to live here," Billy added. "We just wanted to make sure they didn't make a mistake."

"A mistake?"

"Yeah. Maybe Mama and Daddy didn't die. Maybe they're here."

Mrs. Jones texted Missy's number, hoping someone from the family had the phone. *Your boys are at the house, getting ready to lose it.*

"Andy, Billy, come sit by me." She sat on the sofa and patted the cushions beside her.

The boy obeyed, and she put an arm around both of them. "I'm so sorry about your mama and daddy. The whole town is sorry. We're on your side, and we'll be there for you, but you don't need to be here right now. Let's find some toys and go back to your grandpa's house. I'll come with you."

They were heading for the stairs when Julie and Rook arrived.

"Hey, Boys," she said. "Are you getting some of your gear?"

"Yeah."

"How did Mrs. Jones know you were here?"

"We were fighting."

"She heard it?"

Mrs. Jones whispered, "They were crying, too."

"Oh," Julie said softly.

"Let's get going," Rook said. "Don't take too much, maybe your tablets and some ball equipment."

They got the items they wanted and walked out to the car.

"We'll be back," Julie told Mrs. Jones, "just not for a while."

"OK."

As they drove off, Julie said, "We forgot to thank her. We can push redial to do that. Maybe I can get her number and use my own phone. I don't know if I can send a message using a dead woman's phone."

• • • • •

Back at the house, William sat down with the boys. "Thanks for checking the house. How was it?"

"I didn't pour out my cereal," Andy said. "It's thick now."

"They call that clabbered."

"It was gross. I'll always try to do what mama tells me…I mean, told me."

"I had socks on the floor," Billy said.

"That's OK. At least it means you change your socks."

"Mama said we should always pick them up."

"You still wear socks, so you can do that."

"I guess."

"Yeah. We can always improve," Andy said.

"Someday," Vivian said, "your grandpa will get the sock thing right, too. Maybe it can be a contest."

"I don't think I want to move back over there," Andy said.

"It's too early to make that decision."

"We have a list going," William said.

"Should we make our own list?"

"If you want."

"Why don't we ask Rook and your sister to go back to the house and get the Xbox or Gamer Boy, then you can teach Grandpa to play? You can stay with us and help me weed the garden."

"OK."

"Great. Go to the garage and get some tools. I need to change clothes."

They followed Grandpa outside to get tools, but no one was sure which tools they needed.

Vivian turned to Rook and Julie. "I'm sorry to ask, but can you check the house for some games for the boys. We also need clothes for the funeral. It can be just a nice shirt and pants, not a suit. We can buy new if we have to. Would the clothes they wore at the wedding still fit?

"Also, could you look for clothes your parents might want to be buried in? The funeral place can provide clothes, but you might want them buried in their own. Perhaps Missy had a favorite dress. Emily needs an outfit, too. If we need to shop, we'll do that later, but I know there should be plenty of clothes at the house."

"Will they need shoes?"

"No. Nobody will see their feet," Vivian said. "I assume you mean your parents."

Julie nodded.

"If you want them to have shoes on, I'm sure someone at the funeral home will help. FYI, when I die, I want my feet bare. Try to remember a game, so the boys won't guess your mission. I love you." She hugged them both.

Julie and Rook left, and Vivian turned to check if Lucy was OK with the baby, then she went to the garage to see if the men found the tools.

"OK, let's get going. William, could you check Emily? We'll be outside, sweating."

"Sweating? It's almost sixty degrees."

"Hard work makes you sweat." She winked at him.

"Thank goodness I've got a non-sweaty job."

The boys followed Grandma into her beautiful backyard to work on the flower beds.

"Where are they, Grandma?" Billy asked.

"I don't see them, either," Andy added.

"We're installing them today. Where should we put

them?"

"Usually people have them around the sides. Is that where we should start digging?"

"I was thinking of using that corner." She pointed to the far left corner of the lot. "I always wanted a fountain and a stone path to the house, so my feet won't get muddy all the time. I expect the deliveryman to bring the flowers in an hour. We need to remove the sod and prepare the beds. There'll be a cement truck, too."

The boys' eyes lit up. It wasn't a sissy weeding job after all. It was construction, and there would be a cement truck!

They dug up the grass in the corner, and Grandma brought over the wheelbarrow. She would save the sod and plant it along the trench where the water line would be.

The kids had boundless energy. They filled the wheelbarrow four times before the deliverymen arrived. One brought out a ditch witch.

"What will you do with that?" Billy asked.

The man's shirt had the name *Leonard* on the breast pocket. "This is for digging a trench to put in the water line for your grandma's fountain. Can you help me?"

"Sure, Mr. Leonard. What should I do?"

"We need to run this machine down the lane to make sure we won't dig up anything important, like the gas line."

"OK."

"As you run it, it'll paint the ground to show where you've been. If it makes a noise, the paint stops, and you move the obstacle. You can go any way you want and give it an artistic flair."

"I don't know what that means."

"To make it as pretty as your grandma."

"OK."

Another man carried several loads of lumber into the backyard.

"What are you doing, Mr. Jake?" Andy asked, seeing the name *Jake* on his shirt.

"I don't see a name on your shirt. Who are you?"

"Andy."

"Hi, Andy. Nice to meet you." He shook Andy's hand. "Today, we need to prepare a foundation for the fountain. First we need to make a mold, then, once the water lines are in place, we'll set up the fountain. I see you already had a crew digging up the corner. Good job."

"That was me and my brother, Billy."

"Wow. You did a really good job. Can we hire you?"

"I doubt it. We have to go to school next week."

"Maybe next summer. OK, let's get started."

One group hammered, while the other ran the paint sprayer. Vivian went to the patio to rest, while William carried Emily outside, so Lucy could take a nap.

"This was a great idea, wasn't it?" William asked.

"I had no idea that the thing we planned to make would happen during such a tragedy, but the boys can use the distraction. We can dedicate this to their parents."

"There are plenty of things to do. Should we send the boys to school next week? Should we move back to their house or stay here? Would Rook and Julie want the house?"

"She's got one year of nursing school left. She can't move here."

"That's right, and if the boys could return to the same school, that would be good for them, too. Maybe the teachers can watch them."

"They will, but I think it's too soon for that."

"Why?"

"Maybe we should leave Bishop and find a bigger house in Corpus Christi. Having the boys at a new school and in a new house would help erase the pain of seeing their old home every day."

"Lucy could return to her house, but she'd be close enough to help."

"She's been wonderful, hasn't she?"

"Yes. That's a good idea. They have fine high schools. I'm sure walking in their old school halls would freak out the boys."

"They freaked out just sneaking home. I don't know why they wanted to go, or I don't want them afraid at school. Let's call Julie and make sure she comes in through the backyard."

Vivian dialed the number. "Julie? We're doing some construction in the backyard. Please come back through the front door when you get here."

"We took the car, so no problem. We're looking out the back window. It's a great distraction to have the boys occupied."

"I'm glad Leonard and Jake could come over. They're counselors, not handymen. They're evaluating the boys, and we're getting our yard done, too."

"They aren't professionals?"

"Their dad did this for a living, and they helped him. They chose psychology and work at the children's hospital in CC. I met them when Emily was in the hospital. Luckily, I listened. Pretty soon, their dad will come by to make sure they're doing the job right."

"Honey, you're amazing!"

After the mold was set and the trench dug, the water line was laid, and the plumbing for the fountain was installed. The sound of a large truck made the dirty little boys jump to their feet, as a huge cement mixer backed up the driveway. The chute on the back was reached toward the far end of the backyard.

"Billy, Andy, we have to haul the mix to the fountain," Leonard said. "Can you do that?"

"Sure." They didn't know what that meant.

"Hold the wheelbarrow handles real good when the mix falls in."

Grandpa stood, getting ready to help, because he didn't think the boys could do it. He came over to assist. They got the job done. Rook came to help, too.

The fountain was finished quickly. They let it set while they started work on the stone path. They had a load of stones ready. The older men set them down in the path, and the boys had to step on them to make them level.

It was fast-drying cement, and the women left the porch to go inside and prepare lunch. Grandpa came out with a massive plate of sandwiches and drinks.

"When you're done," she called, "you can wash your hands and come eat."

They did, sitting on the edge of the porch to look at their work. After the concrete dried, Vivian moved the dirt the boys dug, placing it between the walking stones to cover the exposed concrete. Leonard and Jake got up to help.

"Why don't you sit this one out?" Andy asked. "We can do this."

The first three sat down on the porch and watched the boys work, quietly reporting their evaluation of the boys.

"We might need to come back to do another job later in the year," Jake said, "but they seem like tough little guys. Just keep an eye on them."

Julie decided to act silly. She put on Grandpa's wellies and stomped on the soil the boys deposited between the stones. Andy and Billy watched, telling her when she missed a spot or had to stomp harder.

When the workers were ready to leave, Vivian paid them, and the boys rushed up to hug them good-bye.

Vivian eyed her construction crew. "I've never seen you boys so dirty. It's time for a bath, but you have to hurry. You can use separate bathrooms. Don't leave the bathrooms too dirty."

"OK."

Everyone went to bed that night exhausted. The following day would be difficult, and they needed a good night's sleep.

• • • • •

Morning began with breakfast.

"Why are we eating cereal today?" Billy asked.

"We have a lot to do today," William replied.

"You used to love cereal," Julie said. "What happened?"

Grandma walked up with Emily in her arms. "Billy, I'll wash the dishes before we leave. You can help."

"OK, Grandma. Thanks." He began eating.

Julie and Grandpa exchanged a look, having forgotten how upset Billy was when he found his cereal bowl after his parents died. Grandma hadn't.

They took a limo to the school, because it held all of them and was customary. They were lucky, because there were no parking spaces left available when they arrived.

Several policemen led them inside, and they found their seats in the front, recognizing several relatives. It was comforting having them there. The gym filled quickly. Many people wanted to thank the family for Andrew saving the rest of the school. The other person who died was a first-year teacher, who left a husband and baby son six months old. It was her first day back after having her baby.

The service was quick, though it seemed long to the boys. Emily slept in Julie's lap. Many people cried. The boys saw friends and family crying, too.

After the service, people came up to offer their condolences. It was almost too much for the boys to handle. Lucy took Emily to relieve Vivian and Julie.

Finally, they got into the limo and headed to the graveyard, which took time. Andy and Billy were soon hungry.

"Look," Vivian said. "The driver brought you some snacks."

The boys devoured the crackers and drank some soda.

"Try to finish that soon," she added. "We're almost there."

The boys finished just as the limo parked. Seeing the funeral tent, they walked in with their grandparents and sister. Rook had the baby. It was a smaller crowd, mostly family. Some of the boys' friends were there, and several of William's friends came. Lucy followed the limo in her old Victoria with her daughter and grandkids. Her family nicknamed Vivian "Auntie V."

The deacon gave a nice sermon, and all felt a little healed from it. It seemed everyone in the audience heard something different and felt comforted.

Then they went to the church to eat at four o'clock. It was a long day. The boys ate heartily, then asked Grandpa if they could use the playground.

"Certainly you can," William said. "Lucy, would your kids like to play, too?"

"I'm sure they do."

All the kids went outside to play, run, and slide.

"Kids need that," Lucy added. "Gloria, can you go out there occasionally and make sure they're OK?"

Gloria was her oldest grandchild and too old for toys, but she knew what to do. Sometimes, kids lost control after an emotional event. Her job was to get help if one of the kids freaked out.

They were doing OK, so Gloria went to bring the baby outside for fresh air. She sat on a bench and talked with the kids.

"Are you going back to school?" she asked.

"I hope never. I don't want to face my friends or teachers. They make me uncomfortable."

"They keep reminding us about our mama and daddy, and that makes me sadder than ever."

"Maybe you need a new school. Ask your grandma. Maybe she can home school you."

"She'd make a wonderful teacher. We could learn how to make cookies."

"But she's old, and she has to take care of Emily."

"The baby will get older soon. They don't need as much attention then."

"That's not true. When they start walking, they get into everything. I remember when you were a baby," Andy told Billy.

"You do not!"

"Hush, Boys," Gloria said. "Play nice or come inside."

"Do they have any more cake?"

"You can go check."

They went inside, but the Queen boys didn't eat. They looked worn out."

"Grandma, Grandpa, can we go home yet?"

"I'm sure we can. We've had a long day."

They stood and thanked everyone for such a fine dinner and reception. There weren't even any scraps for leftovers.

The final limo trip back to the house was a short one. Lucy followed once again.

When they were back at the house, Vivian invited Lucy into the kitchen to talk.

"I will," Lucy said. "I'll call in the morning. Get some rest."

"Thanks, Lucy. I will. Your grandkids are growing fast. Gloria's really pretty."

"Thank you, Auntie V," Gloria replied. "Did I tell you the boys are dreading school?"

"I was afraid of that. What did they say?"

They talked a bit more. Nodding, they returned to the living room.

Julie said, "Let me put Emily to bed. Me and Rook need to leave. Unfortunately, I have school, and he had to get back to the shop." Life went on. The boys went to the guest room and played quietly with their games.

"William," Vivian said, "we need to move soon. Gloria said the boys were talking about it when they played. I don't want them traumatized any more. I asked Lucy to find a Realtor to look for a house for us in Corpus Christi, where we'd be close to Julie and Rook."

"I agree, but we need to close the house."

"Yes. We need to go through it and take what we want. The boys should have mementos for when they're older."

"Maybe I can sneak over there tomorrow while the boys are sleeping or playing games."

"We had a lot of people offer to help. Maybe we could ask their friends to take them to a movie or something. We could take them to Julie's house for the weekend while we wrap up things with the house."

"Maybe your RV man could help with the house problem here after we move."

"That's a good idea, too. For tonight, we need to sleep before the baby wakes us up. We should have a bottle ready."

"Sounds good."

"The first one who hears Emily can tend her."

"You don't hear anything when you're snoring."

"I don't snore."

"Oh?"

"Hmmm. Let's go to bed. We're tired."

• • • • •

Vivian had always been an early riser. As she drank coffee, she checked the fridge for leftovers and remembered she had to return dishes to the neighbors. Lucy put their names on the bottom of each plate, so Vivian would know, but she wasn't sure who all the people were. Some she knew by sight. Her kids had plenty of friends in town.

She decided to wipe the table in the screen front porch and put most of the clean, empty dishes there with thank-you notes in them. She made a hand-painted, faded sweetheart in the upper left corner of each envelope. Many people thought that was sweet. Few understood what it meant.

Walking out the front door, she retrieved the newspaper from the lawn. Bill liked to read the paper as he ate breakfast. She walked back inside and saw Billy on the couch with Emily on his lap, carefully feeding her with the bottle. She enjoyed his attention.

"Does she need to be changed?" Vivian asked.

"She's OK. Could you read the funnies to us?"

"Sure, but wouldn't you like breakfast first?"

"No. I'm OK."

She sat on the sofa, looking for the cartoons in the paper. Billy set Emily on the floor. She couldn't crawl yet, but she still enjoyed herself.

Faded Sweetheart

"Which one should I start with?" Vivian asked.

"How about that one?" He pointed to Beetle Bailey. "Can we stay home and not go to school? Maybe you can teach us. We can help with her." He gestured to the baby.

"We'll investigate that idea, but let's have you read one to me."

"Sure. Pick one."

"Let's try Blondie." Vivian saw Emily on all fours, rocking, and said, "Look. She's doing what you used to do."

"How do you know?"

"I saw the videos."

"You've seen videos of me?"

"You were a cutie."

"Can we see them?"

"Sure. Maybe we can do that tonight. Would you like that?"

"Yeah."

"Are you ready for breakfast now? I could make pancakes."

"Emily can eat a few bites, too."

"She's getting bigger, isn't she?"

"We're all getting older and stronger. We'll help get through this."

The others in the house got up. With Bill's help, they soon sat at the table, eating Cheerios. A stack of pancakes was placed on the table, along with a platter of bacon and sausage.

"Billy wants to watch home videos tonight," Vivian said. "What do you think?"

"It's got a great cast," Bill said. "We can do that. You know, Boys, one of the reasons we go to church is to find comfort. Losing someone you love isn't final. They're in heaven, looking down at us. They can talk to God, because they're with Him."

"We can always talk to God," Vivian said, "and your parents. Remember Elijah? He waited in a cave, and, when he heard quiet, he knew it was God."

"As time goes by," Bill said, "you might be in a crowd and

think you see Mommy or Daddy. It won't be them, of course, but maybe they pointed you in that direction to remember them. Sometimes it'll hurt really bad, but later, it gives a warm feeling of deep love. Longing hurts, but it also feels good. It makes you human and makes you feel.

"You'll both become better men that way. You'll have compassion for others who might need your help. You can be proud your dad was a hero. I'm very proud of him. I miss your parents a lot, but life goes on. We have a job to do."

The boys ate while the adults talked.

"What should we do first?" Andy asked.

"Dishes," Billy said.

"Did I hear that?" Vivian asked.

"Yeah, because my little sister needs a bath. Look at her."

Emily finished her pancake and used the remains as an art project on her tray, then in her hair.

"What a messy baby!" Vivian scooped her up, and Grandpa followed behind, picking up fallen scraps and taking the tray to the sink.

"Guys, clean the dishes," he said. "I'll take care of the mess. I remember when you did this, Andy. You were twice as bad."

"What about me?" Billy asked.

"We withheld pancakes from you for a year. Then your grandma took you for a day, and you attacked her kitchen."

"My grandma?"

"Grandma Ellis."

"Oh."

The kitchen was cleaned up, so they went looking for Grandma. She lay with down Emily for a nap, who was clean and happy, sucking on a bottle.

"Will she remember Mom and Daddy?" Billy whispered.

"Absolutely. You'll remind her. All the good times will make her happy and warm. We have each other."

• • • • •

The family did fine until a solicitor came to the door with a summons. It seemed Grandma Ellis wanted custody of Emily.

"Why would she want our baby?" Vivian asked.

"She's a tad bit crazy," Bill said. "I don't know when it happened. It might've been when she kicked Missy out of her home or maybe before. Once when she took Billy out for pancakes, we had to get Depew's dad to bring him back."

"Was his dad a policeman, too?"

"Yes. That was the first time we had to call the law on anyone."

"Why'd she do it?"

"She was off her meds. She thought she could get money from us. I would've paid, but her demands were constant. Maybe I could have paid for her to be permanently placed in a mental institution, but people aren't kept in there indefinitely. I would've had to press charges and send her to jail."

"Did you?"

"No. We got a restraining order against her. Every month or so when she forgets, we call the cops again. Coach Depew has been a good presence. He knows how to remind her."

"We should call him about this."

"It's a lawyer thing. We'll need one of our own."

"Do you have one up your sleeve?"

"I do."

"But?"

"It's a woman."

"Then I'll talk to her, or I'll call my lawyer. He's a man."

"Let's call Sylvia. She knows the history about this."

"I'll get evidence that Missy and Andrew wanted us as caregivers for their children."

"They might tell us that if we want Emily, we'll have to take the boys, too."

"There's always Julie and Rook. They've got a Doberman and a bunch of pit bulls."

"As well as snakes and the growing rabbit and rat population to feed them."

"Are you talking about the boys or the reptiles?"
"Could be both."
"Are her children crazy, too?"
"No. They're OK. They once testified against her. None of them are blood. All are either her husband's kids, adopted, or foster."
"She did foster care?"
"Until she was fired. All the kids were taken from her."
"Oh, my!"
"That's what we said, too. Missy helped the kids when she leaked some of Grandma Ellis' unusual practices."
"Such as?"
"Read the court testimony."
"I will, but, first, I have a diaper with somebody's name on it. Come here, Missy! I mean, Emily."
"It's OK. I've called her that, too." He hugged her for a second, then they went after their crawling granddaughter.

• • • • •

The document Missy signed when her baby was taken to Corpus Christi with Grandma held up in court despite Grandma Ellis' intentions. A copy of the document went into both lawyers' files for future reference. Bill and Vivian didn't know why it might be an issue, but they didn't worry about it.

As weeks passed, everyone began healing. Miss Lucy called to say she found a few houses Bill and Vivian should see. Bill packed up the boys, Emily, and Grandma in the van, and they drove to Corpus Christi.

The houses seemed large, but, with three kids, they needed a lot of space. Their favorite was within walking distance of a small private school. Vivian knew about it and felt the boys would be protected. The family moved in the following week, and the boys started school a few days later.

It was time to make a list and ask favors from those who offered their help. Rook had to pick up the boys from school

Faded Sweetheart

a few days a week, and Miss Lucy took care of the baby. Bill and Vivian worked with the RV men and a few neighbors to clear out their homes in Bishop.

They owned a lot of possessions. It wasn't easy dividing what to keep and what to sell or give away. Kid's clothes were easy, because they'd be outgrown soon. Vivian hoped Bill would know which baby toys and other things the kids might want. Anything in question was placed in storage, though Bill and Vivian agreed it should be only one large storage unit.

Then they gave in and rented a second unit for future use for the boys, either when they grew up or went to college, which would be within seven years. Dishes and furniture would last that long. Extra linens and towels were donated to charity.

They decided to leave the appliances in the houses to help with their resale value. Will agreed to sell those houses, but his renters were safe. He didn't want them to get stuck with a greedy landlord. If they remained honest and worthy, he was considering giving them those houses someday. Most were. The dishonest ones never stayed for long, so he sold those houses.

Having rentals was a good tax write-off and was also good for the community. He understood how some people struggled with their finances.

It took three days a week for eight weeks to get everything in Bishop organized. The kids' house and Vivian and Bill's houses sold, and the money was placed in a savings account for the boys. Emily was given the money from the rentals that were vacant and sold. Bill and Vivian felt she had more time to gain interest. Julie and Rook were given the money from the estate sale.

They thrived in Corpus Christi, living with family. Life was full. As years passed, the boys grew old enough for high school, and Emily turned three. The document the lawyers kept on file was requested by Emily's preschool program. Some of the teachers wanted the details of her situation with her grandparents.

After a casual conversation with the principal, they were told they didn't have to provide that information to everyone at the school. The principal saw how upsetting it was.

Emily was a good student, though she didn't always follow the teacher's rules. At home with her grandparents, she had plenty of free range. She liked being her own boss. Vivian and Will, blinded with love, felt Emily could do no wrong.

The boys went to high school. "Grandma, we made the team!"

"Andrew, why wouldn't you?" she asked.

"Well, our old school was so small, not enough competition?"

"There isn't enough of that here? And look at your grades. Both of you are either doing it or changing the grades. You two boys are great! I hope it rubs off on Emily."

Walking in with jeans, a tula, and a princess crown, "What? Did I hear my name?"

"No, honey, got back and play." Billy said.

"Or, do your homework!" Said Andrew.

"That's the way boys!" added Grandpa, sitting in his chair, reading the paper.

Emily got better at school but didn't like the school's basketball games, though. The family tried to attend every game to support the boys. Gradma said, "Emily, don't forget your bag!" Filled with crayons and books, it made a big difference."

CHAPTER SEVEN
Basketball

"Grandma," Andy asked one night, "would you sign this?" Handing her a piece of paper, he thought she wouldn't bother to read it.

Without her glasses, she asked, "What's this, Son?"

"It's a permission slip." He unloaded his book bag to start his homework.

"Where and when?" Grandpa walked into the room from the bathroom.

"It's on the paper. It's for spring break. I think we're going to Bishop."

Vivian got her glasses. "This is a mission trip to Bolivia! Did you get this from school or Sunday school?"

"Some kids at school were passing them out for their church. It'll cost about $1,000, so they're looking for kids who can afford it. He said we might need passports."

"Andy," Will said, "I could give you a thousand dollars, but that's not the point. There are plenty of needy people right here. You can do more good here than without an expensive trip to a country where people speak a different language, have lots of disease issues, and where the situation may be dangerous. They have a lot of guerrilla warfare and black-market crime. It would be better to give a donation to folks who live there and know what to do with it."

"They asked for that, too."

"Tell that boy your grandparents said no thank you, but we'll give a nice donation to Food for the Poor, which puts money into existing programs in South America. For spring break, I can take you and Billy to St. Vincent De Paul and work for them for a week here in town. They can always use the help. Maybe we could volunteer for Habitat for Humanity. Would you like to help build a house?"

"Can we do it in one week?"

"I don't know how fast it goes, but, since this isn't basketball season, we could do it after school for a few days a week. Maybe you could Google it and ask some of your friends who won't be going to Bolivia to do God's work. You can still sleep in your own bed at night."

"That sounds good. Should I do that now, or start my homework?"

"How much do you have?"

"Not much."

"Then get on the computer, so we can see. I'll watch, so we don't miss anything."

Once again, Bill saved the situation. He was glad the kids wanted to help people. They already did a lot of things like that during grade school, which had a service-hour quota required for graduation. Public high school was different, but that didn't mean the kids had to stop.

Vivian and Will agreed that keeping the boys safe at home was very important. They knew kids went on mission trips, but why not do similar work at home? Spending money for a trip seemed a poor use of resources. Traveling, especially with people they didn't know, was a bad idea.

The computer offered some information about Habitat for

Faded Sweetheart

Humanity, but they needed to call the local office by phone, so Will offered to do that when the boys were in school. It turned out that helping building a house would be a great summer project. He called Vincent to offer the boys' services during spring break. There was a big project that needed kids for that week, but they had to agree to work and not mess around.

One of the parishes was remodeling its gymnasium, and they needed people to prepare the floors for resurfacing and plumbing. Will, knowing about such work, offered to help.

All the men in the house went to work. They met the priest, who wore jeans and handed out T-shirts with the words *Work, Pray, Play*. His own shirt had the word *Priest* on the back. He also handed out tools to anyone who didn't bring his own, including shovels and pickaxes. Several trash cans and brooms stood to one side.

"Thanks for coming," he told the assembled group. "We have a lot to do in only three days. First, we need to remove the wood from this floor." He pointed at the old basketball court. "We've got a few master plumbers in the group, who'll choose a few of you to help get the bathrooms up to par. I'll introduce them, and they can pick a few people to help. The rest can come with me to confession.... I mean, work on the floor here. We need to get down to the bare floor like we did in this area." He pointed at the space directly under him.

Grandpa, one of the plumbers, chose a few people to help him, but not the boys. He assumed they didn't want to be bossed around by him, though he wondered if he was right.

Billy and Andy got tools and started working at the corner of the court. The boards weren't hard to take off, but the hard part was stopping at the base.

• • • • •

At the end of the day, the floor was finished, and the plumbers needed parts. As they drove home, they discussed their day.

"How'd you do, Men?" William asked.

"Well," Andy said, "since our grandpa didn't want us, I guess we did fine. When we dug too far, we had Father Leonard look it over. He assured us it wasn't a problem. A lot of the kids went too far."

"That's good. How was your day, Billy?"

"Except for taking stuff to the Dumpster, it was fun. Tomorrow we clean up and have pizza."

"They want us done by morning, so they can lay the floor. Thursday we go outside for landscaping."

"How are the bathrooms coming, Grandpa?" Andy asked.

"My help could be better. I should've chosen you two, because I can yell at you. I mean, you can read my mind better. I had to do a lot of explaining, but they eventually got the point. They really didn't like pulling the toilets out."

"Yuck! Me, either, but I can," Andy said.

"Great. I'll switch teams tomorrow. I want my boys back."

"Will we get pizza?"

"Yeah. With you two helping, I expect to get the ladies' and the men's rooms done fast."

"What about the locker rooms?"

"I don't think they have toilets, but we'll check. Maybe we can do them, too."

• • • • •

William arrived early the next day with supplies. Ralph, the other plumber, was happy to see them. Each plumber assembled his team and started work.

After 4 days of work, they played basketball with the Texas A & M Islanders team.

"This is so exciting. They ever had TV camera's here!" Andy said.

Both boys made good shots! John Jason, from the college team complimented them. Grandma and Grandpa enjoyed the game. "We are so proud of you too!" they said.

Rook asked, "How can they play against the pros?"

Running back to the game, Andy yelled, "We are just that good." He was leaping for joy.

Emily put on a cheerleading outfit that once belonged to Julie and led cheers for the team, and some of the other little sisters joined in.

"Dunk that ball! Dunk that ball! Do you hear me? Dunk that ball!" She jumped up and down with pretend pompoms. "Go, team!"

After the game, there was an awards ceremony. Father Leonard took scraps of the old floor and had a parishioner brand *St. Anthony wins again 2007* on each, with the boy's name below.

Each boy was called forward. When Billy and Andy were called, Vivian stood to take their picture. It looked like they had tears in their eyes, but that was probably sweat from the game.

"This is beautiful Father," Billy said, accepting his plaque. "Thank you."

"What all you young men did while other kids were sleeping is great. Look at this place!" He pointed to the left and right. "The bathrooms have been redone, and you even managed the locker rooms. Our volunteers worked overtime, and our supplies mysteriously appeared." He looked at Grandpa.

"We really hit the jackpot this year. Thank you and all the adults who helped us. Let's give them a big hand!"

People stood and applauded.

• • • • •

At school the following week, the boys were tired but proud of their work. The kids at the poor parish now had a great place for games and other activities. Father Leonard said they would host several intramural games, too.

Andy and Billy helped out with other repairs at that parish. Grandpa taught them well. If there was a problem, they brought him along, though sometimes he called in an expert.

CHAPTER EIGHT

Boys Grow Up

Both boys went to college. Andrew wanted to become a lawyer, while Bill wasn't sure about his career. They stayed at a house they repaired with Grandpa's help. It was Emily's ninth birthday, and Julie would bring her toddler to help celebrate. Emily hoped she would be old enough to baby-sit soon.

Spring passed quickly and ended with great sadness when Grandpa became ill. He had a stroke and could no longer walk. Emily and Vivian spent many hours in his room, keeping him company. His once-sharp mind faded, and Vivian became sorrowful.

• • • • •

That Easter, they celebrated the funeral Mass of a fine husband and father. There were no tears, just half-breaths, as

Faded Sweetheart

if the family were holding them back. The kids felt very sad, though they knew Grandpa had never been happier. Vivian held onto them as if fearing she would fall. Miss Lucy came with her family, and the church was filled with people Grandpa's life had touched. One of the young men who helped them dig Grandma's garden after their parents died celebrated the Mass.

"That guy looks familiar," Andrew whispered to Bill.

"Father Leonard was the *Work, Pray, and Play* guy. I asked him when he gave me my award," Bill whispered back, pointing. "His brother's over there." He pointed at someone they recognized who read Bible verses at the Sunday noon Mass.

"What are you two talking about?" Julie asked.

"We know those guys," Andy said.

"OK, but stop talking. We're in church."

They turned their heads toward the center aisle. Grandpa's body had just arrived, and someone removed flowers to put on the ceremonial drape.

Vivian hoped all would receive grace and comfort from the funeral. She wished for some for herself, too.

After Mass, the drape was removed, and the flowers were put back. The congregation came forward to offer their condolences to the family. It was humbling seeing all those kind people expressing their thanks.

"He let us live rent free until I got back to work," one said.

"He took me in as his apprentice so I could make a good living."

"He kept me out of the bar."

"He never judged me. He just stood by my side when I went to jail. When I got out, he was waiting for me."

"He loved you a lot, Vivian, as if he knew you all his life."

"Boys, he was proud of you for conquering your fears."

"Julie was all we heard about until her brothers came, then he loved them, too."

Many people hugged them. The funeral was exhausting

and exhilarating. The family wanted it to end but never end. Finally, the body was taken to the cemetery.

• • • • •

Summer was almost over when Emily received a letter informing her she'd been accepted as a foreign exchange student. She worked hard to earn that award, but she didn't want to go, because that would leave Grandma alone.

"Emily, you worked hard for this," Vivian told her. "You need to go. Maybe I'll fly over during one of your breaks to visit you. It's only for one semester. You'll be home by Christmas.

"I can find something to do. Your sister will have a baby in the spring, so I can help her. Grandpa would want you to go. We've been so lucky having you close to us for all these years."

In the third week of August, Emily boarded a plane for France, where she would live with a French family. She would finally get to meet Renee and use the language she fell in love with many years earlier.

• • • • •

Miss Lucy came to visit Vivian, worrying the empty house might be difficult for her.

"It's not that hard living by myself," Vivian explained. "Emily calls every day. I've been thinking, though, that I never gave Richard a chance."

"You mean Mr. Roscoe?"

"I never tried to love him."

"You were with him for almost forty years. What do you mean?"

"I was stuck in the past."

"Did you ever tell him about Missy? Did you ask him to help find her?"

"Absolutely not. I tried to pretend I was a virgin when we

married. That's what my aunt said I should do."

"He didn't know the difference?"

"I don't think so. My aunt insisted we get married during my period, so he wouldn't notice. I tried to love him, but...."

"But what?"

"He wanted to be successful and show off all the nice things his hard work bought."

"Like that house and you?"

"What are you saying?"

"Mr. Roscoe may not have had the loving wife Bill had, but either he didn't know the difference, or he didn't know how to love. Different marriages have different priorities. The couple works together to make it a success. Richard had a beautiful wife who supported him, never cheated on him, and never embarrassed him. He spent his money well. I never heard either of you yell at each other. He never went out the door angry, and he never hit you. It was a very proper marriage."

"I guess you're right, but I feel bad. With Bill, I know how a perfect marriage really is."

"You're lucky. I wasn't that lucky."

"What do you mean?"

"Remember my son George?"

"I thought he was your nephew."

"He's the illegitimate son of my husband. The mother threatened to kill him if he didn't take him. I had to raise a baby who didn't belong to me."

"He seems like a wonderful son."

"He is, and he *is* my son. I'm just glad his dad left him when he moved out. My husband wasn't a winner, either. Like we both know, we put up with things for the children and the family's honor."

"Have you seen that woman since?"

"I think she died a few years later from a drug overdose. At least she didn't leave me with another kid. My womb worked just fine."

"Wow. We sure kept our secrets well."

"Yeah. We're good together, aren't we?"
Vivian held her friend's hand. "Yes, we are."

• • • • •

School in France was very different and exciting. There were times Emily couldn't go along, though. Some of the things Renee suggested weren't appropriate, and she refused to do them. Instead, she went to her quarters for a video chat with Grandma and friends at home. She tried not to let Grandma know what was happening.

"Can I come home early?" she asked.

"Without any question. We'll get you a ticket by the weekend."

Grandma bought a ticket to fly to France and see her baby before taking her back home.

Emily was glad to see her again. "When do we fly home?"

"I wanted to tour France first, and take a train to England before flying home. You can show me around."

"That's wonderful!"

They apologized to the host family for leaving early. Vivian said, "My husband recently died, and I need Emily at home." They believed the story and hurried to help Emily pack. It wasn't a warm, touching departure.

Vivian didn't know what was going on, but she was glad to have her *roo* back.

"Why do you call me Roo?" Emily asked.

"When you were born, we took you to a big hospital, where they put you under my sweater to keep you warm. The outfit was called a kangaroo, and it helped your heart rate. You slept that way many a night."

"Hmmm. What else should I know?"

"When we get home, I have a box to show you. We can go through it then." Vivian didn't know how much longer she might live, so she wanted to give Emily mementoes of her past.

"Also, when we get home, I'll teach you how to drive, so

you can get your license."

"Shouldn't one of the boys or Rook teach me?"

"I taught your brothers, but they're a bit heavy on the pedal. I'll show you the right way."

"I want to do it right."

"Of course you do." She patted Emily's knee.

• • • • •

Driving classes went well.

"You're doing a good job," Vivian said. "What kind of car would you like to drive?"

"What do you have?"

"I'm thinking we should ask Rook to find a good one."

"Let's drive by there."

"Now?"

"Why not?"

"Let's wait until you get your license. We can try tomorrow if you're ready."

"Let me cram tonight."

"OK. You need to return to school next week. I spoke to the counselor about your returning early. She mentioned you could write an essay about your trip. I suggest you be positive. You should write the family a nice thank-you letter, too. Don't mention any of the negative stuff. Then you can write them out of your life."

"OK."

"What's good cramming food?"

"How about baked potatoes?"

"Coming up. Start working. It looks like it'll be a long night."

• • • • •

"Dinner was good, Grandma," Emily said when they finished. "Can I study in here with you?"

"Sure. I'd love to see you working."

• • • •

Emily got up and dressed in the morning, ready to take her driver's license exam. After breakfast, Vivian followed her to the car and let her drive to the building.

"I brought your paperwork if you need it," Vivian said. "Do you have that school paper?"

"Yes."

"Honey." She touched Emily's hand on the steering wheel. "If you don't pass this time, we can always do it again. Don't get upset."

• • • •

Emily passed her test. They drove to Rook's garage to see what kind of car he might have for her. Julie and Rook knew what kind of car Emily wanted, and they bought her a new one. They also arranged a little party with cake and balloons. Andrew and Bill, with his new wife, were there, too.

Some of Emily's friends who came by reminded her that the law said only one teen passenger was allowed in the car with a new driver. That made Vivian happy, because it helped stop joy riding.

It was getting late, so Grandma let Emily take one friend home, with Grandma in the back seat. The friend offered to sit there instead.

• • • •

On Monday, the buses were running for school.

"Will you drive to school?" Grandma asked.

"No. I don't want any scratches on my new car. I'll drive after school."

Putting butter on her toast, Grandma smiled, happy Emily had good sense.

Grandma helped Emily choose her prom dress and offered advice on how to act at the prom.

At the event, Grandma stood with several other parents to watch. Though it might have been a bit embarrassing for Emily, she was used to it. She remembered the relatives lining up when she graduated from kindergarten. They all wore matching T-shirts at her softball games. She knew she was loved and cherished. Miss Lucy's family attended with everyone else when Emily graduated from high school.

CHAPTER NINE

The Memory Box

The morning after prom, Grandma walked into Emily's room. "Are you up yet, Roo?"

"Yes, I am. I had a lot of fun yesterday. What did you have in mind for today?"

"Remember I said I had a memory box for you? Would you like to look at it today? Do you have time?"

"That would be great. Where is it?"

"In the closet. Can you help me move it?"

"Sure. Let's pull it in here."

Inside the box were lots of papers, baby pictures, doodads, and pressed flowers.

"OK," Emily said. "Where should I start?"

"First, let me tell you why I did this. I'm pretty old, and I don't know how long I've got to talk to you about when you were a baby. I wanted you to know my impressions, hoping they're accurate. I have a notebook about how your mom and I spent your gestation. I loved your grandpa. I made a box for your mother, too. Luckily, I found her, and I was able to give that to her. I was making a baby book for you, but your mother didn't have a chance to read it."

Emily placed her small hands on top of the papers and books. "What should I do first?"

"Right here, when your grandpa and I married. Then go to your mom's pregnancy, then your NICU time." Vivian dug around until she found a white wedding book. When she opened it, they saw pictures of the backyard in Bishop.

"I'll bet Julie would like to see this," Emily said. "Should I call her?"

"If you want. Let me start breakfast."

Emily called Julie to ask if she wanted to go through the box with her. She had the day off and arrived in fifteen minutes.

"Rook wants to see it, too, but he's working today. He'll come by later. I need to sit beside you, Little Sister." She scooted her over on the bed.

"OK. Grandma, sit in this chair. Let's get a table and put the box up higher." Emily moved the furniture around until everyone was comfortable.

They started with the wedding pictures, and soon, they were talking and laughing.

"I remember this!" Julie said.

"I don't," Emily said.

"You weren't born yet."

"Grandma, did you make a box like this for my babies?" Julie asked.

"I've started one, but I doubt I'll be here forever."

"You're not going to be here forever?"

"Julie...."

"I never thought you'd leave us."

"Hopefully I'll always be in your prayers and thoughts."

"You'll be the faded sweetheart who always lingers, reminding us that our lives were better because of you."

"Where'd you get that line?" Emily asked.

"It's in this greeting card Grandpa sent to Grandma in 1961."

"How long did you two date?"

"About four years," Vivian said. "My mother didn't approve, because he was older, but I knew even at that young age he was the one."

"Like I knew Rook was the one," Julie said.

"Yeah. Your mama and grandpa were anxious to keep you away from Rook, even though I knew he was an upstanding young man."

"I'm glad he pursued me. He was the only one who ever rang my chimes."

"Love is funny."

"Yeah, but it doesn't pay the bills," Emily said.

"What does that mean?" Julie asked.

"We need to get back to the box. Your kids will be home from school soon, and Grandma promised me breakfast."

"Yes, I did. What would you like?"

"Do you have any doughnuts left?"

"You want stale doughnuts?"

"Just to get started. I've been waiting eighteen years for this."

"OK. Let's get those doughnuts and some coffee."

"Thank you, Grandma. I could start those, so you can stay in here," Emily said.

"No. You girls start on your box. Julie was there, so she can give you a younger play-by-play. I don't mind making coffee."

The two girls spent the day in their pajamas, looking at memories in the box. Julie talked a lot, because the items brought back many memories. They often looked to Grandma to ask questions. It was a lot of fun. Grandma was

Faded Sweetheart

glad the box worked for the girls. Seeing her husband on their wedding day, Emily as a newborn, and other events was fun, but Grandma soon became tired and went to lie down.

The girls were reading about their school days when Emily left to get drinks. She passed Grandma's room on the way to the kitchen. She found sweet tea and cookies.

"Julie, would you rather have milk?" she asked.

"Bring both."

Emily walked past Grandma's room on the way back. "I'm being a waitress. Do you want anything?"

She didn't answer.

Emily went back to her room and set down the drinks before placing a cookie in her mouth. "I need to check Grandma. She didn't answer just now."

They both walked into Grandma's room.

"Grandma, are you OK?" Emily asked.

She didn't respond.

Julie grabbed her wrist.

"Is there a pulse?"

"I'm not sure. Call 911 quick!"

Emily ran to the phone and called. She turned on the porch light, so the EMTs would be able to see the house.

Emily called her brothers next, and they arrived just before the ambulance. Rook came, too.

The EMSA people arrived and told the family to give them space, so they could work, but there was little they could do. Vivian was dead. Someone called the coroner to pick up the body.

Julie sat in the loveseat, with Rook holding her tightly. The boys and Emily sat on the sofa.

"We need to call Miss Lucy," Emily said.

• • • • •

The following day, they called the priest to discuss the funeral.

It was a beautiful funeral for Grandma. People were very kind to the family. After everyone left the house, all the family members went through the box together. Andrew and Bill cried. The kids, who rarely cared about adult stuff, hung around the table and touched old baby clothes, asking questions about them.

Grandpa and Grandma had a big house, but with all the grandkids and great-grandkids, it was a tight fit overnight. Those who owned dogs let them out in the morning, but the dogs didn't like the backyard very much. Finally, people went home.

CHAPTER TEN
Emily's New Chapter

No one thought Emily, as the baby of the family, could live alone and take care of herself except Grandma. She didn't tell Julie that before she came over the day Grandma died, she handed Emily a letter, saying it should be saved and read after the girls were done with the box. The letter was one of encouragement, telling Emily she had plenty of skills to fulfill her dreams.

When Grandpa died, his money was split four ways for the kids. Grandma's letter informed Emily that she would inherit the Roscoe money. The other children were already taken care of. Emily had to learn to live independently, but

Grandma didn't tell her exactly what to do, deliberately leaving it open.

Emily spoke to Julie, Andrew, and Bill. They suggested she get a good education, so she could have a job to pay for whatever she liked. Julie recommended nursing.

"You'll always be paid well, and you can choose your shifts," she added.

Emily wasn't sure she wanted that career.

"Don't waste your time on music or drawing," Andrew said. "You'll never make any money at it."

Since Emily was the new owner of Roscoe Enterprises, she decided to visit.

• • • • •

Entering the corporate building, she asked for the manager. She found Mr. Howell, the corporate president, a friendly man who sat down with her and explained how the company worked. "When Mr. Roscoe was alive, the firm was very strict. After he died, Vivian made it a bit more human and friendly. She promoted me as president, my present position, and I knew ownership would eventually pass to you."

An older man, he hoped Emily would take over, so he could retire. She learned that Roscoe Enterprises was a huge banking and telecommunications company that reached almost every country in the world. Keeping the headquarters in Corpus Christi was a battle.

"Thank you for the information," Emily said. "I need to start college and can't run the company yet. What classes would I need to take to become the best in the business? Can you stay on until I'm ready?"

"Let me introduce you to our team. I know they want to meet you. Yes, you should finish college and get a degree in accounting, engineering, or management, but that takes six years. Are you ready for that?"

"What do you suggest?"

"If I were in your position, I'd travel and see the world.

We have offices in many countries. You could see how we operate, when you could come back you could work here to see if this suits you or go to college. You could also just be the money behind the business and do whatever makes you happy."

"Wow. That makes sense. I wish I asked Grandma before she died."

"Are you sure she didn't tell you?"

"I need time to think. There's a lot to do."

Mr. Howell stood and patted her shoulder. "Your future is in the palm of your hand, but there's time. We await your decision."

"Thank you for your time."

"Here's a brochure about our European offices. It was nice meeting you. Please keep in touch."

Emily didn't know who to talk to. Finally, she drove to the big yellow house where Miss Lucy lived. She knocked, and Miss Lucy answered.

"Miss Emily! I'm glad to see you. How are you?"

"Miss Lucy, do you have some time? I need some advice."

"I'll do my best to help. Have you spoken with your sister or brothers?"

"I don't think they can help me. Do you know Mr. Howell?"

"Is he the man at the Roscoe Company?"

"Yes."

"What do you want to know about him?"

"Is he legit? Should I follow his ideas or just run away?"

"What did he say?"

"He told me I should live a little, then, if I want to take over the company, I can go to school while I learn the ropes, so he can retire. I'm not sure what they do. What do they sell?"

"When Mr. Roscoe was alive, it was all about money. He made deals in banking, telecommunications companies, fax machines, and copiers. When your granny inherited it, she moved toward helping Third-World nations survive. The company started offering loans to widows, helped feed children, and offered medical care. The company not only gives donations, but their debtors pay them back, too. They have a ninety-percent return rate. Mr. Howell is an honest man who wants to protect your investments. He wants to help those who need it most."

"That's more information than I expected. How do you know so much?"

"When my daughter needed a job, Vivian asked Mr. Howell to give her a chance. She lives in England working for the company and loves it."

"Wow. He said I could go to Europe, and the company would welcome me. I'd love to see Rebecca again. Maybe I should take that trip."

"I'll call her tonight. How will you tell the kids?"

"Maybe I'll call them after I'm over there."

"Not the best idea. I could always cover you."

"I hate to ask, but would you do that?"

"Anything for Vivian's kid."

"Miss Lucy, are you OK? I know you miss her a lot."

"Yes. She was a great friend for decades, and she never forgot me."

"You were her best friend. She loved you like a sister. She was my mother almost my entire life."

"I know, Roo. It'll be hard without her."

"She called me Roo."

"Is it OK if I use that name?"

"Sure."

"Well, if you plan to travel, you'd better get some tickets and pack before Julie and the others find out."

"I could use a house sitter. Any suggestions?"

"I could send George. He's a good person."

"OK. Let me get this started and get back to you. Thank you. I love you." She hugged Miss Lucy, who was old and frail. She was part of Meals on Wheels and had a weekly visit to clean the house and buy groceries. If Rebecca had stayed home, that would have been her job.

Faded Sweetheart

• • • • •

Emily lived alone in Grandma's house for a month, when she bought a ticket and prepared an itinerary. She spent most of her time going through Grandma's possessions and sorting things into piles. Julie came over occasionally and helped decide what had to be thrown out.

Emily didn't want to be ruthless, but she had to clean up the house. She saved items that had sentimental value, in case she bought a smaller house for herself. At times, Julie asked where those things went. Emily tried to remain poker-faced.

The valuable items went into a storage locker. She trusted George, but if something Emily loved went missing, it might be to one of her siblings or a thief. She didn't want to blame anyone if that happened.

She held a nice dinner for her family. There were plenty of chairs and tableware to accommodate all. They ate Emily's favorite meal of steak and spuds, something she got from Grandpa.

After dinner, she told them about her upcoming trip during dessert. Because she planned to see Rebecca, who everyone knew and approved of, there wasn't much they could complain about. Mentioning George as the house sitter went over OK, too.

Though it was near Christmas, Emily said she needed to leave before the weather turned, and the others agreed. They had a rush celebration combining Thanksgiving and Christmas. Julie took a few days off work to help make the dinner Grandma always prepared. Since Emily helped Grandma cook, Julie asked her to help her, too, assuming she knew how to make some of the dishes.

Emily knew how to make deviled eggs and how to mix the stuffing. Both of them forgot to thaw the bird in time, so they made chicken and stuffing instead, with all the trimmings. Once the turkey was defrosted, the others fried it for Thanksgiving.

The kids loved having Christmas early. The family wasn't able to buy much on sale due to how early it was, but at least they could wear their Christmas clothes during the holidays. Usually, cute Christmas clothes went into a drawer and were forgotten. They didn't know if that was a blessing or a curse.

They got silly, and April found Christmas songs on her phone, which everyone sang along with. Angela was pregnant and laughed, saying she almost had to deliver her baby right then. Emily felt sad about leaving, because she would miss the birth. The family had always been together, but life was changing.

Maybe she would hate England and would return in two weeks, like her last trip out of the country. She hoped her visit was worth the price of the ticket.

"Do I have to wear this shirt in England?" Emily asked, holding up a yellow long-sleeved shirt with a Texas flag and some holly around it.

Another person gave her cowboy boots, something Julie tried to get Emily to wear since she was a baby. Emily always made her give up, but not that time.

"You can use these for protection," Julie said.

"What do you mean?"

"See these toes? They can kill, or at least hurt, any guy who won't behave."

"How do you know so much about mauling men?"

"What are you two talking about?" Rook asked, coming in from outside.

"These boots," Emily explained. "Julie is an expert at protecting herself."

"Yeah. She's got me." He smiled at his wife.

"Trust me," Julie said. "Take the boots. I need to keep Killer at home with me."

Emily got out a larger suitcase to accommodate the boots, and April dropped in the yellow T-shirt.

"I saw that!" Emily said.

Faded Sweetheart

"What?" April removed one ear bud, as if she hadn't heard.

Emily smiled and gave up.

• • • • •

On the day of Emily's departure, Rook and Julie drove her to the airport. They found Andrew and Bill waiting for them. It was the middle of the day, so the children were in school. Emily looked for school buses, but it probably wasn't an approved school trip.

In addition, Andrew said he and his wife were going to Italy in a month, and he hoped to see her there.

• • • • •

As Emily flew away, she knew she would miss her family. She already did, but she kept that a secret. Putting on a happy face, she tried to have a happy heart.

Her family let her go, though they couldn't have stopped her, either. As the baby in the family, she was always spunky. Grandma always told her that was what made her tick.

CHAPTER ELEVEN
Emily Takes on England

She flew to France during high school, which was a long, boring trip. On her way to England, though, she brought a book someone at BAM recommended, probably because it cost $25 and was a bit sexy. Maybe the sales guy thought she needed an education.

After twenty pages, though, she had enough sex education. She brought along a few magazines, too, and there were a few sexy things in those, but she liked the decorating information. She must've been hungry, because even the ads looked good. She either had to start cooking more or find Mr. Romance in the book, who was apparently able to cook without a stove.

She shook her head. She liked cooking with Grandma. She helped Emily a lot, but she never cooked anything alone except eggs.

As she drifted off to sleep, her imagination wandered. She saw herself being chosen for the Bachelorette Show, to be wooed by ten very available, handsome men in all shapes and sizes. The first one she dated was Hans, who was almost twice her height with the same color hair. She suspected he colored his. He said he liked to cook, so she asked him to show her.

Emily always thought cooking meant food. Hans thought it meant dancing and removing clothes. She didn't dance, and she didn't carry any sandwiches under her vest. Neither did he. She sent him back to wherever it was he came from. She doubted it was Denmark.

The next contestant was a black firefighter from Arizona. He claimed he fought huge prairie fires, but he couldn't even start the charcoal for their steaks. At least he brought meat, though she didn't like it raw. He claimed he only put out fires, not start them. The boys at the local firehouse had great tailgate parties, but all the food was already cooked.

Emily wondered if she should look at one of those single guys, but she wasn't that desperate. She was still young.

The next two contestants liked each other better than Emily or the program coordinator, so they were quickly checked off the list.

Number five was a geek. He wasn't very virile, and his hair went every which way, as if he never saw a comb. He wore a plaid shirt with a colored T-shirt under it, tucked into his jeans. She didn't see his feet, but she assumed he wore loafers or maybe flip-flops. His cell phone would probably fit into his back pocket, but he was constantly using it in one hand, though he looked at her a few times. Maybe she needed to send him her email address, so he would talk to her. When she tried talking to him, he acted like she scared him off. Though Emily didn't eliminate him, he stayed in his trailer for the rest of the show. Maybe he thought she'd eliminate the others, and he would win by default. He might have been playing a computer game and wanted to reach a higher level before the next commercial.

She had the impression the show organizers were worried she might not find her knight in shining armor, which would be a shame. Out of ten great guys, she couldn't seem to find one. It was a good thing she wasn't a mail-order bride.

How had those women done it? It was easy enough to get along with people, but to marry someone who wasn't even on the same page? Her dream began sliding downhill.

The next two men weren't bad. One was a preacher, which she assumed meant he was a tame date. It turned out she was wrong, but at least she had self-defense training. The producers didn't air that scene.

The last man was wonderful. He held her hand, cooked her an egg, and talked to her. He was tall, dark, and handsome, but he was also married and had to leave when his wife went into labor. Had someone forgotten to screen him?

In desperation, she visited the geek's trailer and found him sitting on the couch, pushing buttons. Emily sat beside him and asked, "What are you doing?"

He said, "I was writing a song for you on my tablet." He put an ear bud into one of her ears. It was a catchy tune that sounded original, though she doubted even Taylor Swift or James Taylor would make any money from that one.

It was touching, but she wondered if he used the same song on every girl he met. She studied him, wondering if there was a heart behind those glasses that she could love. How could she admit to her friends and family that she went on a game show and fell in love with him? He might have been the best they had to offer, but she couldn't do it.

She was too young to marry, and it wouldn't be easy competing with a machine. She knew how to use a computer, but she never considered taking one on a date or to the bathroom.

• • • • •

"Do you need a blanket?" the flight attendant asked.

"I'm OK. Well, maybe I need one." She checked the screen and saw they were halfway, so she had six more hours to go. "Do you have anything to eat?"

"Certainly. I can bring you something right now."

Finally, she had a winner—not to marry, but at least something tasty. She'd been told most airplane food was good.

The sandwich was on a croissant. All sandwiches tasted good on those buttery, flaky buns. She didn't recognize the meat, but the crunchy part and the ice-cold Pepsi were yummy. The stewardess brought a hot chocolate brownie with ice cream.

"Can I stay on the plane longer for seconds?" Emily asked.

The stewardess stared at her.

"I was joking. That was really good."

"Oh." She bowed slightly. "I understand." She walked backward down the aisle, nodding to Emily.

After her snack, Emily dozed without dreaming of a game show or finding a mate.

• • • • •

The plane landed, and Emily found her friend waiting for her at baggage claim.

"Hi, Rebecca!" she said.

As Rebecca gave her a quick hug, she whispered, "We need to pretend you're my boss, and we don't know each other."

"OK."

They walked side-by-side down the concourse. Unlike usual Southern charm, Rebecca displayed a very professional attitude. She had the driver take them to Emily's hotel.

Not knowing any better, Emily asked if Rebecca would like to check the room with her. She got out of the car with Emily.

Once in Emily's room, Rebecca became the friendly person Emily remembered. "The driver was watching us," she explained.

She called the driver and told him Emily needed a tour before going to the office. He arrived in less than ten minutes. Emily and Rebecca put on their formal expressions and went out. It was fun. They used to play like that when they visited Miss Lucy.

Rebecca's office was preceded by hundreds of cubicles eight across in double layers. Each space had a phone, a computer, and files. A few had personalized their spaces. Nicer offices for the managers were around the outside of the room.

"We try to be a happy group," Rebecca explained. "There's a lot going on, and we need accurate, positive people. If you wanted to get a feel for the business, I'd recommend starting here. This desk is for a woman on maternity leave. You can sit here. I don't want you working as an intern for years, just long enough to get a taste for what we do.

I have a great trainer. I won't tell him who you are. If he does a poor job, let me know. I don't want any bad apples here."

"When will this lady return to work?"

"Usually they're given a year, but she called and said she would be back in six weeks. Do you want to work for six weeks? We work four days a week. That leaves you with long weekends to visit Paris, Ireland, or other tourist places. We occasionally take bus trips ourselves. You could join us."

"What should I do after six weeks?"

"You could go to another office, or you could stay here and transfer me."

"You want to be transferred?"

"Yes. Grandma isn't getting any younger."

"Well, hire me, and let's see who gets fired first."

"OK."

"I intend to do my best. I always do. I may be the baby brat, but I didn't like it. The older ones never saw me as a grownup."

"I was the last of eight, so I was a baby brat, too."

Faded Sweetheart

• • • • •

The following week, Emily started her first job in the corporate world. She dressed professionally and thought she looked right for the job. She faced a bit of a language barrier, because the English didn't speak Southern, but Emily was put on the French side of things, and she communicated with them very well. Eventually, everyone spoke English, too.

Her trainer was interesting. He did a good job, but he called her strange names like "Lovey" and "Dear." Rebecca told her that was local slang, and Emily ignored it.

Andrew and Billy met for lunch at the Panera's, "I'm worried about our little sister. She had no business going to Europe."

Andrew responded, "She doesn't have a job or anything! Maybe, surely, she's come home when we met her in Italy."

"You think?" Billy said.

They both shook their heads. They didn't know.

Walking out the door to get back to work, "Why did we go here for lunch?" Billy asked.

"Cause Angie thinks I need to lose the baby fat."

"Does she know you had a double brownie with that salad?"

"What eats at Panera, stays at Panera." Andrew answered back.

"It that written down somewhere?" Billy asked.

"No, it's a company secret, yours and mine." Poking his little brother, "And we may have to postpone that trip a few weeks. Angie needs to get clearance from her ob before she can travel."

"Great, maybe we can look at prices too. I'll tell Julie too."

"Ok, Drew but don't tell Emily. She probably won't come."

"We just didn't train her on the fear of Brothers, did we?"

They laughed as they boarded their trucks. They thought

they still had it.

Working was a new experience for Emily. She liked it. Luckily, with long weekends, she found lots of things to do.

The first weekend, she went on a bus trip to Stonehenge. It was a long drive, but the bus had snacks available. During the trip, her trainer kept hitting on her.

"Beck, he's serious," she told Rebecca.

"Either dump him or accept a date."

"I don't know. Should I accept?"

"If you have to ask, dump him. You can find Mr. Right without those fears."

"Good idea. Will you tell him?"

"He's not hitting on me, Girlfriend. Cowboy up."

"I can't believe I'm hearing 'Cowboy up' at Stonehenge."

The trainer walked up to them. "What are you talking about, Lovey?"

"James, do you have a girlfriend?" Emily asked.

"Yes, I do. Why?"

"Then why are you hitting on me?"

"I'm hitting on you? My wife wouldn't approve."

"You've got a wife, too?"

"Emily, I don't have any time for a wife or girlfriend, but I like talking to pretty girls, and you certainly qualify. Let me be your tour guide. I'll tell you the truth about Stonehenge."

"What's that?"

"It's made of plastic. They take it down at night to keep it clean. Sometimes, the workers don't put it back in the right place, and it ruins the whole solar thing. That's why we have global warming. The guys are a little off, just like me. Do you like me any more?"

"I didn't come to England to find a boyfriend. I've got plenty of time for that later. My grandmother told me that, and she knew a lot. Please find someone else to hit on. I'm tired."

Emily and Rebecca walked away.

"An eighteen-year-old girl is tired?" Rebecca asked.

"What's he doing now?" Emily asked without looking

back.

"Why do you want to know?"

"I hate dropping my options."

"Emily, where'd you learn all this?"

"I get around. I had older brothers and sisters to learn from."

After a day of tramping around Stonehenge and listening to an energetic gray-haired man in a red plaid kilt tell them its history while he walked back and forth, they walked back to the bus. Emily feared a big wind might come up and show them more than they paid for.

"Are you still tired?" the trainer asked.

"No. I'm ready to play again. Instead of chitchat, why not take me out to dinner?"

"Dinner? I don't think...."

"...you've had any good fish and chips since you got here."

"OK. I know exactly the pub."

"You're taking her to a pub?" Rebecca asked.

"She's in England."

"It's time for the Southern belle to get drunk," Emily said.

"No."

"Well, OK. I'll find her some virgin beer."

"Do they make that in England?" Emily asked.

"Maybe at the day care."

"I just changed my mind," Emily said. "Both of you are a little insulting. I'll need a new best friend and new boyfriend." She looked around and saw a stranger sitting on the bus. "Will you be my friend?" She studied the handle hanging from the ceiling of the bus. "Do you need a new girlfriend fresh from Texas? You look like you might have a big heart. It seems I could trust you to not steer me wrong and be there for me."

"James, it looks like our work is done," Rebecca said.

"Yes. We do good work. Who should we call?"

"She needs a doctor."

"Doctor Who?"

"I know him," Emily said. "Let's find the Tardis."

"I'll knock you up around seven," James said.

"That'll give me time to call my big brothers."

James looked at Rebecca. "What's she talking about?"

"It's an American thing."

"It has to do with shotguns," Emily added.

"What?"

"Don't worry. It'll take them awhile to come after you," Rebecca said.

"Stop scaring him," Emily said, pointing to the strap. "My boyfriend here doesn't do much. He just hangs around. You might be more fun."

The bus ride was long and bumpy. When it was over, the obvious man was acting a little less. Rebecca stepped back and watched the young people mix, not mate. James might be fun for Emily, but he wasn't the one. She just arrived in England, and she was worth a fortune. She had the whole world ahead of her.

"Do you want to get fish and chips with us?" Emily asked.

James bit his lip and waited.

"No, thanks," Rebecca said. "I've got work to do. Day trips wash my work time."

"You work weekends?"

"If we're going to Paris next week, I am."

"Don't believe her, Emily," James said. "She works all the time."

"Sorry I haven't been better company since I got here."

"You've been here for ten years."

"Yes."

"You're a workaholic. You need a vacation, and not to Paris. Maybe you should go home."

"That would be great, but how long could I be there?"

"I'll check my crystal ball." Emily winked at her, then turned to James, as the bus stopped at her hotel. "I live here."

"Really?"

"I just got here and haven't found a place yet. Do you want to come up, so I can change for our date?"

"Sure."

James didn't own a car. Few people his age did. They walked, biked, or took public transportation.

When he saw her room, he said, "This is bigger than my flat. How do you afford this?"

She thought fast. "I won a contest for a month in England. I even got a little spending money."

"Where?"

"A TV show called *Let's Make a Deal.*"

"Amazing. I'm impressed. I'd guess you're trying to get all the glitz in fast."

"I was thinking I might find a place to stay after a while. I want to keep the job. Rebecca's grandma is my grandma's best friend. She's like a big sister. I'm the baby. I have lots of big brothers and sisters."

He believed her. It was clear Rebecca and Emily were old friends. He had no idea she inherited the company he was working for. If they were equals, they might hit it off, or at the least, they'd have fun.

"Just sit over here, and I'll be back in a sec." She hurried to the bedroom, locked the door, and chose a cute summer dress and boots.

He looked up as she came back out. "The streets are paved here. You don't have any cow pies to walk around."

"You don't like my boots?"

"They'll grow on me."

"Great. I've been waiting for something special to wear them. Maybe we can find a place to dance."

"There won't be any square dances here."

"Let me get my American flag shawl from the closet." She looked at him, but he didn't get the joke. "I don't have any shawls. Let's go."

They walked to a nearby pub. The tiny, dark room was painted brown. Cute round tables with three or four chairs clustered around them occupied by young men and women. Two spaces opened at the bar, so James led his lady to a stool. She sat and crossed her legs. Before James had a chance to sit down, two young men came by to compliment her legs, though they said her boots.

Emily blushed and laughed. *Is this a great place or what?* she wondered.

James put his arm around her, trying to get her attention. She turned, but before she could speak, he asked, "Love, do you want a beer?"

A little perplexed by the form of address, she recalled he'd been using "Love" since they first met, so it didn't mean much. She calmed herself and said, "Give me what you're having."

"Really?"

"Yes, but make it lady-sized, and don't get me drunk...with alcohol. Drunk with other things would be OK, but don't expect anything."

James ordered two fish and chips and two pints. He tried to start a conversation, but young women kept coming up to ask Emily about her boots.

"Where'd you get them?" one asked.

"I'm from Texas," she drawled.

One of the women looked at James. "Did she say she comes from Texas?"

"Yes, but she speaks English. Why did you ask?"

"We just wondered where you got this one," the other woman blurted.

Emily looked at him. "Do you have a closet full of women I don't know about?"

"Only dead ones."

"You kill me." She knew Rebecca would never let her date a killer.

"I just want to kill you with affection."

When the drinks and food arrived, Emily looked at the table.

"What are you looking for?"

"Catsup."

"Really? We have vinegar."

"Will they bring us a salad?"

"No. It goes on the fish."

"Show me, and I'll try it."

The crispy fish and hot potatoes were good. They didn't need catsup, but that would have classified as a vegetable. The beer was very dark. Emily took small sips, reminding herself it wasn't soda.

James talked, while she listened. He was a good conversationalist. "I lived in a four-room flat with my mum and brother. When we were kids, we took the bus to school. We had to wear uniforms and ties, but we dropped the ties the moment we left campus. We always had hours of homework."

"How often did you not do your homework?"

"I'm working at the computer desk. What do you think?"

"Not often."

"Yeah. I didn't go to college. I started work at sixteen."

"Did you drop out?"

"No. You finish school here at that age. Every man in England had a band. I played guitar and drums. The Pips never made enough to buy a round of pints, but we had fun. We had nowhere to practice. My bloke, Robbie, had a spot, but his wife kicked us out, then he got kicked out. He tried to take turns living with his friends, but luckily, they got back together. He works for the government. When they have a party, we try to get a gig there. Sometimes we do, but really, we aren't very good."

Emily thought about her dream on the plane. Was he a real geek? Was the dream a warning? She shook her head and laughed.

"What did you do in Texas?" James asked.

"I lived a very sheltered life. My parents died when I was a baby, so my grandmother raised me. My brothers were still home, but they grew up when I was still in grade school. Then it was just me and Granny. She was a wonderful woman. I'll tell you about her someday."

He glanced at the wall clock. "I need to get you back. It's late, and we work tomorrow. How do you like working here?"

Looking at her mug, she saw a little splash left. "I find it interesting. Do you like working with Rebecca?"

"She's everyone's boss, but she's OK. She started when I was hired. We had to teach her correct English, but she gives everyone a fair break."

"That's very important. Nowadays, people can't be fired unless there's a ton of documentation. My grandpa warned me about good ol' boys."

"What's that?"

"Worthless people who depend on your friendship, so you can't fire them. He told me never hire a relative unless you trained him first. He was a plumber who eventually got into real estate. He made a lot of money."

"Why are you here working?"

"Grandpa and Grandma thought everyone should have a skill to support herself. They didn't approve of good ol' boys."

"You're too beautiful to be a good ol' boy."

She looked at him and thought, *How many beers has he had?*

"I'm not drunk," he said. "We learn to drink early. It's like water."

"That's good to know. Are you ready to go?"

"Sure." He stepped down and stumbled a bit. "My leg fell asleep." He slapped his leg a few times. "That's better. Which direction is your flat? I mean, your luxury hotel room?"

They walked to the hotel, but they didn't hold hands. The narrow cobblestone walkway forced them to stay close together.

"Do you want to walk me up so I'll be safe?" she asked nervously.

"Of course." He knew the hotel had a doorman and good security. It was an excuse to spend a little more time alone with her without everyone talking to her about those ugly boots.

They walked to the elevator and rode to the fifth floor.

Her room was to the right. They walked down the hall, and she opened her door.

"Go ahead and have a seat," she said. "I need to get these boots off."

She took awhile, because she wanted to wash her feet after wearing the boots. That was the only problem wearing them.

When she walked into the living area, she saw James passed out on the sofa. She placed a blanket over him. She considered removing his shoes, but she wasn't his mother or girlfriend. If he stayed asleep, she didn't need to worry about misconceptions or conceptions.

She realized she was thinking funny, probably from the beer.

She went to her room and locked the door. Since she was tired, she fell asleep fast. She liked James, but she didn't want to start anything yet. She was still too young.

Someone banged on the door.
"I need to go!"
"It's the middle of the night!" she called. "Go to bed."
"I need to go. Where's your loo?"
"My what?"
"I need to take a piss."
"Oh. It's over there." She jumped out of bed, forgetting she wore only a nightgown, and unlocked her door to point. "Over there."

He raced into the bathroom and slammed the door so loud, she hoped none of the neighbors heard.

She went back to bed, fell asleep, and dreamed he joined her to make love. Instead, he returned to the sofa after closing her door.

She knew if the story ever got out, she would have to tell her brothers they slept in separate rooms, though it was possible James saw her wearing her nightie.

• • • • •

He woke in the morning and went to check the fridge for breakfast. All he found was blueberry yogurt. "Do you eat this or put it on your face?" He sniffed it. "Yuck." He closed the fridge door.

Emily came out of her bedroom. "What's going on?"

"I was going make breakfast, but your fridge is empty."

"Did you eat my yogurt?"

"Oh, you *do* eat that."

"What did you think I did with it?"

"It's beyond me."

"Let me call down for breakfast. What do you want?"

"Can you afford room service?"

She thought fast. "It's part of the prize package."

He gave his order, and she called. "We'd like two orders and a diet Pepsi with ice." She glanced at him. "What did you want to drink?"

"Tea?"

"Hot or iced?"

He put his arms around her waist and came close to whisper. She expected something romantic.

"They don't make iced tea in England. It's always hot with milk."

"Yuck!"

He thought she meant she didn't like being held, so he backed off, as she finished the order.

She turned toward him. "I've been wondering why they brought milk every morning. I thought Grandma called ahead and told them to give me lots of milk. I could tell that the hot tea and glass of ice wasn't American iced tea. I was good, because I drank that milk every day."

"It's usually cream."

"It *did* taste funny."

"Now you know."

"Thank you, Dear."

When breakfast arrived, it resembled hot dogs and mashed

potatoes.

"Did they get the order wrong?" she asked.

"This is traditional English breakfast."

"Is this grits?" She poked at the white stuff.

"What's grits?"

"We have a lot to learn about each other. It tastes like potatoes."

"Good. It's supposed to."

They finished breakfast. James wondered if anyone would notice he wore the same clothes as the previous day.

"You weren't at work yesterday," she reminded him. "We were at Stonehenge."

"So just the folks who went will notice."

"You wear almost the same thing every day, so you'll be fine. Let's go."

"Are we taking the limo to work?"

She smiled. "Just get in. We'll be late."

The driver addressed her by name, and she did the same in return, making him smile. That was the first morning he picked her up with a friend. She seemed happy.

At the Roscoe Corporation, the driver opened the door and offered her his hand.

James dug in his pocket for a tip. Emily knew it wasn't necessary, but she let him do it. Surprised, the driver accepted the quid. "Thanks, Mate." He tipped his hat and closed the door, then got behind the wheel and drove off.

They walked inside.

"A very interesting weekend," James said.

"Yes, indeed-y," she replied.

"What?"

"That's Texan."

"I might need lessons."

"It will ruin you. Your mother won't understand."

"Me or your language?"

"Has she ever understood you?"

"Oh, I forgot." He touched her shoulder and turned toward his cubicle. She went to find the ladies' room.

She couldn't wait to tell Rebecca, but that had to be in private. Like her life, Emily wanted her new love to be discreet.

It was hard staying focused on work. She wanted to talk to her grandma about everything. She might need to talk to Julie, too.

CHAPTER TWELVE
Emily Calls Home

Emily called Julie, but she got the time change wrong. Julie usually worked the evening shift, when Rook could be home with the kids. They had ball practice and were already home when the phone rang. By then, the kids were in bed.

"What's going on?" Rook asked. "Have you found a boyfriend?"

"Why do you ask?"

"You sound just like your sister when we first met. Tell your brother-in-law about this guy. What's his name? How'd you meet? Is there anything I need to worry about?"

Should I tell him? she wondered. *Not yet.* "His name is James. I don't know his last name. He works with me at the Roscoe Corporation. Oops. I wasn't supposed to say that."

"You're working?"

"Yes. I ran into Rebecca, Miss Lucy's granddaughter. She suggested I hang around to, well, learn about life."

"She hired you?"

"Yes. She's the boss of the England branch. One of the ladies is on maternity leave, so they had an opening."

"What do you do?"

"I'm on the computer a lot. Since I speak French, I correspond with the French division."

"Wow, Little Sister. I'm impressed. Should we keep this our little secret?"

"That would be great, and the same goes for the boy. I don't want all that advice from Julie and the brothers."

"OK, but at least get his full name and birth date. I want to Google him and make sure he isn't a rapist."

"Oh, he's good. He didn't mess with me last night when he stayed over."

"He what?"

"Oh, nothing."

"Go ahead and spill your guts. If you don't tell me, I'll call Julie. Better yet, I'll call Bill and Andrew right away. If they get a call at this time of night, you'll be home tomorrow morning."

"OK. We went to a pub."

"A what?"

"To get fish and chips. We both had pints."

"They put food in canning jars?"

"No. It was dark beer."

"Very funny. I knew that."

"OK. When we walked home, I suggested he walk me to my suite for my safety."

"I thought you were in a high-class place with a doorman."

"Yes, but...."

"Go ahead."

"I wore my boots. When we got back, I asked him to sit down while I changed out of them."

"Only the boots?"

"Of course. I thought my feet might smell, so I washed them. When I got back to the living area, he was passed out, so I covered him with a blanket and went to bed with my door locked."

"Locked doors are good."

"Around four A.M., he started banging on my door, because he needed a bathroom. I let him in, then I went back to bed and passed out. I was really tired."

"And?"

"He went back to the sofa."

"You think?"

"What? I'm sure. Surely, I would have woken up if...."

"As your adopted father, I have to tell you that you never invite a drunk man whose last name you don't know into your bedroom."

"Yes, Dad." She laughed.

"Please be careful. You're awful young."

"I'm the same age as Grandma, Mom, and Julie."

"Look what happened to them!"

"Yeah, they lived happily ever after."

"You're making this difficult. Does Rebecca think he's OK?"

"Yes. I asked her."

"At least you're checking references."

"Rook, do you talk in your sleep?"

"No. Why?"

"This needs to be our secret until further notice."

"I can keep a secret, but keep me in touch. I won't even say you're working."

"OK. It's mainly so I can gain some knowledge."

"Did Grandma give you the corporation?"

"How would you know about that?"

"I knew her before you did. She was very active in managing that company. She didn't flaunt it, even to the people who worked there. She knew her stuff, though. I think she picked the right person for the job."

"Thank you. That's another secret."

"OK. I'll tell the others that you called, saw Stonehenge, and had fish and chips."

"That's perfect. You can add that everyone loved the boots Julie made me bring."

"Good. Wear them often. They're a good defensive weapon."

"Good night, Rook. Thank you."

"Good night, Emily. Glad you're having fun."

She hung up and fell asleep, glad she had someone to talk to.

• • • • •

The following weeks were interesting. James thought Emily needed a less-expensive place to live, so he became her real-estate agent.

"Is this a safe neighborhood?" she asked, looking around.

"There are locks on the doors."

"Can I walk the streets without being robbed? I'm from a small town, where I knew almost everyone. I knew the police, and they looked after me."

"Sweetie...."

"Where'd you get that word?"

"You've called me that. Do you prefer what I call you?"

"Maybe we should use our given names. Hi. I'm Emily Queen."

"Your last name is Queen?"

"I was born in Bishop."

"Like a chess game?"

"Yes. What's your name, Sir?"

"My name is Colin James Parker. I was born in Liverpool, and my mum moved us to London to find a better job. Dad was a sailor, but he died at sea when I was twelve. Mum barely made enough to keep us in our flat. I had to work early to help support Mum and my brother. If I hadn't been so tired by working, I could've finished school and gone to university.

That didn't happen. I was lucky enough to get a job with Rebecca, and Mum now lives in a nice place. Rebecca helped with that."

"I didn't know that."

"She said she'd never tell anyone. Mum's place is a safe neighborhood. It's just around the corner from here."

"Let's see what she has."

"It's an apartment above a bakery."

"Yum!"

"She works there and does pretty well."

"Was she always a baker?"

"No. She started that job when Rebecca got her the apartment."

"Is she a wonderful cookie maker?"

"No. She's an accountant. She worked for Roscoe, but then she had kids, so Rebecca found a place where she could work from home."

"Doesn't she like going to work?"

"My brother needs care twenty-four hours a day. She can watch over him while she works, though she bakes, too. She has time for both. Do you want to meet her and my brother?"

"Don't you think you should call first and make sure that's OK?"

"She knows you're coming. I told her all about you."

"OK. I'll need my boots."

"Really?"

"My sister said they were my weapon against bad guys. I can protect you with my pointy toes."

Emily's phone rang. "Hello?"

"Who is it, Luv?" James asked.

She covered the mouthpiece with her hand. "It's my brother." She talked into the phone. "So, Andy, what's going on?"

"We're packing our bags. We can't wait to see you."

"You're coming to London?"

"No, we're going to Rome, and you're going to meet us, remember?"

"Oh, yeah. When will you arrive?"

"Emily, it's been six weeks! We're boarding our plane in

three hours. I thought you'd want to see me, Angela, and the kids."

"The kids are coming, too?"

"We rented a villa. You can share a room with Christina."

"Wow. You've got it all planned. I can't wait to see you again. How long will you stay?"

"Two weeks. Isn't that great? Maybe you can get a ticket to ride back home with us. Have you had enough of Europe yet?"

"I haven't even seen Paris yet."

"What the hell have you been doing?"

"The usual."

"Sleeping and shopping?"

"You got it, Bro. I'm eating right now. Let me get a plane for Rome, and I'll call you by tomorrow. How about right after you land, so I can find you?"

"Why don't you rent a car so you can pick us up?"

"I'll send a car for you and your family. We shouldn't drive here. They do it all backward. Love you. Can't wait to see you. Send me the name of your villa. *Ciao.*"

She closed the phone. "I need to sit down."

"What's wrong?" James asked.

"I forgot all about them coming to Italy. They think I'm just sitting around Europe, sleeping and shopping, and I'm probably pretty lonely."

"I don't understand."

"I need to talk to Rebecca."

"OK."

She called Rebecca. "Rebecca, I'm in real trouble."

"Oh, no! He didn't!"

"What? No, not that! My brother and his family are flying to Rome tomorrow, and they expect me to meet them."

"So?"

"They'll be in Europe for two weeks. They think I have the time to stay with them, and they want me to go back home when they do."

"Is that what you want?"

Faded Sweetheart

"Well, no. I have the job you gave me. I'd like to finish that. Then there's James."

"Answer yes or no. Is he standing beside you?"

"Yes. We're on speaker phone."

"Well, then, you can fly to Rome right after work on Thursday and tell your family you can stay until Wednesday morning. Then you have a special trip planned with me to go to...I don't know. How about Scandinavia?"

"That sounds good."

"OK. Problem solved."

"What about James?"

"Is he still on speaker phone? Maybe I can get a few good days' work out of him."

"He just walked away."

"OK, but...."

"He's back. What were you saying?"

"He's a great guy. Maybe I can plan a business trip for him to our Rome office."

James grabbed the phone. "You'd do that for me?"

"Whose phone is this?" Rebecca asked.

"It's mine," Emily said, "but I guess we share."

"Cute."

"Later, thanks. By the way, if I'm returning on Wednesday, who'll cover for me?" Emily asked.

"You'll get a PC hookup at your place, and you'll work there next weekend."

"Oh. Thanks, I guess."

"Happy to assist."

CHAPTER THIRTEEN

Going to Rome

Emily looked at James. "We've got a lot to do. I need to book a flight to Rome for Thursday night and return on Wednesday morning. I'll have to pack, then I have to buy gifts for my nieces and nephews."

"How many are you expecting?"

"I'll bet they're all coming. They plan to take me home with them when they go, too."

"Why do you think they're all coming?"

"Because that's how my family does things. I'm surprised they didn't come the first time."

"I thought you said this was a prize from *Let's Make a Deal.*"

"We need some pillow talk—on the sofa, that is."
"OK. Let's pick up some food and get started."
"I thought we were going to meet your family?"
"Sure, but we have to leave early, because there's a lot to do."

"I'm so happy to finally meet you," James' mother said. "All he talks about is you."
"It's a pleasure to meet you, too," Emily said. "What a lovely home you have."
The steps leading to the second floor were steep, but the living room was bright and filled with flowers.
"You must love flowers." Emily looked around. "They're on the wallpaper, and you've got plants and ceramic figurines."
"I do, but I hate the wallpaper."
"Do you have permission to replace it?"
"Yes, but I'll need help."
"Next week, I'll be out of town to see my family, so James can help you."
"I don't know how to do that," he said.
"I can show you. Can we start now?"
James looked at her. "You said you had to buy plane tickets and pack gifts for your nephews and nieces."
"Yes, but...." She found a Chore Girl plastic scrubber on the sink. "May I borrow this?" She took a dishrag, too. "If you wet down the paper, then move the scrubby in circles, it peels right off. Get something like this spatula to peel off even more. There are chemicals that do the same thing, but this looks pretty easy. Do you want to repaint the walls or have them repapered?"
"I was thinking of different wallpaper, but paint might be OK. James' brother, Joseph, like to draw. That's his talent."
"Mom, we really have to go. Where's Joseph?" James asked.
"He's working downstairs."
"What does he do?"

"He cleans up."

"Oh."

"It's the perfect job for him. He can stay in the building and gets to be his own person."

"When does he get off work?"

"He'll be gone for a while. He just left. Maybe you can meet him later. He can help you take down the wallpaper. Thanks for your help, Emily."

Emily shook her hand. "It was nice to meet you."

"My pleasure. Hope you enjoy your trip."

"I'm sure I will. Good night."

Emily and James returned to her hotel room to go online and order plane tickets. James ordered room service, because they were both hungry, and Emily needed to sort through her clothes.

"You don't have many clothes, do you?" he asked, standing in the closet, trying to help.

"Is that a joke, or are you serious?"

"I've never been in a girl's closet before. I didn't know what to expect."

"I have clothes back in Texas. I didn't know what to bring. I hadn't planned on staying a long time."

He looked sad. "Do you think you might want to change your mind?"

She gave him a light kiss on the lips—their first kiss. "You're sweet, but I don't know what I have in mind. I just lost my grandmother, who raised me since I was a baby. I finished high school and might have all my brothers and sister waiting for me in Italy. There are plenty of emotions going through me. You're my Stonehenge. You're amazing, but I can't answer questions right now."

He kissed her again. "Then let's get back to work."

She put her arms around his neck, while they stood in the closet, and they kissed a few more times.

"This is almost my favorite room," she said.

"I never knew about girl's closets."

"I never even played Dare."

Faded Sweetheart

"What's that?"

"It's a party game where couples go into closets for a few minutes."

"You're kidding."

"I went to very few parties. Grandma and I didn't do parties." She thought about that, knowing very few young people would party with their grandmothers. "I had friends my age, and we had fun. I guess when Grandpa died, I spent more time with Grandma. I was afraid she'd be lonely."

I hate being so honest with him, she thought. *Why does he make me so comfortable?*

Smiling, she touched his hand. "I had friends, but we never went to parties." After patting his hand, she released it.

He waited until she finished talking. "The only parties I went to were ones I played for. I saw a few wild ones but never participated."

"Are we having our own party right now?"

"Yes, but we need to stop. I mean we should postpone this until we have more time."

After a final hug, they separated and looked at the outfits in the closet.

"Where can I find good things for kids?" she asked. "It could be British."

"We can do that tomorrow after work, or we could ask at work if they'd be willing to part with some of the stuff they hand out."

"OK. Our food just arrived. Let's eat."

After they ate, it was late.

"I have to go home," James said.

"I'll see you at work tomorrow. Thanks for all the help in the closet."

"Anything for you, Luv."

She held his lapel and pulled him close. "Here's a kiss for the road."

"It's a long way. I might need more." He kissed her again.

"Time's wasting. You gotta go. I love you."

Her words surprised her. She hadn't expected to say

anything like that. When she was with her family, she said that often. She hoped he didn't notice.

He did. He looked in her eyes, smiled, and walked away looking really happy.

• • • • •

As the week passed quickly, the two young lovers tried to control themselves. She had to leave for Rome in the morning, and he didn't want to go home.

"You have to go, James. I've got to get some sleep before I find out how many relatives I have to face."

"I could stay here and send you off."

"Would you let me sleep?"

"What kind of sleep did you have in mind?"

He stayed.

• • • • •

In the morning, James was very helpful. He called room service for breakfast and added catsup. He also called the driver to come get her bags.

Emily walked out of the bedroom and saw everything was ready. "Wow. You got everything done. Thanks."

"I told you I'd be helpful. The driver's downstairs with your luggage. Let's go."

She checked her purse. "I have my ticket. Thanks, James." She hugged him. "I'll miss you."

He kissed her hand. "I'll miss you, too." Dropping her hand, he held her tight.

"Wow, that's a good one!" she said.

"Aren't they all?"

"Yes, but that was *really* good."

"Thanks. When you're back, they'll all be like that."

"How can I leave after hearing that?"

"Should I call your brother and tell him you aren't coming?"

"No. I'd better go. It'll only be for a few days." She pushed him away. "Love you."

He smiled and opened the door for her. They rode down in the elevator and saw the chauffeur waiting in the lobby.

"Coming with me?" she asked.

"Maybe the driver can drop me off at the office."

"OK."

"Maybe we can smooch on the way."

"You're so embarrassing."

After the driver dropped James off, he drove Emily to the airport. Emily carried her bags to the check-in counter. When she opened one, she saw a note from James.

Emily my Luv,
I hope you have a great time with your family, but I'll wait every minute until you come back to me. You make me full.
Love, James

She folded the note and put it in her purse, wiping her eye with her free hand. She heard her flight announced by the loudspeakers, and she hurried, arriving just in time.

She found her seat on the plane and relaxed. *I'm having a wonderful, interesting time in England. This trip was a good idea. I've been living on my own, kind of.*

What's going on with James? I hardly know him, and I keep saying I love him. Do I? Grandma, I wish you were here. What's going on?

• • • • •

She landed in Rome after a short flight, her mind so full of thoughts, she had no chance to sleep. She thought about Grandma, the person who'd been her entire world, and how she was making a new world for herself.

This is almost a pity party. Why did I lose everyone I loved? My parents died when I was young, but Grandma hung around for almost eighty-five years. She was sharp until the day she died. She even made breakfast for us that day! She was a wonderful person, and now I'm getting off a plane to face my family, and I don't want to discuss my love life.

She looked for a familiar face, as she entered the baggage claim area. Then she saw several people trying to get her attention. One was Billy. Julie was waving frantically. Rook held onto the boys looking guilty. Andrew, holding the baby, got up from a chair with Angela.

Emily took out her phone and snapped a picture, wanting to let James know who was waiting. *I hope they got a large villa,* she thought. *I don't want to share space with anyone, except maybe a certain guy from England. I have to remember I don't have any love life.*

They helped her find and carry her bags, one holding clothes, the other full of gifts. They went outside to a large van. Luckily, it came with a driver.

Driving in Italy was scary. People in Europe didn't seem to have any road sense. All of them were crazy drivers.

After everyone was sufficiently shaken to induce nausea, the van finally stopped before a beautiful, white, six-foot wall with ornate iron gate. It opened, and they drove in, then everyone got out.

"This is our place for the next two weeks," Julie said. "Andy, get those bags. Billy, tip the driver."

"We don't have to tip him," Rook said. "He's already been paid. He's self-employed."

"OK, but we might need him for sightseeing, and I want him to know we appreciate his help."

Angela, Andrew's wife, said, "I already told him. I speak Italian." She was also the one who rented the villa for them.

It was an amazing place, with high ceilings, chandeliers, sconces, crystal, and iron work. The back of the house had an outdoor eating area with tables. A vineyard grew along one wall.

"We've been sitting back and drinking wine here since we arrived," Andy told her.

"Since when have you started drinking wine?" Emily

asked.

"Since we have so much of it. It's good, too."

"There's no air-conditioning," Billy added. "This is the only place that's cool."

"You need to open the windows," Angela said. "That's how they do it around here."

"Let's show you your room," Julie said. "There's enough space that you can have your own."

"Thank You, God," Emily whispered.

"What did you say?" seven-year-old Becca asked, slipping between Emily and Julie.

"Your little hand made me happy I'm here. Family is special. I can't explain it."

Emily's room was small, but a balcony overlooked the grapevines. When Julie opened the windows, a hot blast of wind came in. "This will get better in the evening. The temperature drops pretty fast. I'd suggest wearing cotton, because it's cooler."

"I had some cotton outfits, but I couldn't bring everything. I'll just have to sweat."

"Maybe you can borrow something from Angela. She's gotten skinny after having the baby. Another feature we can offer you is the bathroom. Expect it to be terrible."

She was right. Emily saw a toilet and an old sink.

"Wasn't this room hit during World War One?" Emily asked.

"It probably was, but they thought it still worked."

"They were wrong, weren't they?" Emily bent down to see Becca eye-to-eye.

"This makes my messy room look good, Aunt Em."

"I'll try to clean it. That might help," Julie said, walking back downstairs to the others. "Best of luck. We're getting ready to make dinner. Are you hungry, or did you want to unpack and chill for a while?"

"Let me change, and I'll come down with you. I don't want to waste family time being alone."

"Great. Rook didn't think you'd say that. He thinks he's

an expert." Julie and Becca sat on the bed, while Emily changed.

"Do I have to give you a show?" Emily asked.

"Oh, we'll leave you alone. Listen for the voices when you're ready."

"OK. Thanks."

Emily was glad to see her family again. They'd always been close, but it seemed odd to reconnect with them in Italy. They all took time off work to make the trip, because they missed her.

If I decide to stay in England, will I get new neighbors who eat potato chips with their wine? I hope none of my family have tried that.

She let her mind relax. The women were sophisticated enough, though the men met her at the airport in blue jeans. She almost expected them to have cowboy hats. James would flip out.

"Did you say something?" Tre, Billy's son, asked.

"I wondered if your daddy brought a hat with him."

"You bet. He wore it on the plane, too. They made him take it off at check-in to have it X-rayed. They said they never saw one that old and beat up. Uncle Andy had his baseball cap checked, too." He snuggled up close and asked, "Do you think they're getting bald?"

"I don't think so. I hope not. I'll go check just in case."

They walked down a long staircase. In its prime, the villa must have been magnificent, but she noticed wear on the steps. If someone came down in the dark and hit that chipped marble, he might fall the rest of the way. The banister wasn't that sturdy, either. At least Grandma wasn't there. She stopped using steps shortly before she died, because she feared breaking a hip, even though the doctors could repair a broken hip as good as new. It was hard for some people to change their minds.

"What are we having for lunch?" she asked.

"I'm grilling hamburgers," Bill said.

"We're in Italy, and we're having hamburgers?" his wife

asked.

"Sounds good to me," Andy said. "We can't eat pizza all the time."

"Ladies, we need to find a cook to make local food," Julie said.

"Let me make a call," Emily said, dialing Rebecca's number. "Does the local Roscoe have a chef who works small dinner parties?"

"Is your brother grilling hamburgers?"

"How'd you know?"

"You're asking for a cook, and I know your brothers. I'll call. Expect someone to call you within the hour."

"You're the best. How's it going over there?"

"It's only been one day, but someone really misses you. I'll tell him you called and asked about him."

"Thanks, but don't have him call me yet. They don't know."

"You don't think so, but you might be glowing."

"It's the heat. There's no AC down here or a pool."

"Is this BillyAnn or AndyBeth?"

"I'm sorry. You know how us Texans are. You were one, too."

"I still make ice in my office and the flat."

"Go, Cowboys! I'll have some funny stories to tell later. Thanks, 'Bye."

CHAPTER FOURTEEN
Eating Italian

The women watched Emily call and handle the situation.

"Wow," Julie said. "Our baby has grown up."

They converged around her.

"Did you find a cook?"

"Yes. Someone will call in an hour or so. Maybe they can tell us how to shop around here, too, which would help. We're too big a group to go out to eat too much."

"It would be healthier for the children to eat here."

"This is a beautiful place. It's old, but it's lovely."

"I'm glad you could get off work."

"You're working?" one asked.

"Why?"

"Just to see how the business works."

"Why'd you need to go so far away to figure it out?"

"She wanted to spread her wings," April, Julie's oldest daughter, said. "You guys love her so much, she's almost suffocated. Nobody thought she'd last a week in England, but look at her. She loves it."

"Really, Honey?" Julie eyed her daughter, who was the tallest female there. "You may be right." She looked at her little sister. "You're growing up right in front of us. If you want to stay here awhile, we'll have to let you go. Maybe we could move to England until you're tired of it."

"Actually, my job is only to cover for a woman on maternity leave."

"So she'll be back in a week or two?"

"Most of the women are gone from there months to three years."

"OK." Julie turned away to hide her tears. "That must be nice for them." She turned back, but her lip quivered. First, they lost Grandma, and now Emily lived so far away.

"We need to go shopping," Emily said, hoping to break the tension. "Let's get dressed for it." She even wore her boots.

"You're wearing my boots," Julie said.

"I've gotten lots of compliments on them."

"Are they comfy?"

"Yes, except I worry about smelly feet afterward."

"There's boot spray for that."

"Not in England."

"That's why we have eBay."

"Of course."

"Let's do some local stuff. Who wants to drive?"

"The driver. Will you leave the baby with Daddy?"

"I guess. We need to shop."

• • • • •

They found wonderful things after looking around the stores. Within thirty minutes, the chef called Emily, but he didn't speak much English, so she handed the phone to Angela. He suggested they meet him at the market.

They found him easily, but he wore shorts and a T-shirt. He apologized, because he was home when he got the call, and he didn't have time to change.

"What would you like to eat?" he asked in Italian.

Emily spoke a little French to him, which he understood, and they compared ideas. He showed the ladies what to look for when buying fish, a staple in that area.

In the seasoning section, almost everything was fresh and smelled wonderful. They would be in Italy for only two weeks, so they knew the fresh herbs and spices would keep.

Looking serious, the chef asked, "Do you have a pasta machine?"

They looked at each other. None of them had checked the cupboards.

"I'll be there around seven to start dinner," he promised.

They thought that would mean a late dinner, but they soon learned that late meals were the norm in Italy. He sent the ladies to the bakery to buy snacks or tapas before their dinner.

They loaded all the food into the car and went back to the villa. The men were hungry and complained about having poor TV choices. It was all in Italian, and there was no baseball, only soccer.

As the women unpacked groceries, the men stood across the kitchen island and asked what was for dinner.

"Why so much fish?" one asked.

They ate the bakery items and the tapas. The men thought it would be a good time to nap afterward, even in the heat. Their wives reported the men stripped down to their boxers and slept, while the wives placed new clothes on the dressers for the men to wear that evening.

Faded Sweetheart

The women wore their new dresses. The doorbell rang, and the chef arrived with an assistant.

"Are we supposed to wear special clothes for this dinner?" Emily asked in French, the only foreign language she knew. "We bought new clothes for the men, but if they should wear suits, please tell us."

"If you were eating in my restaurant," the chef replied, "Yes. Here, it's OK to wear what you wish. I just hope you enjoy the meal."

"Anything beats hamburgers," Angela said.

"Oh, no! That's what I planned to make."

"Really?"

"No. Where's the kitchen?"

"Over here. Can we watch?"

"I don't usually have an audience, but if there's space, I can make you into scullery maids." He poured wine for everyone and started work.

"This will be a seven-course meal," he explained. "First, we start with antipasti."

"What's that?" Rook asked.

"It's a starter, usually sausage and olives and peppers in olive oil. Here. Help yourself and share with the others."

The assistant passed out small plates and forks, and everyone tried it. It was so good, the men cleaned their plates, and then came soup.

The group realized they'd paid so much attention to eating, they missed the soup preparation.

"This is delicious," one said. "Do I see shrimp in here?"

"Yes," the chef replied. "It's a typical fish soup."

The men finished their bowls eagerly. The main course was next. Grilled fish, vegetables, and wonderful bread. The men felt really full, but they finished their plates, then it was time for pasta with red sauce and meatballs. It looked familiar but tasted much better than at home.

"You've had us stuffing our faces so much, we missed most of your cooking," someone said.

"It was delicious," Andrew said.

"We still have dessert," the chef added.
"You're kidding."
"I promised seven courses. We need dessert."
"I guess we'll need to man up," Bill said, looking at Andrew and Rook. "OK. Give it your best shot." He sat down on his bar stool.
"This looks like ice cream," a woman said.
"Actually, Young Lady, it's sorbet."
They ate the final course, and Rook asked, "When's breakfast?"
"Are you kidding?" Julie asked.
"I can't be ready for breakfast," Andrew said. "I'm stuffed."
"Usually, we eat fresh fruit," the cook explained, "and maybe a croissant for the first meal of the day."
"Sounds delicious."
"Where's your restaurant, so we can make reservations?"
"Here's my card. It's been a pleasure to serve the Roscoe family." The chef handed business cards to them, collected his assistant, and left.
The men looked at each other. "Where'd that guy come from?" one asked.
"Well...," Emily said.
"Well what?"
"Since we're in Italy, I called Rebecca to see if she knew how we could have some authentic food. She called the Rome office, and they sent their best for Mrs. Roscoe's kids."
"I feel bad using Grandma's previous marriage to have dinner," someone said.
"You may not know it, but during our life with her, she was the head of that company," Emily said. "The man who's the current head said she was the one who really improved the business. Her husband wasn't that good at it. Mrs. Roscoe 'put the human element' into the company."
They felt even prouder of their grandma.
"We were so lucky to find her."
The boys looked at Julie, who held Rook's hands.

"Thanks for running away, Sis."

"I wasn't running away," Julie said. "I was trying out my wings before school started."

"Mom, you never said you went joy riding at eighteen," her son said.

"There's a reason for that," Rook said. "Girls fall in love with the first guy they meet."

"I had previous boyfriends," Julie said.

"That doesn't matter. I'm talking to our daughter. Do what we say, not what we do."

"You're so funny."

"That's why your mom fell in love with me."

"You two need a room, and the rest of us need to go to bed," Andrew said. "Emily, thanks for a great dinner. We need to get out more."

"Yeah. You used your resources wisely."

"They were yummy, Aunt Emily," Lot, Julie's son, said.

"Any time. Good night."

• • • • •

Emily's phone rang in the middle of the night. "Hello?" she asked sleepily.

"Hi, Honey. Were you sleeping?"

"I just put on my nightgown, and I'm looking at the stars. It's so quiet and peaceful."

"Are you having a good time?"

"It could be better, but family is a duty. My sister cried when I told her I could be working that woman's job for three years."

"She's back, but don't tell your sister. Rebecca can find you another position."

"Maybe we can be office buddies."

"I want more than that."

"Oh, you do?"

"Yes. Don't you?"

"You need to make me an offer."

"I can do that."

"Really?"

"I've got the ring to prove it."

"You've got a ring?"

"Yeah. My phone rings every time you call me."

"Is it beautiful?"

"Not as beautiful as you are."

"All right, James."

The door opened.

"Are you still up?" Julie asked. "Are you talking to someone?"

"It's a guy from work," Emily said, trying to hide the phone. "It's about work."

"They call a temp in the middle of the night?"

"It's not the middle of the night in England."

"Let me talk to him!" Julie grabbed the phone. "I've heard a lot about you, James. Why don't you fly down, so we can meet you?"

"Julie, how'd you know?" Emily asked.

"Rook talks in his sleep. April borrowed his computer and noticed he was snooping on someone."

"Rook checked him out?" Emily was astonished.

"He's like your big brother."

"So how many others know?"

"James?" Julie asked. "You still there?"

"Yes."

"We're going on speakerphone, so you don't miss anything. Rook made me swear not to tell the others. We want you to tell them yourself."

"What do you think they'll say?" Emily asked.

"You proved yourself at dinner. They're impressed with the way you went to England and got a job. They might love both of you."

"That's good news."

"Anyway, I need my sleep. You guys can do whatever you want…on the phone. James, the women in this family usually fall in love fast and get pregnant at the first exposure.

That's important information." She blew kisses at Emily, as she left.
"She was a wealth of information" James said.
"Do you suppose she's right?"
"We'll have to see."
"Is she still listening at the door?"
"I forgot about that."
"You'll be an asset to the family. We always needed a spy."
"Call out, 'Good night, Julie!' and see if she replies."
"Good night, Julie!" Emily said. "No reply. Is she there, or is she refusing to answer?"
"Don't know, but it's getting late. Are you tired?"
"Yeah, but I wanted to say good night."
"Good night."
Emily hung up feeling happy and a bit perturbed.

• • • • •

Emily found Rook the next morning and asked, "Do you really talk in your sleep?"
"Who said that? I've been told I snore, but I don't believe that, either."
"How did Julie know?"
"About what?"
"You mean about whom."
"Whom?" Andrew asked.
"This was supposed to be a private conversation, but I might as well make an announcement. I have a boyfriend, and I think, well, I know, that I love him."
"Yeah!" They applauded, and the kids danced around Emily.
"Leave me alone," she said. "I don't know if I really, *really* love him. How does anyone know?"
"You don't. You have to wait and see."
"OK, People. We have to let Emily and James see."
The kids laughed, unable to understand love like that, but

the adults nodded. Their grandmother told them how precious love was and how, even after years of darkness, true love might fade but would spark when two people were reunited. That's how it worked for Grandma.

• • • • •

There was a knock at the door. Julie, being the nosy one, answered. "You must be James."

"How can you tell?" he asked.

"We weren't expecting anyone, and you're carrying a suitcase."

"Good guess. How do you do, Julie? If I may interject, you look just like your sister. Where's my beautiful love?"

Julie assumed he was from England or France. No wonder Emily was so taken with him.

Emily and James planned to act out a bit for the family. She grabbed him at the doorway, he dropped his bag, and he picked her up in a very long kiss.

"Kids, stop that!" Rook said. "We have children here." He knew the children were actually playing outside.

Lot, April's brother, came in. "What did we miss?"

"Nothing," Emily said quickly, realizing that their little drama meant more to her than she expected. Was she consumed with true love?

"Who's this?" Angela asked.

"Emily's boyfriend," Rook said.

"Uh-oh. What does that mean?"

"Nothing yet," Emily said quietly. "We have to wait and see. Be nice to him."

"That's no fun," Bill said.

"Trust me. If you pick on me, I'll tell Grandma." She used the phrase she once used as a little girl. "We have a direct connection from heaven." She pointed upward with one finger. "Leave me alone."

James, listening to the banter, turned to Julie. "Does this go on for long?"

"It's been a hot topic since she learned to talk," Julie explained. "Billy was the baby for so long, he enjoyed being older. Actually, they're good friends."

"They've had no drama lessons, either," Andrew added.

"I'm getting ready to buy groceries. Who wants to come?" Julie asked.

The adults left Emily and James to watch the kids, including the baby.

"This'll keep you busy," Rook said.

"What if she takes a nap?"

"The other four won't. Have a nice afternoon. James, you can bunk with the boys. Show him his room, Guys."

The kids played in the backyard, while the baby played in her pack. Emily poured wine for James.

"Do you want a snack?" she asked. "Are you hungry?"

"Yes, but we're watching the kids. This will do." Instead of drinking his wine, he got up and kissed her. "I have only a few days. I have to be back at work next week, and I'll work the weekend, too. I was wondering if you'd like to go to Venice with me. We could get over there fast and be back in time to catch a plane home."

CHAPTER FIFTEEN

Venice

"I never thought about Venice," Emily said, "but then, I never thought I'd go to Europe. Venice would be fantastic. Rome's wonderful, and it'll be even better with you. Let me see if we can get dinner reservations at that restaurant."

"Which restaurant?"

"We were eating grilled hamburgers, and I called Rebecca to see if she knew of a cook who could make us an authentic Italian dinner. She sent a chef from corporate to us."

"Wow. She must really have clout."

"Honey, I need to tell you, before my grandmother married my grandpa, her last name was Roscoe."

"You're the heiress?"

"No. I'm just Emily. My grandmother was the heiress. It's complicated. I'll tell you on our honeymoon."

"Oh?"

"Does that sound good to you?"

"Everything about it sounds interesting. Are we ready for that?"

"No. We should try to hold out. We have to make our plans and see if this is the real thing."

"Did you miss me?"

"Yes." She sat in his lap and looked him in the eye, ready for a kiss. "It wasn't easy telling them how I feel about you."

"Seems like they already knew."

"I gave a family announcement at breakfast yesterday."

"Were you fighting with Bill?"

"Yeah, but it's not real fighting. That's just how we talk. Lucky for me, everyone, including this little infant, heard me."

"I hope she can keep this secret." He held her close and kissed her. "Do you think if we gave all the children a nip of this, they'd take a nap?"

"I think they'd tell on us and ask their parents for more."

"Actually, I've heard that Italian children drink wine from the time they're babies."

"We're from Texas. We drink soda pop, but parents frown on giving their kids too much of that, because it causes cavities and obesity."

"Oh."

"You're funny." She picked up the baby to change her, hoping they'd drop the subject. James went outside to play catch with the kids. They didn't have any baseball bats, and there were big balls, but there was no basketball hoop.

"Have you ever heard of soccer?" he asked them.

"Yes."

"Let's play that. That's what these balls are for."

Emily watched from the window after changing the baby's diaper. Her niece was a perfect baby. It felt like being a mother would be easy, but she hoped that wouldn't happen too soon.

Making Kool-Aid for the kids, she encouraged them to come inside and cool down. It was funny to think of the house as cool, when they had all the fans running. Getting out of the sun would relieve the kids from the heat.

They watched TV. James found an English program the others were willing to watch. The baby slept in her crib, and Emily made open-faced sandwiches for the others.

• • • • •

The family returned with bags and baskets full of food.

"Why'd you buy so many groceries?" Emily asked.

"Because we'll be here a few more days and...."

"James and I are thinking about going to Venice."

"Venice?"

"We aren't sure how far that is, but it's closer than Texas. We thought we should go for it."

"I want to go, too," Angela said. "Maybe we should pack up this food and come with you."

"Well, Italian-speaking person, you need to find a place for twenty people."

"I'm on it. Here's the baby."

James held the baby. "She feels wet."

"She probably is. That's one of the things she does. The diapers are over there."

"I'll need help with this."

April rescued him. She liked playing with her cousin and had a lot of practice.

• • • • •

Dinner was very good and tasted Italian. The women bought bakery bread, which was delicious.

"Do you want to sight-see in Rome one more time before we leave tomorrow?"

"Sure. Let's start early, so we can pack for our next adventure."

"Why don't we pack tonight? We could have the driver either take us to the train station or drive us to Venice. We need to find out how far it is."

Faded Sweetheart

"It is only a four-hour drive, but Leo, the guy who drove me over here," James said. He paused because everybody was listening, "He suggested to me the Euro-Tran gives a good information and a drop dead scenic route. We'll see a lot more, including the Grand Canal."

Andrew was googling this. He looked up. "James is right, it says they will tell us when to take pictures. The fare was affordable, and the train has amenities."

Lot asked, "What's that?"

Julie said, "It would be more comfortable for you kids, it has a bathroom."

"April will like that." He said.

"Why did you say that?" asked Emily.

"She loves the bathroom, she asked for one last Christmas."

Emily looked at her niece, "That was a great idea, did Santa bring one?"

"No."

"Bad Santa."

The little kids looked shocked.

"Anyway, I'm excited," April said. "We can tour Rome tomorrow, then go to Venice. This will be a great story for school. I'm looking forward to writing about something other than my horse or going fishing."

"I can't imagine doing either of these things," James said. "I've never been to Italy before. It's a whole different culture."

"I'm glad you're coming with us. Let's start packing."

• • • • •

They boarded the van one last time. Mario, their driver, told them about Rome and its history, including the Coliseum, where Christians were fed to the lions. Driving through Vatican City, they saw hundreds of clergy, nuns, and people who spent all their savings to stand in St. Peter's Square, hoping to see the Pope.

"He's in South America right now," April said. "Those pilgrims will be disappointed."

"Are you?" Rook asked.

"I thought so, but I was wrong. This place is too breathtaking, even better than the pictures. We even have a car and driver who's our tour guide. This is great, Dad!"

He nodded. "That's better." He stared at the Basilica.

Mario knew when the Euro-Tran would arrive, so he ended the tour by taking them to a fine restaurant for a meal before they left. Not the biggest place to eat, it wasn't part of a franchise. The wait staff were clean and attentive, and they sang at the table for a small gratuity. Food was prepared by the owner's mother in the kitchen. She occasionally stepped out to check the dining room. She was a plump, gray-haired woman in a starchy white apron. A few strands of hair fell loose, and a heavy rope of pearls moved against her bosom, as she smiled at the tables of diners. The scent of marinara sauce emanated from her dish towel.

"Do you need more bread?" she asked. "How's the pasta? Where are you from?" She smiled, showing she needed new teeth, but her obvious warmth covered up her imperfections.

"This is *so* good!" Rook, Andrew, and Bill at the table chorused.

Angelia tried to translate that into Italian but forgot a few words. Emily said, *"Merci beaucoup."*

She reacted to Emily's French, which made her wonder if her English questions were simply memorized, and she didn't speak English.

Tre asked a question. Mama sent a kid from the kitchen to help. Grinning he showed Tre where the bathroom was, and the rest of us paid attention so we wouldn't have to ask again.

Mama Roberta patted Rook and Julie's backs, said, *"Ciao,"* and moved on to the same table to repeat her memorized questions.

It seemed she didn't need to understand English, because she was fluent in body language. When she saw the clean plates, she knew her patrons enjoyed every morsel. The children acted like they hadn't eaten in a week. Mario was a genius to bring the family there.

The family got into the van and drove to the train station, where Mario asked a porter to load the luggage. Julia, Angela, and Molly packed enough for only one day, but with that many people, it still meant a lot of luggage.

Mario showed them to the ticket window, then wished them well. All the men pulled out their wallets to tip him for his excellent service.

"Can we call you or your service when we're back tomorrow?" someone asked.

"I'll be waiting for you."

"Thank you, Mario. You're the best."

"I have a cousin in Venice who can help you with a car and accommodations. Do you want his number?"

"Certainly," Angela said in Italian. "Thank you."

"What did he say?" Bill asked.

"He knows a man for us in Venice."

"OK, great. *Gratzi,* Mario."

Julie & Andrew laughed at Bill's attempt to speak Italian. Since he was six-feet-four-inches tall, they didn't laugh at him often.

They boarded the train early enough so they could choose seats and sit together. James and Emily lagged behind, sitting a few rows past the family. During the train trip, most of the walking nephews and nieces visited the young lovers, unaware they were interrupting anything.

"She must be sleepy, because her head is on his shoulder."

"They were happy to see me. They told me to come again. Can I go back now?"

"No," the mother said. "Stay here awhile and look out the window."

"James has their window closed. He says it's too sunny."

"It probably is over there. The sun's on that side."

"Hmmm." Monica snuggled into her mother's lap, where the rhythm of the train sent her to sleep. Her mother put her earphones on again, hoping she hadn't missed too much information.

They reached Florence in two hours. It was a beautiful city, but they remained in their seats for Venice.

The steward came through to offer drinks in the bar car. Bill & Andrew & Rook decided to look. Tre was hungry again, so he ate a Monte Cristo sandwich.

"What's that?" he asked.

"It's a ham and cheese sandwich wrapped in fried bread and dusted with powdered sugar," Billy explained. He popped one-fourth of the treat into his mouth. "Yum!"

Tre cautiously took a bite and said, "Hum!" Before his parents finished looking at the Grand Canal, the plate was clean of everything except a few specks of sugar. The water was gone, too.

"You were thirsty?"

"I guess." He wiped his lips with his hand.

"Ready to return to our seats?"

"Sure. Let's go."

When they returned, Tre told the other kids about the sandwich.

"I'm surprised you could even think about eating," April said.

"Hush, Honey. You know boys are bottomless pits."

"Is that a good thing, Mom?"

"Of course. That's how you grow."

Tre looked at his dad. "I have a ways to go."

"What?" His father suddenly found himself in the discussion. "Do I have sugar on my face?"

His wife wet her finger and traced his lips. "No. You're OK." She licked her finger. "Yum!"

"This place is making you crazy, isn't it?"

"No. Just being with you and the kids is so nice. At home, we are so busy."

"We're busy here, too."

"But we're all on the same page."

"I guess."

"Next stop, Venice!" the conductor announced. "Stay seated until the train comes to a full stop!"

The kids sat and looked at the station out the window, where vendors selling food and souvenirs crowded the platform.

"Remember, Kids and Women," Andy warned, "Whatever you buy, you carry all day long and on the way home."

"What a party pooper!" Julie said.

"What a party pooper!" the kids chorused.

"Wow, Angela," Julie said, "that's a great idea. Now I can shop in peace."

"We really only came to see Emily, but this vacation is starting to be a great idea," Rook said. "This place has so much to offer."

"It's not Six Flags," Lot said.

"Yes, Cousin. I haven't seen any rides. What do Italian kids do?"

"Get up, Kids. We can get off now."

The parents herded their children and carried baby supplies. Angela handed a sleepy little girl to Aunt Emily. She didn't have any parcels, just a bag that hung off one shoulder.

Emily readjusted the baby and looked over her to make sure she could clearly see the steps off the train. James held her back to help. Angela and Julie came in the rear, waiting to see how the young couple did with the baby.

"Hold their hands!" the moms told their husbands.

The kids were ready to run around, but holding their hands was a surprise. They jumped one step ahead only to turn and see who grabbed them.

"Hi, Daddy."

Their expressions seemed to ask, *Am I in trouble already?*

"You're OK. We just don't want to lose anybody." Andrew was a good mind reader.

They walked hand-in-hand, though there were occasional tugs to look at new sights.

"Did you bring your book bag to carry all day?"

"No. Can we buy one, too?"

"Maybe we'll find something. I fear we'll be buying lots of stuff."

"We have the stroller."

"Who'll carry the baby?"

"Maybe she can learn to walk."

"She can't even sit up yet."

"Should we try a gondola before shopping?"

"Who said we wanted to shop?'

"The baby said she needed new clothes."

"Whatever. Here's where you can solicit a ride. How many can fit in a boat?"

"Looks like only one family per boat."

"We can do that," James said, hoping for a romantic ride without so many extra people around.

Andrew and his family took a red gondola. William put his family in a yellow one. Julie and Rook took their kids to a blue one. Finally, Emily and James boarded a green one.

"That's for good luck, you know," James said.

"I'm always lucky. Look who I'm with."

He gave her the first kiss of the day, then turned to the boatman. "Row slowly. We want to lose those people." He pointed at the rest of the family.

"My name is Antonio. Would you like me to sing?"

"Does he know the Ariel song?" Emily whispered.

"Kiss the girl?" Antonio asked, starting a CD player and singing.

• • • • •

People on the gondolas ahead heard the song. Rook turned and called like they were in Texas, "Really?"

Emily waved, and James dramatically pulled her down where no one in the other boats could see her.

"What are they doing?" Julie asked.

"They're playing you," April said. "Sit down. Honestly! She's a grown woman."

"No, she's not. She's my little sister."

"That looks like fun. I wish I had a boyfriend in a gondola in Venice. The thought makes my toes curl."

"What do you know about curling toes?"

"I can dream."

"Good. You can dream all you want, but you still have to finish high school."

"And college," Rook added.

"You didn't."

"I'm a craftsman."

"I thought you were a gas monkey."

"I run a large business with several employees. We're all experts. People depend on us. If we can't fix it, you'll have to buy a new car. We're the best of the recyclers."

"You *are* the best, Honey," Julie said. "Maybe April wants to be a mechanic when she finishes high school."

"Mom, I can't even find the gas pump thing."

"That's because your dad helps out too much. I'll bet you can do all the stuff you need to."

"I hope I never do. I don't like getting messy."

"That's good news to me," Rook said, laughing, "because what is in that gondola is messy. Keep away from that."

"Honey, she won't care about messy when love knocks on her door."

"Oh, my!" Rook turned to the other men for support, but their kids were too young, so they didn't care.

• • • • •

"Do you know Mr. Howell in Texas?" she asked.

"The CEO of Roscoe's?" James said.

"Yes. He told me about my grandmother and Mr. Roscoe. You know they never had kids."

"I didn't know that."

"He made her think it was her fault. He tortured her about her wasting his seed."

"That's not very nice."

"It turned out he was sterile. He had mumps as a child, and the doctor told his family that would happen."

"How did Mr. Howell know?"

"When they went on business trips, Mr. Roscoe drank and chased women."

"That's not nice, either."

"He was a pretty loud guy. He told Mr. Howell he was sterile, and if Vivian ever got pregnant, he would divorce her, because he'd know the baby wasn't his. It was a trap. He told his whores, too, so they couldn't accuse him of paternity."

"What did your grandmother do?"

"She was faithful to him until his death. She changed her maid's hours, so she'd never have to work with him in the house."

"What was he doing to the maid?"

"Nothing, but once when she was pregnant, he got behind her and rubbed her belly while staring at Vivian. He told her he needed the help to get an heir. The next day, Miss Lucy was so upset, she cried in Grandma's arms and said it was a lie.

"Vivian knew the truth, because she knew Miss Lucy's husband. That was when she changed Miss Lucy's hours to make sure she was gone by the time Mr. Roscoe came home from work."

"That's good."

"Yes. Grandma made everything better. I loved her so much. She comes to mind at the strangest times." She began crying.

"Go ahead and cry, Honey. Good people deserve to be remembered."

"I'm OK. Thanks for understanding."

"I don't think I'm sterile, but I'd tell you if I knew."

"There are a lot of things you can do if there's a problem."

"Even back when Grandma was young, there were plenty of orphans."

"There still are, and there are sperm banks and surrogate mothers. Looks like our ride's over." Looking up at him, she gave him another kiss.

He helped her from the gondola. The others got out, too, wondering what the couple had been talking about. Nobody knew that story about Vivian except Emily, and she considered telling them later once they were home.

They went shopping.

"Use control, Ladies!"

The men checked the postcard and video shelves, knowing that despite all the pictures they took themselves, a professional picture might be best.

• • • • •

They walked all day until they were famished.

"Where should we eat?"

"That place smells good. There's a hotel, too. We need to find rooms, so we can finish playing tourist tomorrow and return to the villa."

"Let's see if they can accommodate us."

Going to the check-in desk, they asked a few questions.

"They have one two-room suite and two singles. Would that work?"

"Sounds good. Did they recommend the restaurant?"

"We even get a discount for going there."

"Do they have continental breakfast?"

"Didn't Europe invent that?"

"I don't think so either way."

"It was worth a try. Angela, once you're done feeding her, ask them about the places we want to see tomorrow."

"What are they?"

Andrew took out the tour guide and studied it. "It's called Cortina d'Ampezzo and the Garden of Villa Cipriani."

"OK. Mark the pages, so I can learn to pronounce the words. I don't want to look like a tourist."

"You'll be reading it from this book. They'll know."

"Maybe you're right."

The staff at the Piazza San Marco were very friendly. The

place was slightly expensive, but the hotel offered them a van to use the following day. The cooks could pack a lunch for them to take.

"We'll take it," Angela said.

Going upstairs to their rooms, they decided the brothers could take the singles, and the sisters would have the suite. April could sleep with Emily. James would have the sofa in the living room.

Angela asked Andrew to bring her food while she rested with the baby. She needed a bath and a nap. Just as the baby fell asleep in the middle of the bed, Angela's mother called.

"How's the baby? How are all of you doing?"

CHAPTER SIXTEEN
Angela Calling Home

"We're having a wonderful time, Mom," Angela said. "There's a lot to see. We've been in Rome, renting a quaint villa. We had plenty of rooms, but the place was pretty old. I wish I looked somewhere else, but, for the price, it was a winner."

"You get what you pay for."

"It has poor AC, and the restroom is like something from World War One."

"Hmmm."

"It probably is from World War Two. It's an old place, but the scenery is amazing. The bigger kids play in the yard. The baby's taking long naps even in her baby wear. We had a professional chef cook a seven-course dinner in our kitchen, so it can be done."

"That's good to know."

"We took a train to Venice. Oh, Mama, if you ever go, go there!"

"You didn't like Rome?"

"Look at this!" She sent her mother pictures, as she talked.

In Rome, the family enjoyed the Caracalla Baths, the Coliseum with its arched façades and the huge male statue with its missing nose, as well as the Piazza del Campidoglio. The horses reminded them of Texas, but the curly-headed men needed pants. There were staircases everywhere, old but still strong. The Arco di Settimio was so tall and straight, it was amazing it was built in a tool-poor century.

The Pantheon had an enormous ceiling. They loved Vatican City and Michelangelo's St. Peter's Basilica. I've never seen so many books in my entire life. We walked up the spiral staircase of the Vatican Museum and saw the dome Michelangelo painted of the hand of God touching man. The Port St. Angelo and the Castle St. Angelo shining in the sun, with its Trevi Fountain lit up at night. Rome was all big, though mostly in gray tones.

Venice was different. The Grand Canal was a huge body of water surrounded with Burano. They were similar to English flats, but each was painted a bright color—tan, purple, royal blue, brick red, and even pink. Red shutters surrounded the white windows, and tourists walked along the row of buildings built on the water.

The gondolas were in a variety of colors, and the gondoliers wore traditional costumes and hats. The family enjoyed the smooth ride. There were many arched bridges for people to walk to the other side.

Venice also had the Basilica de San Marco, with detailed golden art and golden, winged lions ready for flight. The Piazza San Marco had large cobblestone fields with streetlights that gave glimmering paths to follow. Eating areas contained yellow tables with four chairs, lined up as if for a large school

Faded Sweetheart

class.

The Franchetti Palace was also on the water, but they didn't have time to go inside the three-story building with its Italian gingerbread stone and arched balconies. The Garden of Villa Cipriani in Asolo was some distance off. We're taking a van to see that the following day and also visit Cortina d'Ampezzo.

It's past dinnertime. The baby was so tired, she fell asleep, and the others are out looking for food. Emily wants us to get up early to do everything we want to see tomorrow. Our train goes to Rome at six o'clock in the afternoon.

"It will be wonderful to view the countryside in the dark," Angela said.

"What hasn't been?"

"That's right. I think the others are back now. Let me get back to you. I'm starving."

"OK, Honey. Enjoy, but get some sleep. Love you."

"Thanks, Mom." She hung up. "Hi, Honey. What did you bring me?"

"A babysitter."

"Oh. Who?"

"April volunteered, so you could enjoy a brief night out."

"That's nice. Thanks."

"Is she sleeping?" April asked. "Enjoy your dinner."

April was a good baby-sitter, but there were times the responsibility scared her. The baby wasn't a good bottle baby. She liked to breast feed. Since they were in Europe, that was probably better for her than adding local water to her formula. Even bottled water might not be OK.

A dinner without the baby was a real treat, and eating at an Italian restaurant was even better. The others had already eaten and went for a walk on the cobblestones. They saw other tourists, but there was plenty of room to walk, stop, look around, and start over.

When the baby woke up and began squalling, Emily offered to help.

"Are you fresh?" she asked the baby. ""April, do you

know where the diapers are?"

"No."

"Look for a diaper bag. Check the bottom of the stroller."

"I found one."

"Here we go, Amy. When your cousin April needed a change, she was glad I was there to help."

"You're only three years older than me."

"Actually, it's more like five."

"You'd better appreciate the fires I extinguish for you two."

Emily, holding the baby, studied her niece. "What are you talking about?"

"Ariel?"

"Oh. That was funny."

"Dad had a fit. Mom called you her little sister. Now I either have to get a PhD or a mechanic's license."

"I remember that speech. I took lots of college classes in high school. Are you doing that?"

"Yeah."

"You need to say you want to do something vague, like political science or art theory."

"That's what you wanted!"

"Exactly. It keeps them off your back, so you can have a nice time."

"Should I try that with my father?"

"You're doing OK, aren't you?"

"Well, yeah."

"They just worry."

"How about when you two have children and they try it?" James asked the girls.

"We'd better remember. If we forget, we'll be ashamed."

"Maybe we should write this down, so we don't forget."

"Like in a diary?"

"That's the first place Julie will look. How about a tattoo?"

"That would last, but our kids would read that warning all our lives."

Faded Sweetheart

"As an infant, if you put it here...." James pointed at places babies liked.

"You're so funny, aren't you?"

"She's better now," Emily said. "If you want to choose one side of the bed, I'll come over when the parents come back."

"OK." April went to their suite to prepare for bed.

Emily put Amy back into bed, then she and James walked onto the balcony to look at the stars.

"You have a great relationship with her, don't you?" James asked.

"Poor April. I was only three-and-a-half years older. Luckily, she's cute. I'm sure she'll make it. Her dad's pretty protective. She's never had to buy gas. Can you believe it?"

"Does she need gas?"

"She's got a car. She's had one since she turned sixteen. He had to follow her with a cell phone to tell her how to get to school."

"Oh."

"It took her three trips to learn the route."

"Yeah. A natural blonde?"

"Just like me."

"Oh."

"I'm better. I've grown."

"I noticed."

"What do you mean by that?"

"It's obvious." He looked at her body. "And...."

"Yes?"

"Didn't you get the family a meal?"

"Yes."

"How?"

"I used my resources."

"You're very talented."

"I appreciate your noticing."

"How could I miss?" James looked around. "It's really quiet out here, isn't it?"

"Surprisingly, there are several people still out walking."

172

"Maybe they're wearing sneakers."
"Sneakers?"
"Isn't that what they're called?"
"The only people who wear sneakers in Venice are my brothers."
"Oh, yeah. I forgot you wear boots."
"You have issues with these boots?"
"I love them."
"Why?"
"Because they belong to you."
"Actually, they belong to Julie. She insisted I wear them for protection."
"Protection?"
"Have you ever been kicked by one of these?"
"She must think it'll hurt."
"I'll bet she's right."

Angela and Bill, returning to the suite, looked around.
"Who's watching our baby?" Angela asked.
"We're out here!" Emily said. "Did you have a nice time?"
"Yes. It was wonderful."
"Just sitting out here is lovely," James said.
"How'd you two get this job?"
"April had diaper duty, but it makes her sick. I suggested she go to bed, and she was happy to leave. The baby took one bottle, but...."
"She prefers it on tap," Andrew said.

Angela hugged the young couple. "Thank you, and good night."

James and Emily left.
"Do you want to go for a walk or go to bed?" he asked.
"I can walk with you, but my bed buddy is April. We need sleep more than exercise."

They went to the room and found the others sleeping, so they sat on the loveseat and fell asleep in each other's arms.

Faded Sweetheart

• • • • •

Rook found James asleep on the sofa in the morning, while Emily was in bed with April. It was almost eight o'clock, and the van would arrive soon to pick them up, so he shook James' shoulder.

"Sorry, James, but we need to get moving."

James looked for Emily.

"She went to bed with April," Rook said.

"How'd you know?"

"I heard you two come in. I had to use the bathroom and saw you sleeping here. You're cute. Are you two serious?"

"I am more than Emily."

"I had the pleasure of being with her grandpa when I courted Julie. He liked me, but I had to win her over."

"Really?"

"Yeah. Maybe I'm wrong about that. She never had anyone else. She was a wonderful girl, and I watched her grow into a woman."

"You're the same age. What do you mean?"

"I already had a business. I was living alone, and I had employees and customers. She lived at home with very protective parents and her grandfather."

"I've been told you're protective, too."

"I was taught by the best. When her grandfather lost the love of his life, he sheltered his daughter and then her daughter as natural."

"It's hard to let go, isn't it?"

"You never do."

April emerged from the bedroom. "Emily snores!"

"Really?" Emily asked, following her.

"Yes. I'm surprised I forgot about that."

"Why don't you go in and try again?"

April walked back into the bedroom and came out holding Emily's new shirt. "I had a wonderful night's rest. It was like you weren't even there. Can I try this on?"

Emily looked at Rook. "Of course. I was going to buy

that for you. Then we could be Twinkies."

"I just checked the size. It's for a woman. I'd drown in it."

"We're in Venice. Drowning is easy to arrange."

The men listening to the banter burst out laughing at Emily's last comment. The sound woke Julie.

"Those two are the sisters I always wanted," Julie said.

"But you *are* my sister!" Emily said.

"I know. You two always mix it up. You used to fight over toys, pizza flavors, and rock stars. Luckily, it was never boys."

Emily grabbed James' arm. "This one's mine."

April took his other arm. "He could be my uncle. Too bad his name isn't Bob."

James caught the joke, but the others didn't. "We'd better get started. The van will be here soon."

They dressed and grabbed some fast food for breakfast. Gathering near the van, they made sure everyone was there, then the driver headed for their first location—Cortina d'Ampezzo.

As the can climbed the final hill, they saw a tower.

"It is a ski resort," the driver explained, "in the winter."

They parked and got out. The kids ran in the grass.

"James, did you bring a ball?" one asked.

"Not today."

Slightly disappointed, the boys ran up and down the hill, then rolled down it. The tour guide was appalled. "Tourists don't act like that," he muttered.

"It looks like fun," William heard him and said. "The boys can't hurt the grass, can they?"

"No, Sir," the driver said.

"Let them run it off. It looks safe here."

"Except for the dung."

"What?"

"They have sheep here."

"Come back, Boys! Watch out for poop!"

The boys were used to seeing cow pies, so they looked for large deposits.

"There's a little out here," Tre said.
"Walk around it and come back down to the car. We're getting lunch at the next place."
"OK."
They slid down the hill on their butts, OK.
The driver worried about the next place they would visit. The garden of Villa Cipriani was a refined, adult, reserved setting. People came to sit and quietly enjoy the fine hotel.
The driver dropped them off, unloaded their lunch, and said, "I'll be right back." He quickly drove off.
The adults looked at each other, hoping he would return and wouldn't leave them stranded.
After they ate lunch, the van returned.
"Boys, I found some kites for you," the driver said.
"Thanks! Can you help us?"
He looked at the parents, who nodded. Using his best English, he taught the boys how to fly kites. The adults sat on the ground, while the kids tried to get their kites into the air, assisted by Emily, James, and April.
After an hour of play, they returned to catch their train back to Rome. The boys were sweaty from all their fun, and tired. All of them were quiet, as they sat in the train.
The night lights were beautiful.

• • • • •

Once they reached the villa outside Rome, Emily and James asked the driver to wait, so they could gather their bags for their trip back to England, where they had to return to work.

CHAPTER SEVENTEEN
Back to Work

The plane ride was a short nap for them. When they arrived in England, they went to Emily's hotel.

"Do you want to come in?" she asked, "or would you rather go home to your family?"

"Both sound good."

Emily smiled. Both were good for her, too. "Maybe you should go home. Your mom probably has lots of questions for you, and you've got that thing to give your little brother. Little kids like stuff like that."

"He's actually older than me."

"Then you'd better go home. He must be getting ancient."

They didn't want to part, but they needed a good night's sleep before work.

Emily walked into her room, feeling lonely. After unpacking, she donned a nightgown and went to bed. She had wonderful dreams until the ringing phone woke her.

"Hello?"

"Were you sleeping? Where's James?"

"He's at his house."

"Really?"

"Yeah. We were tired, and we have to work today."

"I'm proud of you."

"It was hard, but we had so much fun with all of you, we needed our sleep. Why are you calling?"

"The villa caught on fire, and we had to evacuate."

She sat upright, suddenly wide awake. "What? Is everyone OK?"

"Strangely enough, there was smoke detector."

"In that dump?"

Actually, Andrew's a volunteer fireman, and he always brings one with him. It saved our lives."

"That's wonderful. Where are you now?"

"At the Hilton, but they didn't have enough rooms. We're a bit cramped."

"I'm so sorry." She wondered if they were planning to come to England. "Are you going home early?"

"We thought we might want to visit England."

"Oh. Do you know anyone there?"

"I have a sister there. There's a vacant suite that's adjacent to hers. We'll be there in the morning."

"I have to go back to work, so I can't play with you that much."

"At least we can share a meal."

"That would be OK. I have to get some sleep. Can we talk later?"

"Sure. Love you."

Instead of going back to bed, she called James. "How much do you miss my family? They're coming to England tomorrow. I told them I had to work, but they want to eat a meal with me."

"Where will they stay?"

"In the suite next to mine."

"So no sleepovers?"

"Isn't it time to move to a real place?"

"Mom said she got a call from a friend who needs to sublet. You want to look at it after work?"

"Sounds good. Is it near your place?"

"Sort of."

"Let's go back to bed. I'm still tired."

"OK."

• • • • •

Luckily, work slowed down a bit. Emily and James had their assignments. After a long day at the office, Emily returned to her apartment and found workmen there.

"What are these men doing here?"

"They said they were setting you up to work at home," Julie replied.

"That won't work with all of you around. Why didn't you tell them to come back when I didn't have company?"

"Honey, they said Rebecca ordered it for your convenience."

"Did she know you were visiting?"

"No. She was surprised you'd do that with all the work you have."

"Did you tell her about the fire and how you need a place to stay?"

"What fire?"

"What do you mean? The fire at the villa last night!"

"That was just a little kitchen fire. We got our stuff out. It wasn't any problem."

"But you're here."

"We're glad, too. It looks like there's a lot of things to do and see. We were thinking about going to Paris before we leave. Want to come?"

"When would I have time?"

"Next weekend. You're off."

"Did you check with Rebecca?"

"Yes. It was nice visiting with her again. She reminds me a lot of her grandmother. I love Miss Lucy."

"You're changing the subject."

"Absolutely. All of us are going out. You have work to do. You can check if they fixed your system. Should we bring you anything?"

"No. I have room service, and I'd love to be with you, but I'm working."

Julie gave her a big hug. "Love you. Got to go." She had the feeling Emily wasn't completely happy with the family moving in next door. She wondered if Emily understood how the family missed Grandma.

Emily checked the work the technicians did. The computer on her desk was on, and she hoped no one was snooping, because she had the family's picture on it.

"Oh, you did miss us!" Julie said.

"Where is James' picture?" someone asked.

"That's against company policy. We don't date at work. Let me get some work done, so we can go out to dinner."

"Where should we go?"

"If we can find a baby-sitter, we can try the fish and chips place."

"You could bring some back," Angela offered. "I can watch the kids."

"That's awfully nice of you," Julie said.

"Nobody else can nurse the baby, and I'm tired of lugging her around. With the pack-and-play they brought up, she can have fun. It's cool in here, and the boys have TV. It won't be that hard. I might call my mom. I don't want her worrying. Which one of you told her we had a fire in the villa? Does she see someone's web page?"

"I'll call James to bring food for the boys, then we can leave," Emily said, dialing the number.

Angela settled the baby with her favorite toys.

• • • • •

James came over in thirty minutes with several bags of interesting-smelling food. He had a different bag with Dr. Pepper and some catsup in it.

The adults and April left. The kids liked the food, as did Angela. April was excited about visiting a bar. It was legal for her in England, though not back in Texas. She wondered what to expect.

"Do you want to sing karaoke?" James asked Emily.

"What songs would they have?"

"Anything you like, but we're short on hillbilly music."

"Why would you think I like hillbilly music?"

He glanced at her boots.

"You don't like my boots, do you?"

"I'm just not accustomed to them."

They went inside and placed their order. While they waited, April looked at the song list for karaoke and saw a few tunes by Mariah Carey, Taylor Swift, and Carrie Underwood.

"I'm ready," she announced.

There was a prompter to one side with the words on it, but she had the songs memorized. She twirled her skirt and stamped her boots, flipping her hair like she was a star on *The Voice.*

Everyone loved her singing and her sparkle. A few others sang a few songs after she finished, then April got back up to try a few more. She asked Julie and Emily to join her. Perhaps it was the beer, but both women agreed. The pub owner told them it was his best night in weeks. People came in off the street to listen to the new sensation.

Faded Sweetheart

When it grew late, Emily said, "I have to go. I've got work to do."

"Can I stay if Mom and Dad want to?" April asked, looking at her parents. "Well, maybe we can come back tomorrow."

"We'll see," Rook said. "Come on, Taylor," he teased, taking her hand and pulling her along, as she waved to her newfound friends.

• • • • •

All the kids slept in the suite, either in front of the TV or in the playpen. Angela was on the phone with her mom.

"It was really nice in Italy. Here in England, we have a nice, modern place. The furniture is big, the bathrooms are clean, and we've got plenty of hot and cold water, with big tubs and multiple head showers. There's room service, but there are no bugs."

"You hated Italy?"

"Hardly. It was beautiful the last day before the fire."

"Fire? What's this about a fire?"

"It was just a kitchen fire, but Andy was already tired of having cold showers when the hot water ran out right after he soaped up."

"No one likes that."

"He had to wear shoes all the time, because the fourth step was cracked, and he was constantly tripping on it. He never managed to adjust his walk to make the other foot come down on that step."

"Like when you kicked with only your right foot?"

"Yeah. Your gait is hard to alter. We aren't ballerinas."

"I hope I never see your linebacker in tights."

"Mom, you're so visual! He was upset, because he didn't know if we could call 911 or had to call the firemen directly. He plans to write to the owners, so they can add that information to the brochure."

"That won't be a very positive feature."

"He painted the smoke detector red and hung it on the wall for the next family. It even has a tag to remind people when to change the battery."

"That's a bit excessive, but you want your family safe."

"It was pretty ugly against that vintage wall, but he was probably right. We went to a hotel that had a huge grassy yard. It was so tranquil. Imagine sitting on the grass drinking wine, though we had water. It wasn't ice water like we're used to in CC."

"Before we went there, the driver took us to the Cortina d'Ampezzo. We hadn't heard of it before. We were just in Europe to see Emily. The stone mountain bathed in sunlight was an extra. The mountain range was supposedly the home of the Olympics just before World War Two. Maybe it was World War One. It was all set up, but they had to cancel due to the invasion. All the able-bodied men went to war. Now, it's a ski resort in winter. The tour guide said it was a popular place. We came at the wrong season."

"That's good timing."

"You can say that again. Imagine how cold it would be compared to how hot it is right now."

"You little Southern belle."

"I'm feeding this baby, too. It's like pouring milk on yourself and letting it sour all day. They may not use much deodorant here, but I smell just like they do."

"I'll bet my grandbaby likes it."

"Oh, yeah. She can sniff me a mile away."

"You're so funny."

"The day before, we went to Venice. The gondola ride was pretty, because all the buildings in Burano are so colorful. We can't wait to show you pictures."

"I look forward to them and to having you home."

"We finally found the shops. Their Murano glass dishes reminded me of the Burano buildings with their bright colors. We bought a bunch of it and had it shipped to Texas. They're full of Italian flavor. I hope the dishes will keep that fire alive. Maybe it'll diminish, as dust falls on the plates in our buffet at home.

"It was almost embarrassing how much stuff we bought. We wanted a video of some things in case we forgot them. We took pictures of the kids in front of everything, including the naked men standing beside their horses."

"Honey, I don't have that much memory in my tablet. Keep those shots and show them to me when you're back."

"OK, Mom. Thanks for the call. We're having fun, but we're ready to come home. I miss my washer and dryer. The baby's making a mess all the time. It's hard to keep everything clean."

"OK. Talk to you later."

"'Bye, Mom!"

Her husband walked up behind her. "Who was that?"

"Mom called."

"From home?"

"She misses us. She wanted to know how we're doing."

"Does her phone make international calls?"

"I think she bought a card for that."

"Well, it's her money. Did you have a nice talk?"

"Yes. Being here has been a great experience, too."

"Too bad the baby won't remember much."

"We can show her the pictures."

"Except the naked men."

"Of course."

The rest of the family came in, many carrying packages. They dumped them anywhere they could.

"Wait a minute. Don't lose your stuff. How will you get home with all this?"

"Can we mail it?"

"I guess so. You'd better mail all of it. Otherwise, you're carrying it yourself."

"I'll ship back my old clothes," April said. "I'm taking this stuff with me."

"Are you planning to get more luggage, or will you send your parents' clothes in the mail, too?" Emily asked.

"That would work."

"We'll have to try it. We're leaving soon."

"But I wanted to see Paris."

"We're doing that next weekend. We'll take the train through the Tunnel."

"Is that safe?"

"It's new. It follows the safety criteria."

"Will you hang your smoke detectors?"

"No. Like I said, it's safe."

"Good. I don't want to be embarrassed."

"I don't want to die on vacation."

"Let's go to bed, everyone." William yawned so widely, his mouth covered his face for a second.

"You look tired. Who sleeps where?"

They found their room. Emily slept on the sofa. Her bedroom had a queen-sized bed. The other room had another bed, and Rook took the other suite. April needed her space. She offered Emily half the bed, but Emily already had her office equipment in the other room. The sofa wasn't that bad, either.

"Hi, James," Emily said over the phone. "I'm happy to have my family here. It was nice they could take the next suite, so we aren't hopping from one place to another, but it's hard on us, and I have a certain work ethic. I like doing good work."

"I like your family. They fill in your background. I was talking to your father, Rook. He told me how much everyone misses your grandmother. This trip is putting life back into your lives."

"I guess. Deep inside, I love these crazy people, but I still hope they leave soon."

"Tomorrow, they're going to Stonehenge."

"Without us?"

"Yes. I told Rook they had to go, but it was a long trip, and you needed to stay home to work."

"That's great. I can get some work done."

"We can do it together."

"Did you tell them that's where you dumped me, and later

Faded Sweetheart

changed your mind?"
"Who said I changed my mind?"
"Huh?"
"That's funny. You could say I can sing and tell jokes."
"But they're supposed to be funny."
"I'm new at it."
"I like you new."
"Thanks. They just found me. Talk to you later."
"'Bye, Love."
That word turned her on. James had a way with words.

The family got up early and didn't wake Emily, sleeping on the sofa. They took a day trip to visit Stonehenge. Though it would be a long drive, James said they had to see it.

It wasn't as pretty as Rome, but it had lots of history. William and his wife were teachers, so they wanted to see it.

"Should we visit Ireland?" his wife asked.

"No. I'm getting homesick."

Taking his hand, she studied the man she married. "Me, too. I don't think these little guys would be willing to sightsee another rock."

They planned to visit Paris, then return home, because school would start soon. William's parents were teachers, too, but times had changed. A school shooting shouldn't happen. How could parents send their most-beloved things when they were in danger?

• • • • •

The family was away all day and most of the evening. James and Emily worked at the office, and later visited the flat he told her about. Rebecca told Emily she could stay at the hotel until another VIP arrived. The corporation owned the suite and would rather have it occupied than vacant.

CHAPTER EIGHTEEN
The Flat

As the heir to the corporation, Emily considered renting the corporate suite to regular clients, but there was too much red tape involved. She checked the flat with James. She needed to stay in the suite until another visitor could have it.

He wouldn't be able to get her out of there for a while, but, when that time came, it would be with little notice. Maybe they could fix up the flat a little at a time.

"That's a good idea," she said. "I'd like to remove the wallpaper, paint, put down new floors, and increase the AC. Do I have a parking spot?"

"Do you have a car?"

"Not yet, but I might want one."

"Will you give me a ride?"
"I'll teach you how to drive."
"Oh. When should we start?"
"When we get a car."

When the family came home, the driver didn't take them to the hotel. Per Emily's instructions, he took them to her new place.

"It's not finished," she explained. "In fact, we haven't started, but we washed the dishes, and I made dinner for you."

"Isn't this cute?" Molly commented when she saw it. "I love this shabby chic!".

The table was a door taken from one of the bedrooms and covered with a plastic tablecloth. The chairs were mismatched. Some came from a used furniture shop down the street, 3 were lawn chairs, and 6 were folding chairs. They brought in the baby's stroller, so she had a place to stay. Dinner was Southern style, depending on what was available in the market. Emily had to cut chocolate from a large block, because she couldn't find chocolate chips.

"This is kind of like fish, but it's steak," James said.

"It's called chicken-fried steak. There are...."

"Mash?"

"Mashed potatoes and gravy." She looked at her family. "I wanted corn on the cob but couldn't find it. I found creamed corn, but I added more flavor to it."

Grabbing a spoon, Angela said, "This is good. You did great!"

"James' brother made the dinner rolls. He works at the bakery over there." She pointed at the shop below the flat.

"How long has he been a baker?" she asked James.

"He usually just cleans the place, but he picked up on some of it, and he's right. These are good. Does anyone else want to spoil his appetite?"

They sat down.

"James bring in your mother and brother to join us," Julie said.

He glanced at Emily. "Will there be enough food?"

"Of course, or they can snack later. Please get them, but we might need another chair."

He brought in his family. The food was getting cold, but the families felt warm.

"You live close to here?" Julie asked.

"On the next floor," James' mother replied.

"That's not so bad. I like the idea of her having someone she knows nearby when we leave." Julie knew that would be soon. The nursing staff needed their manager back. She was already getting emails about disagreements between the nurses or the nurses and doctors.

"You have a lot of work to do," Julie told Emily.

"Yes. I have a plan. Whenever another VIP needs the suite, I'll be pushed out."

"You can't live at that hotel forever."

"This will be what I do when I'm not working. I always wanted to make my own mark."

"Honey, you did that the day you came into the world," Rook said, glancing at James and his mother. "Her mother had Emily just a few months after we married. Emily came to life early, so she was air-lifted to Corpus Christi, where we live. Julie was still in nursing school. Since her mother couldn't come with her, Grandma took the flight with the baby.

"She was the full-time caregiver until her mother was discharged at the Bishop Hospital. Meanwhile, Grandma and Miss Lucy changed our guest room into a nursery for the time when Emily would be discharged and would need to be close to her doctors for a while.

"I worried that Julie would get the mother bug, but she waited until she got her degree and job. We used most of Emily's stuff before passing it on to Will. We got it back for Lot, then it went to Andrew for the baby."

James hugged Emily, as she set food on the table. Paper plates and plastic ware weren't very cute, but she'd be able to buy her own household items when the time came. Her dishes from Italy would arrive soon, too. She wanted a buffet to show them off. It would go on one wall, and she considered painting it in the colors of Venice. Would that be too much? It was her time to experiment.

They sat down to dinner. It was home in a strange land, and the family enjoyed their trip but was ready to go home, too.

The family offered to clean the dishes.

"James' brother already said he'd do that," Emily said. "He's a professional dishwasher."

The van driver took the family back. Emily made hand pies for him, a Southern version of a pie that was small enough to hold in one hand. He loved them. He ate three of the five on the way home.

Back at the hotel, the family ate snacks and discussed who wanted to visit Paris the next day.

"We could see a soccer game instead," James told the men.

"Hell, yes!"

The men even offered to take the baby.

The ladies agreed to see Paris, leaving early and returning late.

• • • • •

The ladies came to the flat to pick up the baby. James' mother offered to take the baby instead of letting the men take her to a soccer game.

"How'd you like the game?" Julie asked her son.

"It was fun. We ate lots of food."

"That sounds nice. Where'd you eat?"

"At a pub."

"A pub?"

"Yes. They said it was OK. We didn't have beer. We had fish and chips and pop."

"OK." She looked at Rook. "A pub?"

"Blame it on James and Tre. He was so hungry, he said he

couldn't walk any farther."

"Why was he so tired?"

"The kids got to play soccer before the game. It was a kid's game," James explained.

"Did they have those things?"

"We borrowed some. They were told not to kick anyone there."

Both showers in the suite worked overtime, as the dirty boys and the women cleaned up after their day. Shopping was hard work. At least shipping things home meant there was less to pack, except for April, who wanted to take her purchases with her.

"Isn't this cute, Daddy?"

"How much was it?"

"I don't know. I don't do francs."

"It's the euro now, Honey."

"It's confusing. Luckily, I used the card."

"You do that well, don't you?"

"Yes, Dad. Thanks!" She hugged him.

He was so easy to manipulate.

CHAPTER NINETEEN
They're Leaving

When the family left for home the following day, Emily felt mixed emotions. She'd be lonely without them, but she had a flat to upgrade, and she liked remodeling.

She realized she had a home to remodel back in Texas. She liked thinking about this

As she worked in the flat, stripping wallpaper, she talked to her grandmother. She felt bad she wasn't talking to her mother, but Grandma always reminded her about her mother. Emily had pictures, and Grandpa always added facts about the family when the boys were little.

Emily had a vivid history of her past. Family mattered,

despite death having an active hand in their family.

Once she gave her family time to fly home and a good night's rest, she desperately wanted to call them.

How independent can I be if I already miss them so much? she wondered. *I can make a quick call to make sure they arrived in one piece and check if the things they bought have arrived. I can ask someone to check my house. That sounds good. It's not that needy.*

"Hi," Emily said over the phone. "How's it going?"

"Fine, Emily. Thanks for calling," Julie said.

"How was your trip? Are you happy to be home?"

"Yes. The flight was OK, but sleeping in our own beds was great. The kids are happy to be home. How are you?"

Emily broke down. "I...I miss you! It was so nice to have you here in Europe. I love you so much!" She began crying.

"Are you OK?" Julie asked. "When did you start crying for us?"

"Just a few minutes ago. I've been busy with work and remodeling the flat. I've got the wallpaper off, and now I'm trying to choose a color. I've been talking to myself a lot. Sometimes I talk to Grandma."

"We all do that, Honey. You're OK. Do you want to come home?"

"Oh, I'm OK. I guess hearing your voice triggered this."

"Rook kept me from calling since we landed last night. I wanted to call from our stopover. Hell, I wanted to call from Heathrow."

"Right after I dropped you off?"

"Yes. I've been aching for you."

"Oh, Sister. I'll be back someday. I need to check the house. Can Miss Lucy's son watch it for a few more months?"

"I don't know. I'll ask. Maybe you should sell the place if you prefer living over...." She felt herself ready to cry, too. "...over there."

"Oh, good grief. Now you're crying."

"Here comes Rook," Julie said quickly.

"Who are you talking to?" Rook asked. "I know. Let me talk to her." Handing her a tissue, he took the phone. "Hi,

Sweetheart. How's it going?"

"It was fine until I called."

"That's what happens. How's work?"

"Good. I got a promotion."

"Because of you, or because of who you're related to?"

"It was for my merit. Rebecca thought I did amazing work considering I was busy entertaining my family, too. She installed that system in the suite to see if I had the work profile."

"I'm glad to hear that. How's the flat coming?"

"It's coming. I haven't chosen the colors, but I'm finding some neat furniture. I want to paint that, too."

"Looks like you're making a nest. You can do it."

"Thanks. Can I talk to Julie again, just for a second?"

"Sure. Here you go."

Julie was more composed when she took the phone. "How can I help?"

"Could you call Mr. Howell at corporate headquarters and ask him to call my cell? I want to run an idea past him about Rebecca."

"OK. Will do."

"Thanks. When do you start work again?"

"I was there today. I couldn't wait. My desk was buried under paperwork!"

"At least you don't have twenty relatives hanging around."

"Yeah."

"But if they're the right relatives, it's wonderful. You probably need a nap."

"Yes, but there's a ballgame tonight."

"Lot?"

"Yeah. It'll be a short one, and we'll bring home pizza. That's Italian food, you know."

"I remember. Talk to you later. Tell my brothers I called."

"Will do, Sweetie."

After they hung up, both women took deep breaths. They felt good.

CHAPTER TWENTY
The Colors of Venice

Emily finally decided to paint the walls robin's egg blue, her favorite color, and she wondered why she bothered considering anything else.

She called James. "What are you doing? I got my dishes today, and I need a buffet to display them."

"Do you already have the walls painted?"

"No."

"Then I'd suggest you keep the plates in boxes. You never know where paint might fly."

"I probably want to paint the furniture, too."

"Have you bought any paint yet?"

"No. Should I take a bus to buy it, take the limo, or order

it online?"

"If you do the last, they deliver."

"That's why I love you. You're so helpful."

"Boy, am I glad to hear that. I thought I lost you when the family left."

"No. I'm just trying to keep busy. Where have you been?"

"Remember when you told my mother I could take down the wallpaper here?"

"Yes."

"She's making me do it every night."

"It's a little room. Why is it taking so long?"

"She wants to do the entire flat, and then she wants to paint it."

"You can hire someone."

"How much do you charge?"

"Since I don't have my paint yet, let me order it. I'll go visit your mom and get that part started for her. When my paint arrives, maybe we'll be finished at her place."

"I hope so."

"I have to get back to the suite. Do you want to tell your mom we'll start tomorrow after work?"

"Sure. I'll leave her a note."

"She's not there? Why aren't you here, helping me?"

"I tried calling, but you didn't pick up."

"I called Julie. I wanted to ask how her flight was and my house, but...."

"You broke down?"

"Yes."

"Don't worry. Your family is close. I'm surprised you didn't go home with them and leave me."

"I'm finding myself. You don't grow much in the bosom of your family."

"Do I have that problem?"

"Thanks," James answered. "I'm hungry. Let's get some food."

They ate a meal out, but they didn't dance or sing

karaoke. When they walked back to the suite hand-in-hand, they found a note on the door.

Miss Queen,
A VIP is coming next week. You'll need to vacate.

"I've got one week or less to get out," Emily said, "but at least you found me a flat." She kissed him. "Thanks."

"At least you've got some warning. Maybe you'd better order a bed to go with your paint. See if they can deliver this week."

"OK. Let's do that."

She called and ordered a bed, bedding, and several gallons of paint. Delivery was guaranteed to be within three days.

"Could your mom sign for these things when they arrive?" she asked.

"I'm sure she will. She likes you."

"I'm glad. Will she be OK without you?"

"She'll adjust."

"I'm tired."

"Me, too. Can I stay over?"

"You want a beer or anything?"

"I'd like you."

She moved closer. "I like you, too."

• • • • •

In the morning, Emily began packing clothes into suitcases. She needed two outfits until her bed arrived at the flat.

She woke James, so they could drop off things at the flat before work.

"I can tidy up before my time is up if I take things over every day," she explained.

"OK. Then I can change clothes, too."

"Let's go."

Dropping off Emily's clothing, they went to work.

Faded Sweetheart

Rebecca was waiting to talk with Emily. She didn't say why, but she wanted Emily in her office immediately.

Emily wondered what was up. She'd just gotten a promotion, so Rebecca was happy with her work. Had Mr. Howell called?

"How can I help you?" Emily asked when they were inside Rebecca's office.

"I think you already did."

"I did?"

"Yes. Thanks for my promotion."

"Mr. Howell called?"

"He told me about it, but he's coming in person to give me his job."

"He told me he wanted to retire. He appreciated it when I said you were ready. I knew you were ready the day I arrived, but I needed to learn more about the business. I'm glad you could put me to work. I hope you can go home and enjoy your grandma for a few years. She'll love having you home."

Rebecca hugged the little woman from Texas. "This is exciting!"

"Who'll replace you? He didn't tell me."

"We'll have to dress for success that day. You need to issue a bulletin to the staff."

"They aren't supposed to know."

"Let's call it Professionals Day. I had a job back home that did that. We all got dressed up for no reason, and it was good practice. People should look nice for work."

"Would you like to do that email for the staff?"

"Sure. Like they did at Alorica, we can offer a prize for the best-dressed person. It can be a day off with pay. We'll have Mr. Howell decide. We need to add there can't be excessive jewelry or hair, though."

"OK."

"I can order a cake for the day, too, and we'll give out random prizes throughout the day."

"Go for it!"

"I'll get on it," Emily said. "Do you want to review my

work before I send that email?"

"Yes."

"I'll suggest you wrote the memo and had the idea."

"Is that OK with you?"

"No problem. I want your staff to respect you. I don't need glory, and I don't want to present something you didn't approve."

"OK. Keep the real reason quiet. Thanks again."

"Why?"

"For the dress-for-success idea, and your call to Mr. Howell."

"You think so?"

"He mentioned your name."

Emily left smiling.

"Why so happy?" James asked.

"I gave her a suggestion, and she took it. Look for the email."

"OK, Mystery Girl. Lunch?"

"Hopefully."

Emily sent the email. Rebecca waited a few hours, then started working on the idea. Emily called several French customers, glad she spoke the language. She loved her job and being in England. She wondered if Rebecca had any wisdom to impart before she went home.

• • • • •

On Wednesday, Emily's new bed and paint arrived. She was excited until she realized she had to assemble it herself.

"How are you at putting things together?" she asked James.

"We could try, but my brother would be better at this," he said. "Want me to get him?"

James' brother couldn't read very well, but he and James assembled the bed quickly. Emily thanked them and said

Faded Sweetheart

she'd visit the flat the next day to help their mother.

"What does she need?" she asked James.

"Help with the wallpaper."

"Oh, yeah."

• • • • •

The following day was Emily's first day off, so she went to see Loretta, James' mother, and said, "I'm here to help with your wallpaper."

The older woman let her inside.

"Your sons don't strip very well, do they?" Emily asked, looking at the walls.

Loretta stared in shock.

"I meant the wallpaper. I thought they would've gotten farther."

"Oh, that. There's been a game on TV, so they had a hard time leaving the telly."

"Did their team win?" She remembered James looking over her shoulder when they went to get fish and chips at the pub that night.

"I think it's still going on. Seems like it lasts for months with all the playoffs and finals." She looked around the kitchen, where items had been removed from the walls and stacked on tables. "I can barely find what I need to make dinner."

"That's why I'm here. It's my day off, so let's get started."

Loretta found a bucket, which Emily filled with hot water. Having the wall already prepped was great. It gave them room to work.

"Look at all the paper that's been here," Emily said.

They worked hard, and several layers of wallpaper were uncovered. At one point, they reached a layer with faded sweethearts like what Emily's grandma used for her signature.

Emily pulled a piece free. "Can I keep a piece of this?"

"You can have anything you want, Dear. Should we try to get you more of this?"

"No. This is enough. Maybe if we find another, I can send it to my sister."

Loretta wondered why American girls would want a layer of old wallpaper, but she didn't argue.

As they worked, they talked. Emily and Loretta got along well. It wasn't the same as when Emily lived with her grandmother, because she was a grown woman. Was talking like that more like being with one's mother?

Unlike most English women, Loretta wasn't reserved with Emily. The pretty girl from America might take away her son, but she saw a sparkle in her, and, unlike the other girls James brought home, Emily was genuine and willing to work hard.

Soon, the kitchen was finished.

"Do you have paint for this room yet?" Emily asked.

"We haven't gotten that far."

"Do you like robin's egg blue? I have some left. As my grandpa always said, 'It doesn't get better in the can.' He restored lots of houses and tried to use whatever he had. I also have some yellow. If we mix them, we'll get light green."

"Let me look at your walls and see if I like it."

"Good. That'll give these walls time to dry."

They walked down a flight to see Emily's flat. She'd already done a lot. She was young and had plenty of energy, plus she was working off her frustrations. There wasn't much furniture yet, but she hadn't moved in yet, either. The kitchen was a lovely blue, and the cupboards and buffet had nice additional colors, with the dishes on display.

"Your colorful dishes match the blue walls," Loretta said. "It's so happy."

"Yellow is supposed to be a happy color." She found the can of yellow. "Here's the sample." Holding it up to the light, she studied it.

"Do you think there's enough yellow for my kitchen?"

Faded Sweetheart

"Yes. It goes on really well and needs only one coat. I did my bathroom in it. Come see."

The bathroom wasn't completely neat and tidy. A towel lay on the floor where Emily stepped out of the tub that morning, and her hair products covered the sink.

"Sorry for the mess," Emily said.

"You use all that in your hair?"

"Well, no. I get convinced to buy it, but really, I just wash and go. I'm a pushover."

"Your hair is lovely, and so is this color. I'll buy this for my kitchen and will use blue in the bathroom."

"I can't sell you half a can of paint. I'd rather give it away to avoid wasting it. When Grandpa couldn't convince Grandma to reuse the last of the paint, he took it to charity. The two of them painted the Madonna House, a place to help poor single mothers get started in life."

"That was nice of them."

"They loved doing it. They had a lot to give."

They carried paint buckets and brushes back upstairs.

"Is your bathroom wallpaper striped?" Emily asked.

"It wasn't wallpaper. It's been painted, but it's depressing."

"Let's wipe down the walls to remove any dirt, then we can get started. We'll check the walls in the kitchen." She placed her hand against the wall in a few places and nodded. "If we were to grab a sandwich now, we could paint the kitchen first, then the bathroom. You could have your kitchen back today."

"That would be so nice!"

They went down to the deli to have a quick lunch.

"This is a nice place," Emily said. "Why haven't I been here before?"

"James doesn't like cold sandwiches. They have too many vegetables."

"I love vegetables. I wondered why they didn't serve them here. It must be the company I keep."

"Yes."

"My brothers opt out of green stuff, too. They want meat and potatoes."

"It's the same around here."

Going back upstairs, they started painting. The yellow covered the walls well. Emily hadn't mentioned she often helped her grandparents paint other people's houses. She was so good, she didn't need a drop cloth and never got paint on herself -- signs of a professional painter.

Loretta tried to keep up, but Emily suggested she start reloading the kitchen shelves, which was a big chore in itself. Emily understood that placing things where someone wanted them was important to women. No woman could properly do that for another.

She wished she had the power to refuse when people selling hair products told her she just had to try something. Sometimes they promised her brain cells or even her chest would grow bigger.

Emily slipped into her element, painting the bathroom after the kitchen. Soon, the cans of paint had barely a drop left in each. She cleaned her brushes and pans, then hugged Loretta.

"I'll be off for my second shower of the day," Emily said. "Let the paint dry about four hours before you get the bathroom steamy. I had a great day with you."

Loretta thanked her at the door, marveling how much young people could cram into their days. She returned to her new kitchen and finished placing things on the proper shelves. When she walked into the bathroom, she thought the new color was lovely. She needed new towels and wondered about buying some for Emily, since she knew what colors the young woman liked.

• • • • •

Emily put the cans in her flat, then she hailed a cab to the suite. It was her last day there, and James would be meeting her soon. She barely had time to shower and put on the last outfit she left in the suite.

James arrived and asked, "What do you want to do here at the suite?"

"We can go in the closet."

"The what?"

"You know what I said."

"OK."

They walked into the bedroom closet, which was almost totally empty. There were no hangers to hit them on the head or shoes to trip over.

He looked at her and smiled. "You're funny."

"I'm sentimental."

"That you are."

She put her arms around his neck, and he hugged her waist, as they kissed.

"Do you remember our first kiss?" she asked.

"It was here in the closet."

"Yes. This is where it all began."

"I thought you had the hots for me from day one."

"Even when you cast me out at Stonehenge?"

"You were a flirt, talking about your women and wives."

"You were...." He kissed her again. "I fell in love with you on first sight."

They kissed some more, then he looked into her eyes. "Do you want to do it on the bed?"

"No."

"Why not?"

"Because."

"You do love me, though?"

"Yes.

"You don't have a sex problem?"

"I've never had sex, but I think all my parts work."

"You've never? Would you like a lesson?"

"Yes, but Honey, right now I need to prepare the suite for the next person. We'll have our lessons in the flat." Straddling him, she shoved him to the floor.

"Do you think you'll be a quick learner?" he asked.

"That's probably why you Queen women get pregnant the first time you do it."

"I have no idea, but I can barely resist trying out the bed with you."

He rolled over until he was on top, with both of them fully dressed, his body pressing against hers. He smelled her perfume, and he liked it.

Someone knocked on the front door, then it opened. "Anybody home?" the housekeeper asked.

Struggling to get up and compose herself, Emily called, "We're in here trying to make sure I got everything. Oh, here's a sock!"

They came out of the bedroom and saw the maid in the living area, dusting the ceiling fan before she vacuumed. She smiled at Emily, then, when James came out next, she blushed.

"If I missed anything, give me a call, and I'll come get it," Emily said. "There's always something."

The maid nodded. After the couple left, she went into the bedroom and wondered how they could have remade the bed exactly the way she left it the previous day. She nodded slowly, remembering what it felt like to be young. She had five children.

• • • • •

Emily and James took a cab to their place.

"I had lunch with your mother at the deli," Emily said. "Are they open for dinner?"

"You probably won't like it. They serve vegetables."

"I like vegetables."

"Yuck!"

"I just need to make you some you'll like."

"For you, I'll try anything."

They got out of the taxi and found the deli closed.

"I can make dinner for us," Emily said. "I've got something to work with, I'm sure. Is that game still going on?"

"What game?"

"The one your mother said had you and your brother glued to the TV. It's the one you watched when we had dinner last night."

"Oh, that one. Maybe."

"Go to your place and watch it while I fix dinner. When I'm done, I'll call for you."

"OK. What about your lesson?"

"What lesson?"

"The one we discussed."

"Well, I enjoy learning. Maybe after dinner."

James was so excited by that idea it was almost impossible to concentrate on the TV. His mother showed him her new kitchen and bathroom.

"What am I looking at?" he asked.

"Emily finished what you and Joseph were supposed to do. She painted the bathroom herself."

"Wow. How long did it take?"

"All day. She's a hard worker."

"She's pretty amazing." He looked up from the TV. "She said she was making dinner for me tonight, so I'll be getting a call soon."

He watched the game for almost ninety minutes. There were only five minutes of game time left. Why hadn't she called?

He called her.

"Honey," he asked groggily, "is dinner ready yet?"

Her mumbled reply told him she was sleeping.

He turned to his mother. "Did you wear out my girlfriend today?"

"She wore me out. We worked all morning stripping those walls."

He'd been looking forward to that job.

"After lunch," she continued, "she painted the kitchen and the bathroom." She pointed toward both rooms. "She did a wonderful job. She told me she used to paint with her grandparents. She didn't lose a drop on the floor or on herself. She was great. I like her. We had such fun."

"I'm glad you like her, but now she's passed out, and she was going to feed me."

"I can feed you. What do you want?"

"Emily."

"I don't think she's on the menu. Try again."

He ate his mother's cooking and let Emily sleep, hoping she hadn't started cooking before she passed out.

"Should I go down there in case she left the stove on?" he asked.

"Just try to smell through the door."

"OK." He took his key and went to see if Emily's kitchen was safe. When he saw it was, he carried her to bed, covered her, and locked the door behind her.

He had such plans for the night, and he thought she was ready, too, but she was too sleepy. She did a week's work in a day. At least he could go back upstairs and watch the game without feeling guilty about not spending time with her.

• • • • •

The following morning, Emily was upset. "Why didn't you come down last night?"

"I did. I called you first, but you answered like you were asleep. I went down to make sure your place wasn't on fire if something was left on the stove, and I found you sleeping on that dog bed."

"That's a body pillow."

"Anyway, I made sure the kitchen was safe, then I picked you up and put you in bed."

"No wonder I woke up in my clothes. You didn't even unhook my bra."

"I knew I was missing something."

"Next time, wake me up."

"You were pretty out of it."

"I'm sorry. We had great plans, didn't we?"

"Maybe tonight."

"Tonight is going to be late. I have to meet Mr. Howell. He wants me to meet his wife and to see how I'm doing."

"Am I invited?"

"I'm sure they wouldn't turn you away as my escort, but there won't be any sports tonight."

"I thought you already said that."

"I meant on TV."

"Oh. Maybe I should let you go without me."

"That would be OK. Let me flip a coin, so the decision of me versus rugby is determined by fate."

"It's not rugby, though I like that, too. It's soccer."

"Oh. What did you teach my nephews?"

"Soccer."

The car stopped. The driver, having heard the entire conversation, turned to open the door. "The coin now?"

"The coin? Sure," Emily said. "Do you have one?"

He handed her a coin. "Call it, Miss Emily."

"Let James call. It's his game."

"Queen." That meant heads, and he lost, so it looked like he'd be watching the game that night. "Will you call me when you get home?"

"Sure. I've got the number." They shared a quick kiss before entering the building.

"Thanks for remembering the toss," said the driver. "It would have driven me crazy not knowing. Did Mr. Howell suggest you bring a friend?"

Emily said, "I didn't think so. I didn't know."

"Well, have a good day," the driver replied, pulling away to pick up Mr. and Mrs. Howell at the airport. He'd known them for years, and he wanted to tell them how Emily was doing. Normally, such information didn't come from a servant, but Mr. Howell liked to talk to anyone who was intelligent. Mr. Howell was careful not to let Emily know about his information sources.

Emily dressed nicely for the day, so she wouldn't have to return home to change. It was a nice day, and she didn't get dirty or sweaty, though she would probably sweat a bit when she met the boss.

• • • • •

The car was waiting for her at six o'clock, and it smelled good as she sat in the back seat. "What's the nice smell?" she asked Carl, the driver.

"Mr. Howell likes that fragrance," he replied.

"Oh. I should've asked what you had."

"Hmmm."

When the car finally stopped, Emily was surprised to see Mr. Howell opening the door for her and offering her a hand to get out.

"Thank you," Emily said. "It's nice to see you again, and kind of you to think of me."

"I wanted to see how you were. Your grandmother would have expected that. I also have a question I want you to consider, and I want you to answer truthfully, but first, let's have dinner. Madge is waiting."

They went up to the suite, which looked familiar to Emily, though some of the furniture had been moved.

"This is the way I like it," Mr. Howell explained. "They put my items in storage when I'm away."

"I like it, but the way I first saw it was fantastic, too." She sat in a familiar chair, and Mr. Howell took his recliner.

"I had to have this delivered from home," he told her. "It makes all the difference in the world. I can relax here." He pointed at the brown leather handle.

She nodded, remembering how Grandpa loved his recliner. She still had it. Grandma couldn't part with it, and neither could Emily.

Madge came out of the bedroom in casual dress. "Emily,

I'm so glad to see you. When I heard your grandma had you and your brothers with her, I was happy knowing she had a family."

"She was very happy. She practically raised me from birth. I guess I was her second child."

"I read about your parents, and I know it's late, but I'm so sorry about that. I lost my dad when I was just a girl. He was a policeman who was killed on the job."

They sat quietly for a moment.

"That was a long time ago for both of us," Madge said. "I've heard nothing but good things about you, Emily. Howie, did you show her what Rebecca wrote about her?"

"No, *Madame,*" he replied. "That's confidential." He looked at Madge, then at Emily. "I can't show you the document, but she thinks you have great promise. When she leaves to take my place in Texas, would you consider taking her place here in England?"

"Wow!" Emily sat back. "That's an honor, but I've been here only three months. I'm still a rookie. Why aren't you looking for a more tenured person?"

"It's an offer, because you're a descendant. It's customary, but there are so few of you. Most relatives aren't as good as you've proven yourself to be."

"I wanted to try it out, but I'd rather stay where I am until it's time for me to return home. I certainly want to remain part owner, but I like the freedom of going home when I feel ready."

"We expected that answer. Had you said yes, we would've asked more questions. This is your company, but I love it, too, and I'd hate to see it go to the dogs. Though you're young, you have the wisdom of age.

"I see a lot of your grandmother in you. She weighed only ninety-eight pounds, but she was a heavy hitter. When her husband died, things changed for the better. She wasn't just a pretty face. She studied the company and was able to read people."

"Dinner's here," Madge said. "Do you want to eat before

it gets cold?" She smiled at Emily. "Howie likes his food hot. Come on, Emily. Carl told us about James. Is he a good man?"

"I think so. He's the first man I've ever felt this way about. I don't know. It'll take some time to decide."

"That sounds good."

Emily tasted her food. "This is really…. What is this?"

"Pheasant."

"Oh. It doesn't taste like chicken."

Mr. Howell looked at her. "You're funny. Your grandmother said the same thing to me years ago."

He continued talking to her about her grandmother, which made her happy. It sounded like a different person, though Emily knew it was the same.

"Honey, do you remember when Mrs. Roscoe came with this little girl in her stroller?"

"Yes. She ate all your cookies."

"I brought a couple from my lunch. You were so cute."

"Then, Mrs. Roscoe suggested we always have cookies on hand for company, which was a great idea. We had many businessmen and women come to our company to offer large donations, and they always had a cookie in their hands."

"I'll bet you gave her that idea," Mr. Howell said. "You were the idea girl even when you were in diapers."

Emily blushed.

"I heard you started that Dress for Success day tomorrow."

"I wanted everyone to look nice when you came to see Rebecca."

"That's good business sense. People work better when they look professional."

"Everyone needs a shot in the arm sometimes. It can't hurt. We even have prizes for the winners."

"What kind of gifts are they?"

"The best-dressed person gets a paid day off. Other prizes are food coupons and small electronic gizmos, stuff I thought might be interesting."

"Why you? Were you the only one?"

"We had to do it quickly. I really like Rebecca and wanted this to be a special day for her. I felt if we wanted to do it again or to try other activities, we could form a committee of some kind."

"Not just the bosses?"

"We could have a few, but, if the peons join, there's more pride and chances to shine."

"Wow. That's another good idea."

"Thanks. Other companies do this, too, but we can always borrow a good idea."

"I was just thinking.... Since you aren't taking Rebecca's job, why don't we see if the new man needs a personal secretary or assistant That way, if he turns bad, you'll know and can tell me. For now, it'll be Rebecca."

"Don't you trust the people around here?"

"It's not completely that. It's just better to extinguish a fire when it's small. I had an office in another country where the people broke lots of rules. We almost lost contributors. Worse, our clients weren't being served properly. I have people overseeing the computer activity there now."

"You need company-wide policy classes with all employees signing a promise to follow the rules once they learn them. Give them three strikes and they're out."

"Wow. You're a little Vivian. What else?"

"Maybe a suggestion box with a prize for the best submitted idea each quarter?"

"Marge, are you taking notes on this?"

"I don't do that anymore, Dear. Maybe Emily can write a list for us. She can send it to me and Rebecca."

"Actually," Emily said, "some of those ideas are Rebecca's. She didn't want to compromise the company's standards."

"It'll be a long day tomorrow," Mr. Howell said. "I can't wait."

"I can't, either," his wife said.

"May I ask you something?" Emily asked.

"Yes."

"I'm trying to hide my identity. When you come to the office, I want to be in my own office, not standing beside Rebecca when you surprise her. James, my boyfriend, knows who I am, but it wouldn't be good for everyone else to find out. I need a low profile."

"I'll beep you when my car arrives. You can go to your office and get involved with something, but you'll miss all the glory."

"Her workers have been with her longer than I have. They deserve to celebrate her success. I'll come out later when it's time for cake. I like cake."

"That's a good idea. When people are standing around, eating cake, I can talk to you and Rebecca. People won't notice then. You won't be wearing your Queen hat, either."

"We call it a crown in Texas."

They laughed.

"I've been saying that all my life."

"The car's here, and it's late," Emily said. "See you tomorrow."

• • • • •

At her flat, she found James waiting at her door.

"Why didn't you just go inside?" she asked.

"That might've scared you."

"You scare me all the time." She put her arms around him, and he led her into the flat.

After kissing for a few minutes, he looked at her and asked, "How was dinner?"

"It was pretty amazing. We were at the hotel suite. I got to meet his wife, too. They remember me as a baby. They knew my grandma."

He blinked in surprise.

"You can't tell anyone. Please? I want to stay here awhile and have a regular job."

"And?"

"And spend quality time loving you."

"Sounds good to me."

They sat on the dog pad, where they had to lean against the wall to sit up, though they often didn't bother.

"Do you have a nice outfit for tomorrow?" she asked.

"Why?"

"Tomorrow is Dress for Success day. Mr. Howell's coming, and I want everyone to look good."

"OK. I'll wear a tie at least until lunch."

"How about a jacket?"

"Pants, too?"

She looked at him. He was cute, but she was too tired.

"Want me to tuck you in?" he asked.

"I can't wait for the weekend."

"Why?"

"We're off work."

He wanted to stay, but his mother was ready to lock the apartment. Since she thought so highly of Emily, his mother wouldn't approve of his hitting on her.

CHAPTER TWENTY-ONE

The Dream

Emily needed sleep, but she had too much on her mind. Tossing and turning, she eventually fell into a dream. She walked into the office in high heels, a black pencil skirt, and a blazer. For color, jumbo red beads caressed her neck. No one else wore nice business clothes. They wore blue jeans with holes, even in inappropriate places, logo T-shirts, and multicolored bra straps hanging over tattooed ladies. She saw more than the usual amount of spiked, rainbow-colored hair, and everyone had piercings in her nose, lip, and cheeks. It looked like someone poked them with guns. They pulled out cigarettes and dropped smoldering butts behind. Used coffee cups and McDonald's breakfast sandwich wrappers in wads lay near the trash basket. It was like Halloween.

Turning on Emily, they shoved her around so hard, she almost fell down.

"What do you expect after pushing us around?"

"Why'd you give us this crap? We don't dress for success. We dress to express!"

"Do you get the message? Bug off! Go home!"

They shoved her until she fell down among the remnants of Egg McMuffins and cocoa lattes. She braced her arms, but she slipped on the liquids and fell down, messing up her shiny black skirt while she lost a shoe.

Her friend, Marcy, grabbed the shoe and aimed the heel at Emily's face. Security ran in to control the mob, while Emily screamed for help. Everyone in the big crowd seemed strong and scary, their faces twisted in anger. They had hated her all along, but that time, it was worse. She had no idea they felt that way about her.

A big blond football player dressed in black with a gun on his hip plowed through the crowd toward her.

"Lie on the ground with your hands behind your back." His hand rested on his gun butt.

She couldn't believe what was happening, but she followed his demands to avoid being shot.

He grabbed her small hands and jerked the cuffs as tight as he could. Blood oozed from both wrists. He lifted her by her hands until she thought her shoulders were dislocated. Once on her feet, she realized she had only one shoe. Marcy threw the missing shoe at her. Striking her face, it left a nasty gash, then it bounced against the soda machine and broke the glass.

She kicked off her other shoe and tried to walk, as the cop shoved her into a city bus.

"Take this trash to the airport. We've had enough of her here," he told the driver.

She was barely on the first step when the driver floored the accelerator, and she fell backward onto the street, her face bloody, barefoot, crying, and broken. She turned only to see no one nearby.

It started raining, and her tears joined the raindrops. Kneeling on her snagged hosiery, she tried to stand, which in a pencil skirt didn't look pretty.

Where could she go? She walked toward her flat. It was ten blocks away, but she had nowhere else to go. She refused to return to the office building. Her wrists burned when raindrops struck the bloody cuts. She wondered if she could slide her hands from back to front under her legs. She might be able to try that in a bathroom.

It was a long walk. When she finally got her arms in front of her body, her wrists hurt even more. She looked for her flat, wondering where it was. She never walked there before. All the buildings looked alike. Usually, the chauffeur picked her up. Mr. Howell should have seen her walking and rescued her. Where was the love of her life, the man who should be waiting for her? Why wasn't he there? Were their feelings toward each other nothing?

• • • • •

The phone rang, waking her.

"Hey, Babe. I'm all dressed up," James said. "Open the door."

She opened the door and felt the bad dream recede.

"Honey? What's going on?"

"I had a terrible dream. People at work ganged up on me. They were furious with me. They beat me, then Rob, the security guy, cuffed me and put me on the bus to the airport, so I could go back to America."

"Oh, Love, I'm so sorry! I promise that won't happen. I'll protect you no matter what happens. My new line is, 'God save the Queen.'"

"What?"

"You're my queen. I'd never let anyone hurt you." He knelt before her, lowered his head, and kissed her hands.

She held his head, near her stomach, and knelt until they were on the floor, facing each other. Their kisses were different. She had a nightmare, and he said he was her white knight, but where was he in her dream? Dreams always had a catch that gave them away. Not seeing James was a missing component. She wondered if he'd been in the crowd that attacked her but didn't want her to see him.

"I'd love to stay here all day, but this is your day," he said. "Let's dress and shine. If anything happens, I'll protect you."

"Will they like this, or will they be angry?"

"I like wearing my T-shirt and jeans to work, but it was fun dressing up for today. If it was an everyday thing, I wouldn't like it. This is just once in a while. It's like picture day. Is anyone going to photograph people today?"

"I didn't think that far ahead. I expect the pictures in my mind will be enough."

"I have my camera, so we can take some pictures. It should be fun. We can post them on our desktops. People will like that. It'll be good for all the offices. Get ready. I'll watch."

She looked at him, then down at herself. It seemed he'd had a free show already. She returned to her bedroom and started cleaning up. She donned the outfit she wore in the dream and looked at the shoes. Would they be her doom?

Forcing herself to smile, she walked out of the room.

"Wow!" James said. "How am I supposed to work with this kind of distraction?"

"Some people work in clothes like these every day."

"Do they strip?"

"You're a gem. Let's get going. You make me happy."

"That's my job."

On the way to work, Emily paid attention to street signs and distances. She looked for icons that would help her memorize where she lived. Before that day, she just got into a car and let someone drive her.

"Are you reliving the dream?" James asked.

"I'm trying not to, but could you give me bus fare? I want to hide it in my bra just in case."

"Should I get cuff keys, too?"

"Do you have any?"

"Who do you think I am, McGiver?" He kissed her. "It'll be a wonderful day. Are you OK?"

"I guess."

Stepping out, she saw people in the building smiling at her. They stood around, drinking coffee and eating breakfast, but they carefully disposed of their trash in the bins. Every time someone new walked by in a nice outfit, people complimented him or her.

It was like picture day at school or graduation. Maybe it was a good idea after all.

"Everyone has nice clothes," James told her, "but we have nowhere to wear them. You gave them a chance to think about dressing up."

"I hope you're right."

He hugged her without a kiss. They didn't want others to know how they felt.

They walked into the building as if walking into a church. It would be a good day. When the huge cop walked past, he saluted her. He wasn't wearing a gun, and he didn't brandish any handcuffs. Maybe the day would be OK after all. She wondered if executives like Mr. Howell or her grandmother had nightmares like that.

Looking out the window near her office, Emily saw the limo arrive with the Howells. The chauffeur, stepping out, opened the door for them, offered Mrs. Howell his hand, and shook Mr. Howell's hand after he was out.

The three of them admired the impressive, shiny, black-glass tower. Mr. Howell wanted an impressive building and designed it that way. By the way the three talked together, it was clear they were friends. She knew Mr. Howell would give his impressions to Rebecca.

Suddenly, James came up and said, "Boo!"

She jumped.

"Did I scare you?"

"I guess. I was taking a picture in my mind."

"Let's get it on film." He took out his camera and snapped

several pictures outside, then he caught the limo driver and their VIP guests.

He logged on to Emily's computer and tapped a few keys. "Since you want to hide up here, I logged into the security cameras so you can see everything. Here's a spare USB drive. If you see anything you want as a memory, snap it. You can keep this."

He kissed her. "I need to get down there and take some memories, too."

She was alone in her room, and having the cameras showing on her computer was better than TV. Work could wait. Since James signed on, if she changed anything, she'd lose the show.

She felt worried, but it was also exciting. She sat down, sipped her tea, and watched the world go by.

The presentation of Rebecca's promotion was like a royal crowning. The staff looked good in their outfits. All were glad they dressed for the happy occasion, and Rebecca was glad she hadn't worn her regular clothes, even though she always dressed well. That day, she looked better than ever.

She thought of Emily and realized her friend had known all about it. Telling her they needed a dress-up day was just an excuse.

She looked up at the nearest security camera and said, "Emily, come to my office right now."

Emily snapped a picture of that before she left. Seeing a nice bouquet of flowers someone placed on her desk, she scooped them up to give to Rebecca.

Emily went to the party, glad her heels didn't hurt. She felt like she was floating.

Rebecca saw her coming, then she saw the flowers.

Emily handed her friend the flowers. "Today, you're a queen."

"Look who's talking."

"Oh?"

"How do you feel?"

"Like a queen."

"I'm so happy. This is more than I could have imagined."

"We'll need to serve cake and pass out the awards for the best-dressed."

"I got this," Rebecca said. "I asked a couple of my people to make the decisions and hand out the awards, so folks won't know it was your idea. That's what you wanted, right?"

"Yes. That's perfect. You make me so happy. I'll miss you."

They hugged, then Emily stepped back, because the Howells were approaching. They carefully called Emily Miss, not her full name. She was anxious to talk to them, but the party was so loud, they couldn't carry on a clear conversation.

They hugged, and heart-shaped balloons fell from the ceiling, with faded color on the sides.

"I've never seen balloons like this," Emily said.

"It's your grandmother's design," Mrs. Howell said. "We love the faded sweetheart, don't you?"

"That was the first art we ever did. Grandma loved the fact that I loved them as much as she did. I'd love them for my wedding, too."

"When will that be?"

Emily's friends at work came to carry her off to another conversation, so she didn't have to answer. Everyone had a great day while not working.

She waved good-bye to the Howells. Now that she was in the actual party, she wasn't on the security cameras. Someone else could take pictures.

Joel, a friend of James, offered to take over the job. James eventually met up with Emily, and they talked briefly.

Soon, an announcement was made that everyone should move to the lunchroom for cake and prizes. It was a tight squeeze, but everyone fit.

Rebecca stepped forward. "We'll have lunch served, then there are cake and awards. Then we need to get some work done this afternoon, OK?"

They cheered.

"What's for lunch?" someone asked.

She looked at Mr. Howell. "Sir?"

"I found a place that makes Texas barbecue. I hope you like it."

The crowd was silent for a moment, then a voice from the back of the room said, "Hee-haw! That's what I'm talkin' about!"

They turned and were surprised to see the normally quiet production manager from the second floor jumping up and down in a lasso dance. Music started playing, and everyone did the horse.

Emily looked at James. "What's gotten into them? Where'd they learn this dance?"

"Blake," James called, "who taught you to hee-haw?"

"It just comes natural!"

As country music played throughout lunch, people tapped their feet, and they enjoyed the saucy, sweet cuts of beef, chicken, and sausage. Mr. Howell made sure ice-cold sweet tea was served. Anyone who wanted something else had traditional hot tea or a soda.

The co-managers began cutting and passing out cake. Emily hoped the cake was big enough. James' brother made it for them, having been allowed to do more cooking at the bakery.

Finally, at one o'clock, it was time to return to work. Rebecca and the Howells stood in a reception line, while people walked by and thanked them, wishing Rebecca the best with her promotion.

James started walking Emily to her office, but Rebecca stopped her.

"Can I speak with Emily for a few minutes?" she asked James "She can find her own way to her desk."

He looked at Emily, and she squeezed his hand before letting go, then turned to face her boss squarely. "Later, James."

"Later, Luv," he said softly, walking away.

"That was a great lunch, wasn't it?" Emily asked.

"It's been a great day. You did an awesome job. Where'd

you find a barbecue place in London?"

"I've been calling around, but I couldn't find anyplace, so I sent the recipes to the hotel and asked them to work on it. They did a pretty good job, didn't they? I sent my expert to help. She's been working with them all night to perfect the recipe. Luckily, we included a grocery list, so it was a matter of mixing things properly. They've got a great kitchen."

Rebecca nodded.

"Did you know they want to add those things to the menu?" Rebecca asked.

"Another reason why we'll want to visit."

"It might be a good thing for tourism."

"Should I return to work?"

"No. We've got some legal work to do first."

"OK." Emily wondered what was going on.

"Since you're the primary owner of Roscoe Corporation, you need to sign the transfer so Rebecca can go to Texas as my replacement," Mr. Howell said.

"OK."

"We decided to promote Michael Cain as her replacement here," he continued. "He's been here for several years and has proved himself. He'll do a wonderful job, but I want to promote you as his personal assistant. You're fresh, capable, and have proven yourself. If he thinks you need more instruction, he'll call Rebecca. He'll report on you periodically. We won't reveal your identity, but if you can help Michael without reporting any problems to us, that would be good. We don't want you acting as a snitch unless it's a dire condition. Do you agree?"

"Yes."

"Then sign here. We'll take this document back to corporate, so no one will see it. I'll keep it in my briefcase." He put those papers inside, then added Rebecca's paperwork, too. "It's time for me and Mrs. Howell to leave. We're going to Paris, so if you want your suite back, it's available."

"I've got a flat now, so I'm good. Thank you."

"Emily, you can return to work," Rebecca said. "I told

your boss I wanted our help cleaning up the party stuff."

"OK."

The Howells walked outside to the limo. The driver closed the door behind them and started the engine. Their bags were already in the trunk. They would take a train to Paris before returning to the States.

After the balance of the workday, a general email went out to invite people to a pub to continue the celebration.

"Do you want to go?" James asked Emily.

"Is it the place we went before?"

"No. It's bigger."

"Maybe for a few minutes, but I like our place."

"OK. I'll meet you in a few hours. We can go to the party first, then to our place for dinner."

CHAPTER TWENTY-TWO

Sometimes, You Party Too Hard

The first pub was very crowded. Men removed their ties and stuffed them into pockets. Blazers hung over people's shoulders, women removed their high heels, and people drank pints of beer like water. When country music played on the loudspeakers, the men shouted, "Hee haw!"

Emily could barely see James. She had too many pints and needed to go home, so he called a cab for them. She was so tipsy, he almost carried her upstairs.

Faded Sweetheart

"Emily, you need to go to bed."
"Well, then take me."
"Take you where?"
"In the bed, Stupid."
"I beg your pardon?"
"I want you now. I need you. Come to me."
"Are you sure you want to do this?"
"Of course I do." She suddenly became serious. "You do want me, don't you?"
He looked at her. "I love you. I'll be true to you."

• • • • •

The following morning, Emily woke up and shouted, "Where are my clothes? Good grief, James, what are you doing here? Where are *your* clothes? What did we do last night? Oh, my gosh!"

She grabbed the sheet but didn't want to uncover James, so she tossed him a pillow before running to the bathroom.

"Emily? I think it's too late for that."

She poked her head outside the bathroom. "It's too late? Oh, my gosh. What will I tell my grandmother?" She walked back to the bed, the sheet falling away, and began crying. "What kind of person am I?"

He removed the pillow and placed his hand on her bare back. "You're a beautiful person. I love you. You might have been a bit drunk last night, but you weren't about to take no for an answer. You were hot. You almost tore off my clothes. I wondered if you were a pro."

"What?"

"You were amazing."

She blushed. "Well, let's do it again, so I can enjoy it. I don't remember much of last night."

He smiled and obliged.

• • • • •

Two hours later, she looked at the man she loved. "I really did remember last night. I just wanted to do it again."

He rolled on top of her. "You want to do it again?"

"Well," she said, feeling his bare skin against hers, "maybe we should have breakfast first."

"OK, but we should shower first."

"Together?"

"Will we fit?"

"We can squeeze in."

James' phone rang.

"I'll bet that's your mother, wondering what we're doing."

"You made a lot of noise last night."

"I hope not."

"Hello? Yes, Sir. Red alert." He paused. "Report for duty this afternoon? Yes, Sir."

He turned, but Emily had gone to the bathroom. A moment later she returned in her bathrobe.

"What's the matter?" she asked. "Who was that?"

"When I first got out of school, I joined the Royal Navy. I spent four years there and got out, but I'm still in the Joint Cyber Reserve. They want me out there this afternoon."

"This afternoon? Is that a joke? That's no warning at all. What kind of weekend soldier are you?"

"I'm in cyber spy warfare. There must be some hacking that the regulars can't deal with."

"Can you fix it that fast? Why can't you do it at home? Why do you have to leave?"

"I haven't been told everything, but the military prefers us to use their systems, not a tablet in a flat."

"So I have to make breakfast for you and say 'Good-bye,'?" she asked, crying.

"It's not like I'm going to the front lines. People don't get killed with using computers. Will you marry me today before I leave?"

They looked at the clock. It was almost noon on Saturday.

"If we were in the States, we could fly to Vegas, but I

don't think you can hire a British jet for that."

"Probably not. If only we hadn't stayed in bed so long."

"If only you hadn't answered the phone."

"They would've called my next contact, which would mean having my mother banging on the door to get me."

"We need to dress and tell her."

He looked at the pillows, then he grabbed her waist to turn her toward him. "Do we have time?"

She kissed him. "You have government things to do. We have to rise, because duty calls." She got out of bed. "How about that shower?"

The day passed in a flurry of activity. His uniform hung in the closet, but there wasn't time to have it steamed and pressed. Emily shook it out to get some freshness into the fabric.

Loretta sat on the bed, thinking about James' recall. When he went the first time, she was ready, but that time, it seemed too sudden.

Emily tried to make the best of it. "Do you have all our numbers in case they take away your cell phone? Will you get to call us every day? If you're allowed only one call, I would relay everything to your mother."

"I would tell you, too," Loretta said.

"Maybe we should only speak face-to-face to avoid having our information leaked to the enemy." She didn't know who the enemy was, but she heard plenty of stories from Grandpa about such things.

She was under so much stress, she almost forgot they made love. She knew he loved her, and, if it weren't a weekend, they would have gotten married.

Married in a day, she thought. *My family would kill me. He just needs to fix some profiles, test them, and come back. That should take no more than a couple days. He's good.*

He packed his duffle bag and dressed in his uniform. Instead of seeing him off at the dock, the Navy sent a car for him. Emily, Loretta, and Joseph stood outside the bakery to say good-bye. Before James got into the car, he checked the other people's ID, and they checked his. If there was a cyber war, it would be a good idea to kidnap the other side's personnel.

As the car drove off, those left behind went inside feeling sad but hopeful he wouldn't be away long.

Emily received her first call that evening. James was fine, and he had already been briefed on his assignment.

"It shouldn't take very long," he told her. "We've discussed ideas to lock it down. I'll be back in a couple weeks."

"Weeks?"

"We have to go out to sea to tweak the system onboard."

"Oh."

"Call my mom. If I get another chance to call, maybe I'll call her."

"That would be good, I guess."

"Yes, and Honey, you can't mention this trip to anyone. We're on high alert."

"OK."

"That includes your family."

"OK."

"Got to go. I miss you. Plan a wedding for me while I'm gone."

She had no idea what kind of wedding he wanted. She wasn't even sure what kind *she* wanted. That would occupy her time while he was away, though, and it sounded like fun.

Needing to call Rebecca, she checked the time difference with Texas. She hated people who called based on the wrong time zone.

"Do you have a minute?" she asked Rebecca. "It's about Grandma's house."

"It's still in one piece. Do you want us to put it on the market?"

"I've been thinking. I spoke with William and Andrew. Where do VIPs stay when they're in Corpus Christi?"

"We usually have them find a place and reimburse them."

"The boys could set up my house with two nice master bedrooms with en suites, a fully stocked kitchen, and catering available. We'll get a deluxe kid toy in the back. It already has a beautiful deck and outdoor kitchen. We might even put a suite on the second floor. Grandpa never finished it, but we didn't need it then. It was already a four-bedroom house."

"We could have Internet connected directly to the company, so they can work from home. Families could stay with them. It's possible two or three people, once the upstairs was finished, could share the house, so you wouldn't have to boot someone out when another person arrived."

"That sounds like a dream. Would we have to pay for it?"

"No. It's an investment on my part. When the guys are done, you can have a board meeting there with the caterer, and they can decide."

"OK, but why not make one side a big master and the upstairs, and the other side could be a nice apartment with medium-sized rooms for the families or if we're having an in-service and need the space."

"Great. I'll email some drawings to you. Go ahead and add the new ideas."

When Rebecca's revisions came back to Emily, she sent the drawings to her brothers, then called William.

"What do you think?" she asked.

"It looks like a good idea. Who'll choose the colors and furnishings?"

"Isn't April taking something like that in school?"

"Yeah, but she's just a kid."

"Before we did anything, Julie and I would have to approve it. She usually has good taste, and being young is good in design. Young people think outside the box. If your boys want to help, I'll pay them appropriately."

"That would be good for them. We loved working with our hands with Grandpa."

"I remember. Maybe you can add a basketball hoop in front of the garage."

"What about the ball?"

"Keep it locked in your car until you're finished."
"Sounds like talking to Grandpa."
"He was a natural. Send me pictures as you progress. When will it be finished?"
"We haven't even started yet. I'll work up some numbers. Once I look over the plans, I'll get back to you."
"You sound like a professional."
"I am, and...."
"What?"
"What color do you want your room?"
"My room?"
"I'd guess you'll have the master suite when you visit."
"My, my. You can read me pretty well."
"I know. I can also guess the color you'd like."
"What would that be?"
"Crème and sky blue, with yellow in the bathroom?"
"A really light yellow."
"Yes, Ma'am."
"Keep in touch."
"OK. 'Bye, Sister."
"'Bye. Love you."

William, driving to the house, looked around. Emily left everything in it, so they could save money by using that furniture for a while. They would replace it once they found something better, or if the furniture became worn.

In the kitchen, he saw Grandma's best silver was missing, but the rest of the utensils would be fine for everyday use. George did a good job taking care of the place. Maybe they could pay him to stay in the guest house out back to oversee the main house when it was occupied. He made notes for Emily. Once he had the answers he needed, he would propose the idea to George.

Will tried to call Emily back several times without success. He didn't think too much of that and emailed her instead.

Why didn't you call me? she typed back.

Seeing it on paper is better. We can see the first page. Call me. I tried to call a couple times.

When did you call?

Around one.

I was sleeping. I probably didn't hear.

I'm glad we did this on computer.

Can you have April send me some of her shots?

OK. I figure it'll take three months.

That puts it around October. That's good. I'll tell Rebecca.

OK.

I was also thinking that if an employee had a housing problem, we could offer them the house for a short period of time until they're settled. I talked to the son of the man Grandma used to have for the RV supplies delivery system.

Are you buying an RV now?

No, but the guy could stock the house. He's also a caterer. If a guest couldn't or didn't want to cook, we could call him.

That sounds interesting.

When we finish the house, we'll ask the board to have dinner there. He'll cook for us.

If he's good, that would be great.

In England, when Mr. Howell came, they furnished certain items for him, like his recliner.

You'll be the biggest big shot, so we could keep your stuff here.

We might want to keep some baby stuff there and foldaway beds for kids.

Another good idea. How about a car in the garage? That way, it would be under cover and already insured. With built-in GPS, anyone can find their way around.

So unlike England. And....

Another idea?

This could be a template. We could do the same thing on other places and/or sell the homes to other companies.

OK. I need to rest. Your great ideas are making me tired.

Since it's almost four o'clock in the morning here, I need to sleep, too.

You should have told me.

It's on your phone. Did you know that?
I guess I do. Good night.
'Night.

• • • • •

Mr. Howell called Emily later in the day. "What are you doing tonight?"

"It's nice to hear from you, Mr. Howell. I just got off the phone with my brother. Have you heard about the corporate house?"

"Rebecca mentioned it. It's very generous of you to donate it to the corporation."

"When I visit, I want someplace to stay. The hotel was wonderful, but there were many nights I wanted a fried egg or PBJ."

"You've got some great ideas, though you sound tired."

"It's four o'clock in the morning here, and William talked to me for about an hour."

"I'm so sorry. Now that I'm retired, I have a poor sense of time."

"Do you sleep better now?"

"Yes. No more nightmares."

"You had nightmares?"

"Terrible ones. That goes with being top dog."

"I've had a few, too. How did you deal with them? I'm tired, because I had a horrible nightmare last night."

"It's part of being the boss."

"Am I dreaming now, or am I on speaker phone?"

"We forgot to tell you. We're in the conference room, discussing your plan. Sorry."

"Who's we?"

"It's me, Emily," Madge said. "Rebecca's here, too."

Emily was relieved not to be speaking with a board room full of strangers. "Thanks, Mrs. Howell. It's nice to hear from you, too." She tried not to sound tired.

"Emily, you might need to take a sleep aid on certain

nights," Rebecca said.

"Or a drink," Mrs. Howell said.

"Don't drink. That's what Mr. Roscoe did—often. Make sure you're ready those days. Remind yourself of the details, make a list, and check them off as you go. Get a good team and use them. That's what you hired them for. Let them work and shine. You'll still get nightmares, but you can laugh them off. You're strong."

"Thank you." She loved the older man and his wife, and she missed having Rebecca stand from her desk for a *little sister hug.*

"I miss you here in Texas. When you want to come home," Rebecca said, "I'll find you a job, or you can have mine."

"It'll be a long time before I do that. I might stay here awhile. My family misses me, but I need to be alone and grow."

"Good answer. Good night, Sweetheart."

Emily, hanging up, pulled the covers over herself. She closed her eyes and remembered happily leaving Rebecca's office while everyone looked fondly at her.

• • • • •

She kept working on her flat. She bought a buffet for her new Italian dishes, and their pretty colors motivated her to add more color to the place. She used five rolls of painter's tape to make a crisscross pattern on the top of the buffet. She painted the interior spaces white, so the dishes placed inside would show their color, then added lights to increase the shine.

In the crisscross, she painted it blue and white with the same paint she used for the kitchen walls. Next, she bought colorful appliances. It took some searching, but she eventually found cobalt-blue pans, a yellow mixer with flowers on the side, and orange utensils to hang on the wall. She added towels in brilliant colors, dish rags, potholders, and a floor rug. She didn't have a table yet, so she put off buying anything for that.

For the sofa, she bought yellow stretched broadcloth and several yards of blue stars, purple stripes, and solid red. She planned to make lots of pillows, so she ordered five pounds of batting. She loved sewing and hoped her pillows would hold up.

• • • • •

Two weeks passed without James. Contact was limited, and his calls were very brief. Emily understood what he couldn't say. She always said she loved him.

Since walking to work was a long process, she decided to get a Vespa. She could park it just inside the corridor at night, and having it made her feel independent. She took it to shopping and work.

She kept looking for a sofa and found one that almost seemed right, but she remembered the one she saw online and decided to get that instead. A day later, she changed her mind and canceled the order, using the saved money to get the quirky one that caught her eye. She bought more batting to cover it.

She likes being cradle with her early American sofa with wooden wings on the head, but she didn't like the wood. So she would pad that part and have one smooth plane covered in yellow. She made the slipcover and liked it.

She removed the sofa skirt and painted the legs green to make it stand out. When she posted a picture of it on FaceBook, she received many likes, and someone asked for the pattern.

"Who uses patterns?" she asked herself. "If you ask for a pattern, you might as well go buy one."

She ignored that message.

Sometimes, she sewed almost all night, because she felt inspired. She missed James, but she was happy with her projects. Nothing could hold her back. Even Grandma left her alone when the sewing machine was running. She stood

Faded Sweetheart

at the door and watched quietly. If Grandma made a sound, Emily might look up, but otherwise, she was lost in concentration.

• • • • •

The next day, Emily went to rest on the sofa when she noticed the wall with the door didn't look very impressive. She got out a stepstool and pencil to sketch a paisley pattern. From there, she began sketching all around the room.

She looked for her box of paints and made up a pallet of colors. Any she was missing, she could buy on her Vespa the following day.

"That thing sure comes in handy," she muttered.

She took out her paint brushes and set to work.

• • • • •

The wall took only two days, and she added more color to the buffet. In the morning, she spent more time than usual in the bathroom. She had a queasy stomach and wondered if it was food poisoning, but it lasted too long. She wiped away tears and studied the yellow walls, trying to ignore her symptoms.

Emily called Julie to tell her about her remodeling. "I made faded sweethearts all over the bathroom."

"That's probably pretty."

"I started to count them, but there are too many."

"I thought you liked them."

They ended the call, because Julie had to go to work.

• • • • •

When Emily called a week later, she said, "I thought it was too much, so I painted over them, but the paint doesn't cover the lumps from the strokes of paint, so my faded sweethearts became bumpies. You can't see them, but you can feel

236

them."

"Are we talking about your bathroom again?" Julie asked.

"Yeah. What else is going on in my life? How are your kids?"

"They're fine. Where's James?"

"He's out of town on a project."

"OK. No wonder your bathroom is the topic. That's your busy work."

"Yeah."

"OK. Now we can talk about my kids." Julie told her several stories, then she heard soft snoring. "Emily? What time is it over there?"

There was no reply.

"Emily!"

"Yes?"

"Go to bed. You're tired."

"OK. 'Bye, Sister."

Several weeks later, Julie couldn't stand it any longer and called Emily.

"What's going on, Little Sister? You haven't called in weeks. I thought you were talking to Rook, so I asked him, but he said you haven't called him, either. Spill it, or I'm coming over there."

Emily was glad for the call, but she didn't want to reveal too much. "I've been busy. I started my bedroom, and you know what?"

"What?"

"It's your favorite color."

"What's that?"

Emily hoped she was right. "Off white. I got eyelet bed sheets and did French knots in white to decorate the pillows. It's a crème color. It's beautiful. My ceiling has sparkles in it." She felt she diverted Julie.

"That sounds lovely, but how busy are you that you can't call?"

"I was going to call tonight with pictures."

"Really? I'm calling you. What's going on?"

"I'm the executive secretary now. I take work home a lot. We have plenty of projects, and I give my ideas."

"Enough of work. I got all that from Rebecca. How's your love life? Where's James?"

"Oh. He's in Austria, fixing their computer system."

"Has he been there long?"

"This is his second trip. Someone switched the system after the first time, so he had to go back. He's trying to find out who did it, so he can have the person retrained or fired." *Boy, I can come up with some interesting lies,* she thought.

"With him gone, how are you doing?"

"I got a Vespa."

"Can you take medicine for it?"

"It's a little motorcycle. Ask Rook. He can probably find a picture for you. Maybe I'll send you one tomorrow."

"Why'd you want one?"

"I can get to work in five minutes, and it's safer and easier to park than a car. I buy groceries with it, too."

"How fast can it go?"

"I don't think I've gone over forty. Usually, I'm at thirty. It's navy blue, and I have a helmet, too."

"Thank God for that."

"I've got an incoming call, maybe from James. Can I call you back?"

"When?"

"Next week."

"OK, but don't forget. If you don't call, I'll fly over there."

"I'd love to see you, but I'm fine. You can stay at home and take care of your family. I miss them."

"We miss you, too."

• • • • •

Work for Emily was busy, and the new director did a good job. Emily had no complaints about her job, but James had been away for three months, and she began to stress out. She was also developing a bump in her stomach.

One day, Rebecca called.

"It's nice to hear from you," Emily said. "What's going on? How'd the board like the dinner and the house? Are we adding it to the company? I'm not sure what that's called. Anyway, you called, so go ahead."

"Dinner was good. It's a very pretty house. The board was delighted to have a place to offer visiting VIPs. You said you were going to put a car in the garage, didn't you?"

"I thought we could use the Jeep I left behind. It wasn't there?"

"We didn't see it, but actually, I'm calling about something else."

"OK. What?"

"What's going on with you?"

"I'm really busy. I have several projects they're letting me lead. I bought a Vespa, and I finally got the flat furnished. It's cute."

"And you're pregnant?"

Emily paused. "How'd you know?"

"I was checking the insurance payouts."

"Have you told anyone?"

"You mean your family?"

"Yes."

"No."

"Thank God."

"How'd it happen?"

"Are you asking me where babies come from?"

"No, I'm asking where James is. We don't have a branch in Austria."

"Remember my grandpa?"

"Oh." Rebecca assumed Emily was talking in code. "Are you OK? Do you want to move back to Texas?"

"No. I want to stay here. He should be back soon."

"Do we know when?"

"No, but his mother might be getting suspicious."

"You need to tell her."

"I'm not sure. I want to be independent. Maybe I'll go home during my leave."

"You bought a Vespa?"

"Yes. It's nice to be able to drive anywhere."

"Be careful. We had our first visitor in your...I mean the corporate house. They were from Australia, and they really liked the kitchen. They gave Leroy's kid the grocery list, and they were in heaven. The kids loved the jungle gym, and the crib was nice, too. You even thought of linens."

"You needed a bed sheet, and April was the one who bought it. She did a good job. She seems ready to spread her wings."

"It must run in the family. Please be careful. Let me know if I can help in any way. I'm on speed dial, right?"

"You are, and I will."

"Take care of yourself, Little Sister."

"I will. Don't tell anyone yet. I've got awhile to go, and I hope James comes back soon."

"I know he will. Get some sleep."

"OK. It was nice talking to you. How do you like being back in Texas?"

"It's hot, and I can't find a good cup of tea."

"You miss tea?"

"No, but I had to say it."

"You're funny."

"I just got an email. We found the car. The family parked it at the airport. They forgot it belonged to the house. Corporate places usually don't provide a car unless it has a driver."

"OK. Email bills to me for any out-of-pocket they generated."

"Corporate pays, but I'm guessing you want to keep a running account."

"Yeah, so I can use it as a promotion for corporate home-away-from-home packages for other companies."

"Always coming up with good ideas. Thanks! Later."

The call ended, and Emily made a mental note to call her brothers for their figures and to check with George about upkeep of the car.

"I'm sure the family would prefer curbside departure instead of having to park and walk at the airport," George said in agreement. "Always something."

"Thanks, George. You're doing a great job."

• • • • •

Emily had been in England for almost a year. Keeping a house ready for her in Texas was crazy, but going to a charming corporate home when she needed to visit was wonderful. It didn't take much to make her happy.

She thought about every room and what she loved in it. She wanted her box of possessions mailed to her. She wanted the dishes and items in the dining room kept. She didn't care about the bedding or living room furniture, but she wanted the pictures from the walls sent, too. The books could go into storage, but she wanted her art supplies.

She checked her flat. She might need a bigger room, especially after she doubled her family. She patted her belly, hoping the little one was started on her second time with James, when she wasn't drunk, knew what she was doing, and had such a wonderful time. How could she not get pregnant at such a special moment?

He wanted to marry her that day and told her to plan a wedding. She hadn't started yet, because she had so many things on her mind. She hoped he understood and would be happy about the baby.

Loretta knocked on Emily's door. When Emily let her in, Loretta said, "I got a call."

"From James?"

"Yes. He said your line was busy."

"I was talking to Rebecca. She offered to sell my house in Texas."

Loretta glanced down and frowned. "Emily, is there something you want to tell me?"

"What?"

She gently rubbed Emily's belly. "This."

"Yes, it's what you think."

"Does James know?"

"I haven't told him since he left. How is he?"

"He said he's OK, but he misses you."

"Did he say when he'd come back?"

"He didn't know."

"Oh."

"When are you due?"

"In twelve weeks."

"Do you want to go to America to be with your family?"

"I'd like to stay here in case he gets back, but I might go to Texas during my maternity leave."

Loretta hugged her. "I thought you were pregnant. You hid it well, but your face is so radiant, it's hard to miss."

"I'm trying to keep a low profile. Rebecca figured it out when she looked at some insurance reports. I wonder if my boss red-flagged it for her. How could she notice my name out of hundreds of employees around the world?"

"I guess that's what James deals with. There are no secrets anymore."

"Yeah."

"Well, you rest. I won't tell anyone, but if you need something, call." She walked out looking very happy, then popped her head back in. "I'm so happy we're having a baby!"

"Thank you!"

Loretta kissed Emily's cheek and left.

Emily finished her list and sent it to Rebecca.

• • • • •

The following day, Emily received a message telling her that her items from the house would arrive within ten weeks.

• • • • •

One week later, a large package arrived for Emily at work.

"Miss Queen, you received a package today," Mr. Cain said.

"May I open it?" She touched the box.

"Be my guest. Can I watch?"

"I guess." She bent over the large box, her belly getting in the way.

"Let me help." He opened it to reveal a plastic box. "Do you recognize this?" He lifted it by its handles.

"It was my grandmother's. I spoke with Rebecca recently, and she offered to send it to me. It has sentimental value, but it won't fit on my Vespa."

"I can have a car take it there. We can put the Vespa on the back."

"Thank you, Mr. Cain."

"You're a great employee. We all like you. It's my pleasure."

"Thank you."

"I'll put this box in the corner. The driver can load it for you later."

Emily went to her desk and checked her email. The first came from Texas headquarters. Rebecca told her the first box was shipped express to the office. The rest would get there in about eight more weeks.

Emily thanked her and started work.

• • • • •

At two-thirty, the driver came in to pick up the box. Mr. Cain suggested Emily leave for an early weekend, because he knew she felt sleepy in the afternoon and might want to open the box before her energy slumped.

Closing her desk, she left with happy feeling. She patted the box, as the man lifted it. The Vespa was already in the truck. After the man helped her into her seat, they drove off.

After driving for a while, he asked, "Do you know if it's a boy or girl?"

She looked at him. "I haven't asked. I could, but it doesn't matter. It's my first. If I already had a dozen boys, I'd be more concerned."

"My missus had four boys before we had girls."

"How many girls do you have?"

"Right now there are three. The next one was a boy."

"Wow. That's a lot of children. You're blessed."

"Thank you. They're a lot of work, but we're a happy bunch."

"I can see that."

A little while later, she said, "Here's my place. I can carry it up."

"Nonsense. I'll bet you haven't seen your feet in weeks."

She glanced down. "I can see them now. Oops. I'm wearing two different shoes."

"I know. My wife did the same thing. You women are so independent. What does your husband say?"

"He doesn't. He knows better." It was a lie, but she didn't want to admit the truth.

The driver laughed. "I should remember that. We could get a dog for the doghouse I'm always in."

She laughed, too.

He carried the box up the two flights of stairs and asked where to put it.

"On the coffee table. Thank you again. Good luck with that boy."

"Good luck with yours."

"You think it's a boy?"

"I'm a pretty good guesser."

"You guessed all your own children?"

"All but the last one."
"You wanted another girl?"
"I wanted a false alarm."
"Oh."
"But it's OK. It happens. I love them all."
"Good night."
"Good night." He tipped his hat and left, wondering who she was. Why would Michael Cain ask one of the drivers to take her to her house? Maybe it was his kid. She seemed nice enough. He hoped he was wrong.

• • • • •

Emily was consumed by the contents of the box all weekend. Every memory touched her heart. She cried often. When she saw the baby clothes Grandma made for her mother, she wondered if her baby could wear them and set them atop the dresser.

Looking down at her belly, she thought, *I need at least one belly picture.* She took a selfie with her shirt pulled up standing in the bathroom. Without knowing it, she accidentally sent it to James and Julie. Her fingers were getting clumsy.

She examined it and barely saw her own face. With any luck, Julie wouldn't know who it was. James probably wouldn't receive it at all.

She was so tired, she fell into bed, crying a little, hoping to sleep. Instead, she had a pity party.

Her life sucked. Her mom couldn't be with her for the first few days, then, once she had her mom, she died barely a year later. Except for the memories Grandma left, both Emily's parents were strangers. She had no memory of being held or kissed. They never saw her take her first steps, her first run through the daisies, walking down the aisle at her graduation, or seeing her pregnant.

The same day Emily was given the box, she lost her grandmother. She might have been sitting with Emily right

Faded Sweetheart

then, explaining what was in the box and what it meant. Emily loved Julie and was happy to have her discover the box, but what if she hadn't interrupted? Maybe Grandma wouldn't have died if she hadn't gone out of the room to prepare breakfast.

Then she had one night of passion, and she was pregnant without a husband or boyfriend.

"Baby," she said, "this is your mother. You won't do what your grandmother did and what I've done. I want you to be an honorable person. You're my baby, and I'm the one who loves you."

She lay down to rest. "Did I hear you say you wanted a cookie or a brownie? We live at a bakery. Let's see what's left."

Finding two matching shoes, she went downstairs. The store was ready to close, but she banged on the door, and Joseph answered.

"What are you doing, Mama?" he asked.

"Baby wants a snack. What do you have?"

"You can see whatever we have left. If we don't have something, I'll make it for you tonight once I'm home."

She studied the cakes and cookies. "I'll have a dozen cookies, two of each kind."

"OK." He packed a box for her.

She walked over to look at the cakes. "Is this one chocolate?"

"No. It's white sponge cake with a raspberry center and crème topping."

"Good. That's what I want. I don't like chocolate cake."

"Do you want this instead of the cookie or both?"

"I want it all, and I might not be done." She walked a little farther. "Are these doughnuts fresh?"

"We made them this morning. You can taste one to see if it's OK." Breaking off a piece, he handed it to her.

"I'll need a bigger piece to try it," she said.

He halved the doughnut, and they shared.

"These aren't that fresh," he said. "I'll make you fresh

ones tomorrow."

"You want me to wait that long?"

"You have a dozen cookies and a cake. Won't that tide you over for a few hours?"

She patted her belly and thought it over. "Baby, will that be OK, getting dozen fresh doughnuts tomorrow? He said he'd deliver them to us first thing in the morning."

"What kind of doughnuts do you want, Nephew?"

"You think it's a boy, too?"

"I don't think a girl would be that hungry."

"Give me a couple of each kind you make. Wait. Make that one of each kind. I don't want to be a pig."

"OK, Cookie and Cake Lady. Can you carry this upstairs? Would you like me to bring up some milk to go with the cookies?"

"That would be nice. See you later. Please make the milk two percent. I need to watch my calories." She waddled out and went upstairs. Eating was a good way to end a pity party.

The moment she took the first bite of cake, the phone rang. When she saw who it was, she wanted to throw up.

"She got the picture," Rook told her when she answered.

"What?"

"You sent her a picture."

"But you couldn't see my face!"

"It was your phone number. She recognized the wallpaper."

"What wallpaper?"

"The stuff in your bathroom. She was pretty upset. She's looking for flights right now."

"She's coming here?"

"No. She wants you back here. She's worried it may be too late for you to travel, though. How far along are you?"

"That's a pretty personal question."

"Uh-oh. She's coming this way. Be ready."

Julie snatched the phone from Rook's hand. "What were you thinking? You need to be home. How far are you?"

"I'm in England."

"We know that! Can you fly?"

"I never could."

"I couldn't book you a flight, so I'm coming over there. I need to take care of you."

"Will you tell the boys?"

"Maybe later. I'm too upset right now. Where's James?"

"He's not here right now."

"Why hasn't he married you yet?"

"We're busy."

"She's making me angry!" Julie told Rook.

Emily listened, as Julie kept talking.

"I'm sure there's an explanation," Rook said. "When we get over there, we'll figure it out."

"You aren't going. You need to stay with the kids. Obviously, we need to watch them like hawks."

Emily wanted to remind Julie she wasn't one of her kids, but she refrained. "I'll be happy to see you, Julie. Tell me when you're getting here. I love you."

Julie's tone changed. "Honey, I love you, too. I know you're a grown woman, but if you're having a baby, you need me. I'm your big sister. I can get there within two weeks. I'll email my flight plans. Bye for now. Get some sleep."

"Thanks. Can I talk to Rook for a second?" When Rook came on the line, she said, "Thanks for the warning."

"No problem. It's my duty as your brother-in-law."

Emily reboxed the cake, no longer hungry, and went to bed after a very long day.

She dreamed James was away a long time, but he finally returned in time to see her go into labor at the hospital. Loretta told him where Emily was, and he was outraged, because he didn't want children. Emily was just a fling, someone he didn't have any deep feelings for. He didn't love her. Instead, he found a new love while working on the ship.

He had no trouble telling Emily the truth, while she was on the delivery table. She was in labor, and he shouted at her. When she cried, he didn't give a damn.

He walked out before she gave birth. Her little girl had no father, and returning to the flat at Loretta's place wasn't an option.

Julie wasn't much help, either. She suggested Emily give the baby away for adoption and start a new life away from James. She called James worthless, while the beautiful baby was adoptable.

The nurses asked Julie to leave, because she upset Emily so much, but Julie refused, demanding paperwork to start the adoption process. Then she lied about Emily's age.

"Really?" Emily asked. "You're telling them I'm a minor?"

Emily heard her grandmother saying, "No! Don't take my baby! Don't take my baby!"

• • • • •

Emily woke up feeling terrible and vowed to never eat cookies before bed again. She had a few right before that bite of cake, without waiting for Joseph to bring up the milk.

After that, when Emily had trouble, she spoke to her grandmother. She knew some people talked to saints, so why not?

The idea made her feel better, so she looked at more items from the box and remembered her grandmother. Finally, she calmed down.

• • • • •

When Joseph came up with a dozen doughnuts in the morning, Emily asked, "What's this?"

"You asked for them last night along with your cookies and cake."

"Oh."

"Here's your milk. I forgot yesterday. Sorry."

"I wondered where you were. I had to eat them dry."

"I'm sorry."

Faded Sweetheart

"Then I had a horrible dream."
"I'm sorry."
"That's OK. I shouldn't have eaten so many sweets at one time."
"You ate the whole cake, too?"
"No, just a bite. Then my sister and brother-in-law called. She found out about this." She pointed at her stomach.
"You hadn't told them yet?"
"No. She'll be here in two weeks."
"Good. Let's hope James gets home, too. I miss him."
"I do, too. Do you think he still loves me?"
"He'd better There's more to love now."
"You're so funny."
"I didn't eat a dozen cookies last night."
"Yeah."

Joseph had matured a lot since starting the bakery job. She was glad, because that freed Loretta from a lot of work.

• • • • •

A female officer sat beside James on the ship during their lunch break. She was a big flirt, and she made him uncomfortable.

"Who's Emily?" she asked.
"Emily who?" He didn't want her to know about Emily."
"You know I have all the cell phones on this ship. She sent you a picture."

James prayed she hadn't sent a sexy photo, because he'd get into a lot of trouble.

"I brought it. Take a look." She took out the phone and turned it on. "Is this someone you know?'

He took one look, and his jaw dropped. They'd been apart for seven months. Was she having a baby without him?

"I need to call her. I need permission, please."
"We're in the middle of the ocean. I doubt this phone will reach. Maybe you can ask someone to reach her for you."

The admiral aboard wired the naval yard, and they sent a

man to Emily's flat.

Emily, answering the door, saw a Navy man outside. "Hello. Why are you here? Can I help you?"

"We were sent to verify."

"Verify what?"

"Did you send one of our officers a picture of you...and the baby?"

"Yes, but it was a mistake. My finger brushed the send button by accident."

"This baby belongs to one of our officers?"

"Yes."

"Then we'll pass this on to the admiral."

"He's not the father."

"We were pretty sure of that, but he has to know before he can expedite your husband."

"You mean I might get him back before I deliver this baby?"

"We can't promise anything, but we'll report whatever we know."

The second officer leaned closer and whispered to the first, "Maybe we should ask the due date."

"Ma'am, when's the baby due?" the first officer asked.

"In about two weeks."

"Hmmm. That's pretty close. Too bad Stella didn't report this sooner."

"Who's Stella?"

"She had the phone. She was the one who showed him."

"Why'd she have his phone?"

"Classified."

"Classified?"

"Yes, Ma'am."

"We'll say farewell now."

"All right. Thank you."

Emily closed the door and marched up to Loretta's room. "Who's Stella?"

"Stella?"

"Yes. She had James' phone. She showed him the picture

I sent accidentally."

"I don't know why she'd have his phone, Luv. Don't let it bother you."

"Well, it does."

"Sit down and have some tea."

She didn't want to sit down or to drink tea. She wanted answers. She went to the bakery to talk to Joseph.

"Hi, Joseph."

"Hi. What would you like today?"

"I want an answer. Do you know a Stella?"

"Sure. That was a girl James knew when he first joined the Navy. She had the hots for him."

Emily was angry. Stella had been messing with her man all that time.

"He didn't like her. He said that was why he left the service when he did. She was the only woman he ever hated. He never wanted to see her again. Is she on his ship?"

"Yes. She had his phone."

"She has all the phones. It's a security thing. Nobody's supposed to receive messages, so she keeps all the personal items locked in a drawer. You must've made a noise when they got that picture. Is there a problem?"

"Are you sure about all that?"

"Yes."

"OK. Then all I need is a dozen cookies. I still have some milk."

"Do you want a variety?"

She nodded, waited for her box of cookies, and left feeling better.

• • • • •

Work was getting difficult. There were rumors about her pregnancy, and she felt upset. Mr. Cain and Emily never did anything but work, but someone claimed it was his baby. In reality, Mr. Cain was homosexual and already had a life partner. To them, the situation was funny, but his relationship was a very well-kept secret.

Emily wondered who started the rumor. She remembered talking to the truck driver that day and encountered him in the lunchroom. As loudly as necessary, she announced the baby didn't belong to anyone currently working at the company, which was true. James hadn't been there in eight months.

She hoped the truth would be passed around, but it didn't matter. She was preparing for her maternity leave and couldn't wait. She was tired all the time.

Julie would arrive soon, so Emily had to pretend she wasn't as tired as she really felt. She promised Julie that during her leave, she would consider leaving England. She hoped that didn't become necessary. If James didn't return, or if he changed his mind about his feelings for her, Emily would leave for certain.

With or without a husband, she wanted her child to live in Texas. She wanted a house with a yard and swing set, a pool, and a tree house. She wanted a nice room for her son or daughter, with a good school nearby. She wanted clean streets. If Emily's child wanted to ride a horse, he could.

Emily missed home. She liked her Vespa, but she missed her car, family, and friends. She missed shopping at Wal-Mart and the Dairy Queen. If she wanted barbecue, she had to go to the hotel where she first stayed.

If James were with her, she wouldn't miss those things so much, but he'd been gone a long time. It was just her and the baby. She didn't even have a name chosen yet, in case James came back in time. What kind of mother didn't choose names for her child?

• • • • •

The plane arrived on time, and Julie saw Emily first. She grabbed her head in both hands and gently kissed her forehead, then she placed one hand on Emily's belly. "They don't tell you the sex of the baby in England?"

"I didn't want to know. I kept hoping James would get back, so we could find out together."

"Where is he? He's been gone that long?"

"He left the day it happened."

"What?"

"We got a little drunk, did the deed, and then...." Emily started crying.

Julie hugged her. They sat in chairs, waiting for their luggage.

"What happened?" Julie asked.

"He got a call from the Royal Navy Reserve. They said he needed to leave that day. He offered to marry me the same day, but he had only three hours before he had to go, and it was Saturday. It wasn't going to happen."

Julie patted Emily's back. "Go on."

"I can't tell you any more. It's classified."

"Huh?"

"It's a military thing. Besides, I don't know. He hasn't called in months."

"If he's on a ship, maybe they can't communicate."

"Two men came from the service yesterday, asked about me, said they'd tell the admiral the situation. I didn't know why the admiral had to know, but maybe he does."

Julie rocked Emily back and forth, but the motion almost made her sick. "It'll be OK. I'm here. If James doesn't come back, you're willing to come home?"

"Yes. If he doesn't come back, I'll go home and be the failure I am."

"Good grief, Woman! You're far from a failure. You're fully pregnant, and you've managed just fine. You did better than I ever did, and Rook never left me when I was pregnant."

"With April?"

"No, the first one—the one I lost."

"When was this?"

"Long before you were born...and before I was married," she added in a whisper.

"What?"

"Oh. There's my bag. Let me help you up. You didn't bring that Vespa to get me, did you?"

"No." Emily could tell Julie wanted to change the subject.

They walked to a taxi and went to Emily's flat. Julie set her suitcase in the bedroom.

"This place is so cute! You did a lot of work." She walked through the rooms. "That buffet with the Italian dishes is really pretty. Did you paint that yourself?"

When she reached the bathroom, she said, "Wow. So this is the wallpaper with hearts under the paint. What a neat concept."

"I did the hearts first, but I didn't like them and painted over them. I forgot they'd show through, but I like it now."

"I do, too. Honey, let me get you comfy, so you can rest. Are you off work now?"

"Yes. I'm on maternity leave. I can take up to two years."

"Or never come back?"

"I need to work somewhere."

"Rebecca said she'd hire you any time."

"In Texas?"

"I hope that's what she meant. Where'd you get so many cookies?"

"The bakery downstairs. I get them by the dozen."

"And you eat them all?"

"Every day."

"That's terrible!"

"Oh, no. They're really good."

"Not for the baby."

"He likes cookies."

"Emily!"

They laughed.

"Let me call Rook," Julie said, "so he knows I made it."

When she called, Lot answered. "Mama, April won't let me have any cookies."

"Let me talk to her," Emily said. "April? Give your brother cookies. Just ask your dad to buy more."

"Mama, you made them before you left."

Emily looked at her sister. "You made cookies?"

"Like Grandma used to make. I brought some for you, too." She opened her suitcase and showed Emily, who walked to the fridge for milk.

"Finish talking, and I'll pour you a cool one," Emily said.

The last time they ate in a real kitchen together was the time when their grandmother died. They had homemade cookies, too. The thought made Emily cry.

"You're getting to be a crybaby," Julie said. "You might need a nap."

"You might have jet lag. Want to join us?"

Julie looked down at her sister. "Sure. Does he kick?"

Someone else thinks it's a boy, Emily thought. *I wonder who'll end up surprised?*

• • • •

They napped until nightfall.

"Our schedules are messed up," Emily said. "I can fix a snack, then, if you want, you can see what I bought the baby."

As Julie watched, Emily made pizza from scratch.

"What did you want to drink?" Emily asked.

Julie set plates on the table. "What do you have?"

"Milk, water, tea in bags, or Pepsi."

"Let's share the Pepsi."

After they ate the entire pizza, Emily took out the box.

"Is that Grandma's box?" Julie asked.

"Yes. I've been dumping all the baby things in here to keep them together."

"Let me see." Julie carefully opened the plastic lid and touched the first outfit, which was yellow.

"It's a safe color," Emily said.

"You need to know what you're having."

"If or when James comes back, I will. I want us to find out together."

"OK, but I'd really like to know."

"Keep going."

She looked down and saw another yellow outfit. "This is cute, too."

"Thank you. That's about all I have."

"You don't have diapers, bottles, or a bed?"

"If I decide to go back to Texas, I can get all those things there."

Julie held Emily's hands. "You've really been thinking about it."

"I have. I never thought about having a baby, and I never thought I'd do it alone. If I have children with or without a husband, I want my kids to have a backyard, a swing set, a pool, a trampoline, and a tree house. I can't have those things here. I want dance classes or T-ball teams. For me, I'll blend in better in Texas. I have family. I've been missing that."

"Do you want to leave now?"

"It's probably too late. I'll give James another month. If he's not back, I'll go. I need to start building a home for my baby."

"Will you look for him?"

"No. If he wants to find me, he'll have to do it."

"How will you tell his mother?"

"I already have. She's upset but understands. She hopes he gets back in time and can talk me into loving England."

"She must be an amazing woman."

"She is."

"It's morning. What should we do?" Julie asked.

"Let's get enough nappies and a few bottles to last before we ship out."

"OK. Let's get dressed."

They pulled on blue jeans, T-shirts, and started out the door.

ENDING ONE

Emily offered Julie the back of her Vespa to ride on.

"Shouldn't I drive?" Julie asked.

Emily patted her belly. "This little guys wants to be in front."

They boarded the bike and drove off.

"You need to teach me how to drive this, so I can run errands when you're post-partum."

"OK. It's easy. You'll like it."

"I'll see. "We need to order a stroller. A baby can't ride on one of these things."

Maybe we'll be home by then, Emily thought, *and I can get a car like God intended.*

They came to a cute boutique.

"I was thinking about cloth diapers," Emily said. "We could just get a few and wash them."

"Newborns pee and poop about ten times a day. We'd be washing all the time. We can get you some when you're home, but we need Pampers."

They bought Pampers, blankets, and a dressing gown. Back on the bike, Julie let the bags hang off her arms and held tightly to Emily.

"That was fun," she said. "I can't wait to drive my own errands for you."

"Do you want to drop these off so we can get some dinner?"

"OK." She held open the flat door, and Emily insisted the Vespa was safe inside.

"What do you want for dinner?" Emily asked.

"You choose. You're the pregnant one."

"You mean I'm the boss?"

"At least when you're driving and know the way."

They eventually parked in front of a hotel. The valet helped Emily off and said, "Hello, Miss Queen. I'm glad to see you."

"Thank you, Colin." She placed her helmet on the back of the bike, and they walked in.

"What craving did you have to come to a hotel for?" Julie asked.

"Texas barbecue."

"Really?"

"Yes. Mrs. Howell taught them how to prepare it when we sent Rebecca back to Texas, and they kept the recipe on the menu mainly for tourists."

The head waiter smiled at Emily. "Do you wish your usual table, or is this to go?"

Emily covered her face with her hand. "This is getting embarrassing."

Julie laughed. "How often do you come here for this?"

"Once a week. This week, it's twice."

"Do you need a menu?" the waiter asked.

Emily shook her head, but Julie said, "Yes, please."

He handed her one, and she studied the pages.

"I'd like your barbecue combo with.... What are chips?"

Emily whispered, "French fries."

"Can't they give France credit? They don't have slaw?"

"Do you want some?"

"No. Just asking."

Waiters brought their food quickly along with two bottles

of Pepsi in an ice bucket.

"They like to do things fancy," Emily explained. "They used to pour it for me and ask me to taste it. I looked at them and asked, 'Really?' They finally stopped doing that."

She found the bib the waiter provided and started eating ribs with her fingers. Seeing Emily's expression, she knew the food had to be good.

"This is great!" Julie said.

"When we have this baby, you'll need to get a couple orders to leave at the house for me."

"I'm not leaving until I take both of you home."

"Thank you, Sis. That makes me happy."

After dinner, they drove back to the flat.

"Turn on the light so you don't trip over anything," Emily said.

"Here it is." Julie turned on the light and lifted their bags away, as Emily parked the Vespa.

They went upstairs.

"I'm pooped," Emily said. "Where are my cookies?" She grabbed the telephone receiver. "Joseph? Cookies?"

"Coming right now."

"My sister's here. Bring your mom down to meet her."

"OK."

They came down, and all four of them ate cookies and milk, talking for hours. Nothing was said about Julie's quest to take Emily and the baby back to Texas. Loretta knew, but Joseph didn't.

The evening was fun, and they examined the new purchases.

"Where will you put the crib?" Joseph asked.

Emily looked at him. "We'll move to a bigger place."

That made sense, and he didn't ask any more questions.

• • • • •

Emily felt increasingly tired over the next few days. Finally, it was time for her checkup. Julie went with her and met the midwife.

"Where's your doctor?" Julie whispered.

"They don't use one unless there are complications."

"Isn't that too late?"

"Hush. Look at me. It's already too late."

Julie wondered if Emily was considering giving the baby up for adoption but didn't want to bring it up. Her family would keep both of them going. There was plenty of love.

• • • • •

In the middle of the night, Julie awoke to the sound of Emily talking on the phone.

"I need a cab," Emily said. "I'm in labor."

Julie jumped out of bed, wondering where the old Emily had gone. She didn't even groan or cry out with her contractions. What happened to the other girl she knew? A lot of Emily wasn't the old Emily she remembered, but maybe that was because she'd always been thought of as the baby, not a grown woman.

The cab arrived, and they got to the clinic on time. The baby was born without any trouble or any father. Emily was discharged with her little girl the following day. Julie worried about Emily climbing stairs, but she had no trouble.

Julie tried to remember where all the food was stored to make something for the family. When she had to leave the flat, Loretta came to help out, delighted to be there for her only grandchild.

"When we leave," Emily told Loretta, "I'll send you money for air fare, and you can visit us at least once a year. Will you do that?"

"Of course."

"Or you can come with us now."

"No. I have to watch Joseph. He still needs me."

Neither one mentioned James. They didn't know where he was or when he might return. There was no word from the Navy or the admiral. War was like that.

After one month, Julie, Emily, and Sara Queen boarded an airplane for America. No one came to send them off. If James wanted her back, he could find her.

• • • • •

They arrived in Corpus Christi and found the entire family, plus Rebecca, waiting for them. The adults took turns holding the baby.

Everything but the boxes Rebecca sent remained in England. Emily left her flat furnished, and it rented quickly with such cute décor. The new resident, a woman named Harper, didn't change anything, but she wondered what happened to the bathroom wallpaper.

One day, a man entered the flat with his key and found Harper living there.

"I'm sorry," he said. "Where's Emily?"

"I live here. I don't know anyone by that name."

"She used to live here. This is a cute place. Did you do the decorating?"

"No. This is how it came. Can I ask you what's going on with the bathroom wallpaper?" She led him to the room and showed him.

He looked at it. "That's not wallpaper, Emily...I mean, Harper." He fought back tears. "She liked to paint faded sweethearts. Maybe she didn't like it and painted over them. They must've leaked through. Do you like it?"

"No. I hate it."

"Oh, well. You can probably scrape it off and repaint. You could even panel over it. I have to go."

• • • • •

In Corpus Christi, Emily moved back into Grandma's house. It was already paid for, and there was plenty of room for Sara to grow. Emily planned to take the first year off.

Rebecca came to her with a request one day. After playing with Sara for a bit, Rebecca asked, "Can I return to England? I like working at Roscoe's, but since Granny died, my family wants to go back.

Why don't you take over?" she asked Emily, looking into her eyes. "You own the place. You know what it's all about. You'd be a good CEO."

"I'm barely twenty-two."

"You were there when you were Sara's age. Your grandma taught you."

"Do you think I'm ready?"

"You were ready back in England."

"OK."

They hugged, and Rebecca left with a smile.

• • • • •

Emily planned to start her corporate life in a month. The company offered in-house day care, and Sara loved playing with kids her age.

Emily arranged an office in her home, so if Sara was ill, she could still work and care for her.

• • • • •

On Sara's first birthday, Uncle Bill and Uncle Andrew made a castle for the little princess. It was a wooden, two-story playhouse. The first floor was a big room with tiny staircase to the second balcony, where Sara loved to stand and look out. A slide was beside the window, so she could get down easily. During the summer, a pool would be at the end of the slide.

• • • • •

As years passed, the princess wardrobe filled with dresses, wands, and crowns. The little tea set looked lovely on its tiny table and chairs, and Sara had afternoon tea there often, with friends or mama, and, when her grandmother visited from England, with her, too. Sara was proud to prepare a proper tea—sweet, cold, made of Red Diamond tea and served with vanilla wafers. Loretta loved those parties.

One day, Loretta asked Emily in private, "Do you want me to tell her about her father?"

"Certainly, when you think it's the right time."

"I'll do it later, when she's older."

They nodded.

• • • • •

As Sara grew too old for her castle and was ready to learn about her father, Loretta died, the right time never came.

Julie often tried to arrange dates for Emily. "Emily, got a second?"

"Sure. What's going on?"

"We're thinking of having a dinner tomorrow."

"That's good. People need to eat every day."

"No, Smarty. I'm talking about a nice dinner with just us adults."

"That sounds nice, since Sara has issues with her spoon."

"Can you come around seven?"

"Who'll be there?"

"Why do you ask?"

"I don't want or need a boyfriend. Thank you for trying so hard, but you're wasting your time."

"Really?"

"Yes, really. I'm done with men. I saw *Mighty Mike* twice, but as far as something personal goes, I'm not in business, understand?"

"You're too young to say that."

"If my knight in shining armor ever comes to my castle, I might change my mind, but right now, I'm fine. I'm happy and busy. Good grief! I'm late for a meeting. I'll call you later. Are you working tonight?"

"No. Please call me this evening."

"Will you be eating tonight?"

"Ha ha!"

"Later." Emily set down the receiver and stared at it. She didn't have a meeting, just a trip to the daycare center to pick up her princess.

• • • • •

Julie set down the phone, and hearing Rook drive home, she met him at the door. She usually didn't touch him when he first arrived from work, because he was sweating, smelly, and covered in some sort of fluid. It might be thirty-weight Penz oil, transmission fluid, or his lunch. She always said hello and gave him a long-distance kiss.

That day, she placed her head against his chest and put her arms around his neck. "Can you do me a favor?"

"You want me to invite that new guy to dinner to meet Emily?"

"Yes, but it won't work. She's empty inside. She doesn't need a man or want any help finding one."

"She's a smart girl."

Julie released him and smacked his butt, not caring if he was dirty. "Can you find James?"

"Can you get your tired husband something to drink?"

"What would you like—pop, milk, or a beer?"

"Let's have a beer."

She turned to the fridge, got out a Bud in a bottle, popped the cap, drank a bit, and wiped off the bottle with the outside of her hand, because the inside was fragrant with gas-station alley perfume.

Rook accepted the beer and walked to the kitchen table, then he sat with the bottle in both hands, as if someone might steal another swig. Julie sat opposite him.

"His mother never mentioned him," Rook said. "Why would Emily want him back?"

"She needs him."

"I don't think she ever said that. If I were actually able to locate him, I'd kill him. Then I'd end up in jail."

"What?"

"You heard me." He drank from his bottle.

"Emily's a beautiful, wealthy woman. She's a great catch, but she doesn't want anyone, Honey. She's content, and she's only twenty-four."

"I thought so, too, but she's been hurt so badly, she never wants to get involved again. You come from strong stock. Your grandmother was punished by Roscoe for forty years."

"What?"

"He was a lousy son of a gun."

"Good grief! Why do you say that?"

"Because I saw him more than once. I hate talking bad about a dead man, but it bugged me from the moment I married into this family. Roscoe was bad news. The first time I saw him, I was at a bar with my buds, and he was over with some broads, licking them up one side and down the other. Then he started passing out bills, and they got into it. The bartender told them to get a room. He gave the guy some trash about who he was and what he could do to him.

"The other time, his car broke down, and he had Mr. Howell follow him, so he wouldn't have to walk. He talked to Howell like he was a dog and badmouthed your grandmother. We were all underpaid, but we put up with him. He offended me so much, I did some tricks to his car. I twisted a cord, left some oil on top of his radiator, and toyed with the carburetor.

"Once I fixed his car so that it died four blocks from my shop. My guys had a bet going over what he'd do. It was hilarious. He started sending Vivian with the car when it needed a tune up. They never had a problem with Vicky. He didn't have a clue."

Julie remembered who Vicky was. "Emily says she has no spark with anyone."

"Honey, not everyone can be as happy as you."

She gave him an angry look.

"I love you so much, and I love Emily like a daughter, but

I never want to hurt her. She's already had that. Maybe if we leave her alone, something will happen. We have to let her find what she wants on her own." He bent over the table, spilling beer to kiss her.

She let the bottle fall. A kiss was more important.

• • • • •

Emily never regained her spark. The only light in her life was Sara. The sweetheart faded completely, replaced by a Texas rose, a bud plucked early that wilted gracefully until it was pressed in a book.

ENDING TWO

When James appeared at Emily's door, Julie stood beside her sister, holding her up.

"James?" said Julie.

James!" said Emily walking toward him.

He knelt before the pregnant woman he loved and kissed her belly. Taking her hand, he offered her a small box. "I love you. I've missed you so much. If I had known, I never would've left."

"How could you have known?"

"Your sister warned me it would happen."

"You believed her?"

"No, but look at you."

She broke away and turned for him. "What do you think?"

"It's amazing. How big is this baby?"

"This is normal size for a full-term woman."

"Wow. Does it hurt?"

"Did you accomplish your mission?"

"I never want to see water again. We were on that ship for almost nine months."

"Tell me about it."

He knelt down again. "Will you marry me?"

"This is kind of sudden."

"Really?"

"Tell you what. Why don't we get married after I have this baby? I'd like to be a beautiful bride."

"Are you sure?"

"No, she's not," Julie said. "Find a preacher today. Let's get this done, so the baby is legitimate."

She turned to Julie. "I was ready to leave England. I haven't had James with me for almost a year. I want to make sure I love him."

"You do."

"I want to be sure."

"Do I have to call Rook to straighten you out?"

"That sounds like you're threatening me with my dad."

"It's the closest thing you've got to a dad. He loves you like a daughter."

"Does that make you my mother?"

Julie looked at James. "I had no idea pregnancy made her into a comedian. It's bedtime. You two sleep in there." She pointed to the bedroom.

"I'll sleep here." She indicated the couch and matching pillows.

"You finally got a sofa," James said. "It's very colorful. Did you have the cushions made?"

"No. I did them myself. I had a lot of time on my hands." She pressed his hand against their baby, and he kissed her.

They walked into the bedroom and closed the door, trying to be quiet so Julie wouldn't overhear.

"Does she fall asleep quickly?" he whispered.

"She still has jet lag. What did you have in mind?"

"I remember you liked this." He removed her clothes and kissed her neck.

"I do. I remember you liked this." She rubbed his back, though she had to reach at an angle due to the baby.

They lay in bed spooning.

"Do you suppose we should try before the big event?"

"If you're game, so am I."

• • • • •

Though James had very little sleep, being with her kept him awake. He missed her so much. That was the worst part of his mission. When he signed up, all personnel were supposed to be unattached. There had to be no family, girlfriend, and absolutely no children. The reserve didn't want their people distracted. He had no idea his life would change so fast.

"Emily, I love you. I missed you."

"Ouch!" Emily said suddenly, then she moaned with pain.

• • • • •

Julie popped up from the couch like toast from a toaster. "What are you two doing in there?"

She opened the door. "Good grief! Where are your clothes? Do you think this is the best time for this?"

"Actually, yes," James said.

Emily moaned again.

They turned to her.

"Are you OK?" James asked. "Did you hurt anything? What's wrong?"

"You need to describe it," Julie said. "I was an OB/GYN nurse for many years."

"I think I might be in labor."

"You're not due for another three weeks."

"They said I was totally effaced and dilated to two."

"When were you going to tell me this?"

"I don't know what it means!"

"Neither do I," James added.

"It means you're ready to give birth. Lie down. Where does it hurt?" Julie examined her, feeling for a contraction and listening carefully.

"My back and legs. It feels like a terrible bellyache going from front to back."

"That's a contraction."

"Is it serious? Ouch!"

"Was that another one?"

"I think so."

"James, how do pregnant women get to the hospital in England?"

"We can call a cab."

"You'd better call. This might be the real thing."

"I hope it is."

"Emily, it is. Trust me. I can tell by how you're dressed."

"I'm naked."

"Would you be naked with a guy you didn't love?"

"Well...."

"I hope not. Do you have a hospital bag ready?"

"No."

"Clothes for the baby?"

"The ones in the box. James, if you want to know what this baby is, there's an envelope that will tell you the sex. Ouch!" She began panting.

Julie looked in her closet. "What still fits you? Here. This will do." She grabbed a nightgown, slippers, underwear, and socks."

Emily watched. "Why do I need socks?"

"In case your feet get cold during labor."

• • • • •

The cab arrived, and they all got in.

"Which hospital?" the driver asked.

"I don't know," Emily said.

"What do you mean, you don't know?"

"I didn't pay attention."

"Cabbie, take us to the closest hospital," Julie said.

He drove off fast, not wanting a mess in his cab. Emily screamed with the contractions, while James and Julie began arguing over who could take better care of her.

"Emily, you need to breathe," Julie said.

The cab stopped, and Julie threw the bag at James' gut.

"Ouch!" he said.

"Really, James. Pick up the bag. Let's get inside before she drops it in the parking lot."

He hurried to catch up. Emily stopped when another contraction came, and James fell over her.

Julie gave him another dirty look. "I'm sorry, James. We're just a little bit stressed right now."

They went into ER.

"Are you at the right hospital?" the nurse asked.

"Does it make a difference?"

"This is a mental hospital."

"What was that driver thinking?"

"We'll call an ambulance for you. They'll get you to the right place."

The ambulance arrived, and they got in, then they drove to the next hospital in record time.

The nurse took Emily to check in. Julie wanted to be with her, but she was held back, so she sat in a chair beside James. They talked, working hard to be civil with each other.

The nurse came out with Emily still dressed. "She isn't in labor yet. She can go home for now."

Julie looked around. "How will we get home?"

"It's just a few blocks," Emily said. "We can walk."

The nurse nodded. "Walking is a good idea."

Julie knew a walk wouldn't hurt Emily, since she wasn't due for another week or two. "If it's just a few blocks, OK. Is it safe?"

"We don't have guns in England," James said.

"Well, the good guys don't."

"Let's go home. James, we can take turns holding the bag." She took it first.

James held Emily's hand, as they walked together. The walk was nice, except her labor pains returned, so they turned back toward the hospital.

"What kind of shoes are you wearing?" Julie asked.

"My house shoes. Why?"

"Why didn't you wear regular shoes?"

"You rushed me. Besides, they don't always fit."

"You're swollen?"

"Like army boots."

Almost at the hospital, Emily took a few steps, bent over, and screamed. Having a relative on both sides didn't seem to make much difference.

"Do you want me to carry you?" James asked.

"Honey, I outweigh you right now. I should offer to carry you."

"He's a foot taller, though," Julie said. "You just feel big."

The nurse just returned after having a cigarette. "You're back already?"

"Emily almost went to her knees on the last one," Julie said. "Please check her again. If she's OK, could you call a cab for us? That walk really got her going again."

The nurse took Emily to a room, then returned a minute later. "You're right. She's in full bloom. We're taking her to a birthing room. Do you want to join us?"

They got up. Instead of giving James a dirty look for leaving the bag behind, Julie grabbed it and followed the nurse with the wheelchair carrying Emily.

The nurse rattled off instructions without much enthusiasm. James tried to remember all of them. Julie listened, making sure the rules were the same ones she told pregnant women and their ill-informed mates. She remembered how innocent they seemed, even if it wasn't their first child. Nursing was an amazing job, involving life or death. If the situation was appropriate, there was hell for the staff and patients, too. No one liked being sick, and the nurses had to make the situation as good as possible. Her instructor said, "As a nurse, you're here to make things as good as can be."

She hoped the English nurse learned in the same school. She wouldn't let anyone hurt her little sister. Emily had already been through a lot.

James and Julie found Emily in a bed, connected to a monitor on her big belly.

"Do they have to do that?" he asked.

"It's the best way," Julie replied. "We can keep track of

the baby. If anything goes wrong, the staff can intervene before it gets worse."

"In other words, you approve?" He looked at her like all parents did in labor and delivery.

"Yes." She patted his hand. "Why don't you ask the nurse if Emily can have some ice chips?"

Nurses usually had that available, but she didn't know if the English would offer hot tea instead. Drinking hot tea during contractions seemed like it would warrant a lawsuit for burns.

He came back beaming, because he found ice chips. "Here, Honey. Do you want me to hand it to you or spoon some in your mouth?"

She looked at the cup. "I can probably handle that. Thank you."

She wasn't in hard labor yet, but the easy contractions would stop soon. Then she'd become a different person and would probably frighten James. Julie wondered if she should warn him.

"Emily, we'll be right back," Julie said, pulling James into the hall. He didn't want to leave.

"James, you don't know what will happen when the labor pains become intense."

"More than now?"

"Oh, yeah. She may act like a monster. It's a process many women go through. They call it labor for a reason. She might say things you don't deserve that will hurt your feelings, but stay with her. She's never done this before. Cowboy up and let it go past you. She might even bite you."

"Bite me?"

"It's like cowboy movies where someone has to remove a bullet. The guy bites down on something. Get a washcloth. Don't let her bite your skin. I've had patients' husbands end up bleeding."

James became worried.

"Don't worry. They won't let her push that hard for long, maybe an hour or so."

"She might bite me for an hour?"

"No. Some women get the baby out in three pushes. We need to teach her to breathe. First, short puppy breaths, then later, long in and long out cleansing breaths. OK?"

"OK. Keep me informed. Please help us. We've never done this before."

"Nobody has. Every time is new. Every child is a gift from God. It'll be amazing. I'm glad I came here at the right time."

"Me, too. I think."

"What about the pregnant woman?" Emily called, screaming again.

They ran into the room.

James eyed his future sister-in-law. "Is it happening now?"

"Let me check the strips." She put on her glasses and studied the printouts, instinctively sliding her hand into her pocket to get her gauge. She forgot she wasn't at work and didn't have her usual supplies. "I don't have my gauge, but it looks like your contractions are getting closer and harder."

"You think?" Emily asked.

"Can they give you an epidural? I'll ask. That would make it better for you." She walked out and found the nurses talking on their cell phones. "Excuse me. Can my sister get her epidural?"

"Is she a high-risk patient?"

"I don't think so."

The nurse recognized her accent. "Where are you from?"

"Texas."

"We don't offer drugs unless the mother is in danger. She's fine."

"It's an elective?"

"Yes, Ma'am."

Julie walked back toward the room, muttering, "You'll be sorry." She smiled at the thought.

Emily was progressing quickly and screaming frequently. The nurse walked by and asked why she was being so noisy.

If looks could kill, that nurse would have keeled over.

275

Faded Sweetheart

Julie had plenty of experience with patients and her own family.

"It looks like you're almost there," she told Emily. "It's almost time to see our little baby. James, get two washcloths. One is to wipe her off if she gets sweaty, the other is for her mouth if she gets a dry mouth." She hoped he would remember the one in her mouth was also to keep his fingers safe.

He jumped up like a toddler after naptime and went looking for the items.

The staff nurse looked in the room. The woman from Texas was managing a noisy problem patient. After only a few hours, she was ready to push.

Julie was impressed. For a first-time mother, Emily was doing well. The nurses came in to assist.

"Where's the doctor?" Julie asked.

"He's on call. He won't come in unless there's a problem."

Emily went into full labor.

"Did you pay for a doctor?" Julie asked her.

She nodded. She was a cash patient, because she wasn't part of socialized medicine in England.

Julie looked at the nurse in charge. "She paid cash for a doctor, and we want him here now."

Her demand quickly summoned a young man in scrubs trying to finish his last drop of tea.

"Hi, Emily," he said. "I'm glad you called me. Is this James? This must be your sister. Didn't you say she was head nurse at OB/GYN in Dallas?"

That wasn't exactly right, but he wanted the staff to know Julie wasn't just a crazy relative. Julie nodded, and together, they began examining Emily.

The doctor looked up from between Emily's legs. "James and Julie, get on either side of Emily, and let's see what we can do. Emily, I'll tell you when to push. Take a deep breath, hold it, then release."

They repeated twice. Out came Sara, a seven-pound-three-ounce, twenty-one-inch baby girl. She cried initially, then a staff nurse placed her on Emily's chest, and she calmed down.

The doctor finished work and looked up at the baby, glad Emily had family with her. He worried how she'd get through the birth alone. He wiped off his hand and shook James' hand, then he nodded to Julie almost like a salute before walking out with the nurses.

"That's how it's done," the doctor said.

The other staff nodded.

"It's customary for our families to have a little bonding time before we take the baby for evaluation," one nurse told them, "considering her Apgar score was sufficient. We'll return in thirty minutes to complete our well-baby workup. Is that agreeable?"

"By all means," Emily said, once Julie nodded. "Do what you need to do."

After the nurse nodded respectfully and left, James took out his cell phone to take pictures. Emily asked him to find hers next, because she had her family phone numbers on it. They took a selfie of James, Emily, and Sara and sent it to everyone.

The nurse returned to take the baby to the nursery for a workup and returned her cleaned and dressed in hospital garb. Emily went to the post-partum suite, which had several beds for delivered women. It wasn't a ward, but it was close enough for the Americans. Strangely, no other mothers came in while they were there.

• • • • •

At three o'clock in the morning, Rook's phone rang on his nightstand. He hoped it was Julie, because he hadn't heard from her that evening. Rubbing his eyes, he focused on the screen.

"James is back," he muttered. "Look who's here! It's the baby. I wonder what it is. It looks like a girl, but boys are cute, too."

He quickly sent a reply. *Congrats. Is it a boy or a girl? How big? How are you? Have Julie call me.*

Studying the picture, he said, "Hello, Trouble. Welcome to the family." He wiped his eyes, and his hand came away wet. "I really feel like your father, Emily. If that jerk ever hurts you again, he'll answer to me."

The door opened, and a soft voice asked, "Daddy, who are you talking to?"

"Your mom."

He looked at the empty side of the bed.

"Look what we have." He handed his phone to Lot.

Lot studied the photo. "She had her baby?"

Rook nodded, and Lot left to tell his sister.

It wasn't time to get up, but Rook did, anyway. "It's coffee time." He stood by his cup in the kitchen when he heard the kids.

"What are you doing in here?" April asked. "Oh! Get out of my room. Thanks."

Lot went downstairs, following the scent of coffee. "Can I have some cereal?"

"Lot, it's three in the morning. Go back to bed."

"A little Captain Crunch goes a long way. Besides, don't you expect Mom to call?"

"You can have a small bowl, but Mom might be going home to sleep. If she's been up all this time helping Emily, she's probably tired." He set out three bowls, knowing April would come down soon.

Excited, all three of them talked while they ate, wondering what time it was in England.

"I guess we could Google that," April said. She wore her Hello Kitty shorts and T-shirt. Her hair was in a ragged ponytail, probably because she forgot to take it down.

She grabbed a spoon and started eating even faster than Lot. He usually won that game, but April was a strong contender and beat him occasionally.

"We can do that in the morning," Rook said. "We need

to head to bed."

After putting the kids back to bed, he lay down again, but he couldn't find his phone. Back in the days of having only a landline, that wouldn't be a problem.

He walked past April's room and saw the phone on her desk. She lifted her head from the covers.

"At least we got a picture," she said.

"You're right. See you later." He closed her door, which she preferred.

• • • • •

Julie was very tired. James told her which bus to catch to get back to the flat. She boarded and asked the conductor to tell her when they got to her stop. Her accent showed she was a foreigner.

She was asleep when they arrived.

"Miss, your stop is here."

Julie rubbed her eyes. That was the place. She noticed the bakery and knew it was the right block.

Entering through the side door, she saw the Vespa parked inside. Digging in her purse, she hoped she could find the key. When that failed, she tried the knob and found the door wasn't locked, anyway.

"Great. We left in a hurry." She lay down on the blue, yellow, orange, and purple sofa and was instantly asleep.

• • • • •

A few hours later, Rook called. "Were you asleep?"

"Yeah."

"Did you have a hard shift?" That was his standard question.

"You're so funny. How'd you find out?"

"They sent a selfie around three o'clock this morning. It woke me up, then the kids woke up. We ate cereal and went back to bed. They were late for school. I called the shop to tell them I'd be in around noon. I'm heading there now. Give me the details."

"What do you need to know?'

"Is it a pretty girl or a boy with problems?"

Julie shook her head. James and Emily sent the picture without any information. "It's OK. It was a crazy night. First, the cab driver took us to a mental hospital, then we got an ambulance ride."

"I don't know if I have enough time for all this. Is everyone OK?"

"Yes. They're fine. They're a cute couple. When James came home last night, he knelt down and kissed her belly. Did you ever kiss my belly?"

"That was a long time ago. I will when you get back, OK?"

"OK. Go to work. Have a nice day. I love you!"

"Love you, too. Send them my love."

"I will."

She hung up and went back to bed to sleep for a few more hours.

• • • • •

Once Julie was awake again, she wondered where to find Emily. "I need to get back to the hospital. Which one was it? I hate England. I'll have to take that darned Vespa and find it."

The door opened, and James came in.

"Were you on the phone? I heard you talking to someone." He set down his overnight bag.

"Why didn't you leave that at the hospital?"

"Because," Emily said behind him, "we got discharged."

"Already? How long did I sleep?"

Emily walked to the rattan swing she bought at a second-hand store on Ashby. The yellow color matched her funky décor. Since she was so short, she had to hop to get settled in the right place. It was a great basket for laundry, but she didn't buy it for that. Usually, she kept a stepstool nearby to get up and down from the swing, though the stool didn't match. Joseph suggested she hang it lower, but she told him it wouldn't hang properly that way.

"It would be too low," she said.

"Like the owner?"

"It's not my fault."

Julie rushed over to place a cushion under Emily's bottom and held the chair steady for her.

"Thanks, Sis." She used one hand to grab onto the side and carefully sat down.

"Are you OK?"

"Certainly, but I have a few scripts. Can you fill them for me?"

"Sure. Give me a map or put it on my phone. I always forget."

James programmed the address into her phone. "Here you go."

"Thanks. What would you like for dinner? Should I get anything for the baby?"

"The hospital gave us some things," Emily said. "Just come back so I can have all the things they suggested."

"OK. I'll go as fast as I can without getting lost." Julie left on her mission, praying she'd be able to get back before any problems arose.

James helped Emily up with one hand, as he held his baby daughter in his other arm, then he kissed both of them.

"Let's get some sleep," he said.

They walked to the bedroom arm-in-arm and set the baby on the bed between them. Looking up, James saw the ceiling was the only part of the room Emily hadn't painted.

"You know," he said, "once we get the little one established, we should move to the country."

"Oh." She was too tired to reply.

"We should look for a small castle. You could do some great work with that as a canvas."

She turned toward him. "That sounds interesting."

"Yes. You have a year off. We could do it. What do you think?"

"I love ideas like that. We'll have to look online, then we could take the Vespa to see them."

"All three of us can't ride on that."

"Yes, but maybe your mom or Julie can watch Sara while we house hunt. Is it a long drive?"

"We'll figure it out later. Go to bed, Sleepyhead."

• • • • •

The baby woke them.

"I think she wants to be fed," he said.

"OK. Bring her over here. I'm not very good at this."

"It just takes practice." He wasn't certain, but he hoped he was right. Julie could help once she returned.

She walked in with a lot of packages.

"How'd you carry all of that?" Emily asked.

"I have skills."

James looked out the window. "There's a cab downstairs."

"Yes. There were so many places to go, I figured the cab driver who took us to the wrong hospital owed us a favor."

"What is all this stuff?"

"I found a Pack and Play, a stroller, and some clothes that weren't yellow. Let me see." She dug into her purse and pulled out another bag. "Here are your pills and a spray that's supposed to help. I also bought dinner. Joseph will bring you cookies soon."

"Cookies?" James asked.

"He bakes some for Emily every day."

"My brother?"

"Yes. He's doing a lot of the cooking."

"Great."

• • • • •

After a few weeks, they were ready to look for a castle. They found several but really liked one just south of London. It didn't belong to a king, but it soon was owned by a Queen, and they called it Serendipity.

Julie told them they owed her a big favor, so they agreed to have their wedding in Texas. It was a small ceremony in Andrew's backyard. Angela, his wife, had been working on the yard for weeks and did a beautiful job. The rose bushes were in full bloom. Flowers covered a trellis Andrew built with the help of their oldest son.

The wedding day was a bit of a hassle. Emily had to fit into her dress, but the baby wanted to be fed. Rook drove James around town to show off where he worked and the high school Emily attended. He also wanted to show him the big Roscoe Incorporated building and the house Vivian owned.

"Why are you doing this?" James asked.

"I'm keeping you from seeing the bride too early. It's bad luck."

"We've been together for almost two years. I've seen all of her."

"Julie told me to—or else."

"Is she bossy?"

"You haven't learned anything. All the women in the family are bossy, but in a cute way."

"How's that?"

"I play stupid and make her explain her ideas. Lots of times I'll pretend I'm involved in a game or watching TV. Maybe I'll say I have a big project at work. I used to pretend I was on the phone, but the last time I tried that, a call came in during my fake call."

"Do you remember who it was?"

"Julie. She knew what I'd been doing."

"Did you end up in the dog house?"

"No. We kid around. We love each other."

Faded Sweetheart

"Sounds like a good example."

"That's what I've been waiting to hear. Now we can go back."

"Why were you waiting to hear that?"

"Julie wanted me to find out if you understood how marriage works. You just proved it. Thanks for listening."

"So now I know?"

"Not everything, but you can always follow my good example."

"Thanks. We're going home now?"

"Not yet. We may need to buy some umbrellas."

"More good luck?"

• • • •

The wedding was held inside the house. Everyone fit, and the baby slept in a cousin's Pack and Play. Afterward, they ate a typical barbecue dinner and had a huge white cake with strawberries and blueberries cascading down the sides. James' mother and brother thought it was beautiful. They made the cake in Angela's kitchen.

Molly looked out the window at all her work in the garden. "It finally stopped raining."

"Let's get some pictures," Bill said. "Honey, where's my camera?"

"I bet one of your kids have it." Molly looked around and there was her 5 year old taking pictures of the sleeping baby. "Precious, Daddy wants it back. Here you go, Honey."

Bill smiled at his wife and their youngest. "Thank you Peaches, thank you, Little Peaches.", patting the little one on her curly locks.

They all checked appearances in a mirror. Julie put Emily's veil on, and they went outside. The fresh moisture made everything look brilliant green. The wives remembered their own weddings and how happy they were. The kids looked for soccer balls to play with James.

"He can't do that today," Emily told them.

"Why not?" James asked.

They took turns trying for a goal through the trellis, with the 4 o'clocks opening their petals like trumpets. It was fun until the boys started sliding around in their Sunday clothes and making ruts in the grass.

"Stop, Boys," William said. "It's getting late."

"Why, Uncle Bill?"

"I can't see you anymore. Do you have a ball that glows in the dark?"

"They don't have that in soccer, Kids," James said. "That's a joke or a fine idea for an invention. Work on it, and you could get rich."

They laughed. It was a great wedding and party.

• • • • •

Instead of a honeymoon, the English visitors had to return home. Work was calling, and Emily had some serious decorating to do in her castle.

"It'll be so much fun," she told her family.

The Queen lost her title and gained a husband. They had a long, prosperous reign over many subjects—some were short, blond, and boys. Bad dreams stopped.

They built a swing at the rear of the palace and a balcony in front. They lived happily ever after.

ENDING THREE

"Are you OK? Emily, Luv, can you wake up?" James got up from the hospital chair and looked into the hall. "Nurse, I think she's waking up."

The nurse looked down at the hopeful young man and took his hand. "I'll find a doctor."

He went back inside, as the nurse walked away. Emily looked up at him.

"James, is that you? You're back! When did you get back?"

"I've been gone for only a few minutes. I had to speak to the nurse."

"Oh." She touched her flat belly. "Where's my baby? Is she OK?"

"What baby?"

"The baby we made just before you left for the Royal Naval Reserve."

"For what?"

"You had to work on cyber warfare."

"I haven't been anywhere. I've been pretty much in your face for three years."

"Three years?"

"Look at your hands."

She looked and saw she wore no nail polish. An IV entered her vein on one side, and she wore a diamond ring.

"Where'd I get that?" she asked.

"I gave it to you two years ago. We were supposed to get married next week."

"Then why am I here?"

"The Vespa."

"What about it?"

"You drove too fast and fell off."

"I did?"

"You've been in a coma for almost a month. They didn't know when you'd wake up. They said there might be memory loss. Do you know who I am?"

"I love you."

"That's close enough for me. Your family's been really worried. Your brothers are staying with me, while your sisters are in your flat. Here's a test. What are their names?"

"Daddy, Overkill, and Stupid."

"And the women?"

"James, Rook, William, Andrew. Then there's Julie, Angela, and Peaches."

"Peaches?"

"That's what William calls her when she gets sunburned. Her real name is Molly."

"Good. You still have your memory."

"Where are the kids?"

"April's watching them."

"Isn't she in school?"

"She takes online classes this semester, so she can study when she wants."

"She always did. Three years? She must be in college by now."

"Yes. Do you remember her graduation?"

"Vaguely. Tell me more."

"We planned the wedding. Now your sister and sisters-in-law are replanning it."

"How's that?"

"Different dresses, different food, different music, and we almost needed a different bride."

"You're so funny."

"The doctor said when you hit the pavement' you hit your head right about here." He kissed the back of her neck.

"Are you kissing our comatose patient again?"

James lifted his head.

"Hi, Doctor," Emily said. "How am I doing?"

"Well, Miss Queen, it's nice to hear you talking. We had no ETA for that. How do you feel?"

"Pretty darn good."

"Any headaches? Dizziness? Any fopintmernt?"

"What?"

"Nothing. I made that up to see if you were listening clearly. Let me get some tools to examine you." He took a stethoscope from his old-fashioned doctor's bag, then a penlight and a small rubber hammer.

"Let's see if you can sit up." He offered her hand, and she quickly sat up tall. "Feel OK?"

"I feel fine."

He tapped her knee with the hammer, and her leg popped up like normal. He checked in her ears and touched the glands in her neck. "Any pain? Are you dizzy being upright?"

"No. I feel fine."

"Let's check your gait."

She frowned in confusion.

"Take a few steps toward the door."

She got up and pulled down the back of her gown, then walked to the door. Turning too fast, she lost her balance for a second.

"Go slowly for the first couple of days," the doctor said. "Have James or someone steady you." He nodded. "We can discharge you this afternoon if the next tests come back normal. Get back in bed and rest. You should expect to feel tired. You haven't used those muscles for a while, but you'll be back to your old self soon."

He shook James's hand and walked away.

The couple looked at each other.

"Could the wedding still be on?" she asked.

"It looks like it. I'll call the family." He got his cell phone, but she took it from his hand.

"I'll talk to them. Who do you call first?"

"Who do you think?"

She dialed and waited. "Hi, Julie. Are you messing up my house?"

"Emily, you're up!"

"Yes. If I pass all my tests, I can go home today."

Shouts of joy exploded in the background. Julie never learned how to turn off speakerphone.

Andy took the phone from Julie. "Are you sure you want to marry James? He's kind of messy."

"Have you been giving him lessons?" she quipped.

William took the phone next. "They're both bad. I pick up after them all the time, just like my kids."

"I'm glad they brought you, Billy. How is April holding up with your destruction crew?"

"I don't know. They're at your house."

"Why'd you pick that place?"

"It had more space. You also asked April to paint some rooms."

"I did?"

"Yes. The living room's purple, and the bathrooms are chalkboard black. She whited out the kitchen and bricked up the bedroom."

"What?"

"April Fool's!"

"It's not April."

"That's what we call her."

Julie grabbed the phone back. "I've been hearing that line from my brother for twenty years."

"It never gets old!" he shouted in the background.

"Yeah, yeah. Go away. Honey, do you want us to come over there? Should we just move our stuff away, so you can get back in here?"

"I don't know where we'll stay until I get there. Then we can decide."

"OK. Talk to you later."

Emily ended the call.

"How have you been able to work with all those people around?" she asked James.

"I worked at home before they got here. Now I bring work with me." He moved aside, and she saw a makeshift office near the bay window. "It's not great, but at least I can do payroll. When you were unconscious, it helped pass the time."

He looked at her and placed his hand on the side of her face. "I'm so glad you're back." He stepped forward and gave her a real hug. She felt him gulping for air, as if he were crying. She put her IV arm and her free arm around him.

"I'm lucky I was able to come back. This is much better than my dreams. I was lonely without you."

"You can tell me all about your life when we get back to Texas. The office is ready for our transfer. It's been on hold. Your sisters added to the guest list at the wedding, so everyone from here is invited."

"Maybe they can wear nametags or drape stethoscopes around their necks so I'll know who they are."

"We can ask," he said, smiling, wondering how much she remembered, or if she was just being hospitable. Wanting to ask if a person could fall back into a coma once she came out, he hoped to find a doctor or nurse safely out of earshot.

His marring a Queen had become a big pub joke. His blokes had a good time with it. Staying with her brothers was like living at the pub. They cursed, burped, farted, and made terrible jokes. They acted like they were always drunk, but they weren't.

They loved their sister very much but hadn't visited Europe since the time she first moved to England. They figured it cost a lot less for them to visit her at the hospital than it would if their wives went shopping like the first time.

The bills took months to arrive at their bank accounts. UPS and FedEx deliverymen soon knew them by name and brought the paper to the door if it was on the sidewalk when they arrived. Some of the things the packages contained were items Julie, Angela, and Molly couldn't remember buying, or so they said.

Loretta had been in the hospital, too, for an infection after a knee operation. That happened at a different hospital, and Joseph rode the damaged Vespa to take care of her. He liked the new houseguests. They felt like brothers.

The ladies took turns sleeping on the multicolored sofa, which was the worst bed in the flat. It was too short, it was lumpy, and the colors were bright enough to keep them awake. Julie had nursing hours and could go to the kitchen in the middle of the night to make a pot of coffee and call April. They had to search town for a decent coffeepot, and beans were difficult to buy, too.

"We want only regular coffee, not the stuff you sell at Starbuck's," Julie often said.

When Julie turned on the lights, whoever slept on the sofa woke up, too. If it was Angela, she walked to the bed, hating the smell of coffee.

"Who hates the smell of coffee?" Julie asked. "It's like sex on a plate."

No one knew where she got that line, but she used it whenever the kids were absent. When she had her cup, she carried it to the bay window and let the steam drift over her face. She loved the scent as well as drinking it day and night. It was a wonder she slept at all.

She stared out into the darkness, seeing an occasional walker on the street below under the lamplight. When the bakery owner was dropped off by his wife, Julie knew it was time for bed. In a couple hours, they'd wake to the smell of fresh bread, something that was impossible to sleep through.

She finished the last drops, set the cup on the coffee table among all the stuff people left from the previous day, and fell asleep on the sofa. Emily's glass tabletop had pretty things

Faded Sweetheart

under it, but it was currently hidden under a pile of receipts, newspapers, and underwear. According to Milly, Julie drooled while she slept.

• • • • •

The following day, the women in James' life were finally coming home. Everyone made a special effort to clean up. James had his mother stay with her sister for a while, because there were no stairs. He didn't think she should climb three flights so soon after surgery, and she agreed.

Emily, ready to return to a full life, couldn't believe she fell off the Vespa. She always considered herself an awesome driver. She never even fell off a horse, but that was just a stick pony. She never rode a real horse, and she hoped James never found out.

Their welcome home was amazing. James and Emily never hosted a party with nine people in their flat before. All the chairs were removed, the old bed was back, and one of her brothers wanted to try the yellow rattan swing chair until another warned he might break it.

Julie bought barbecue from the hotel for their dinner, which was the only way real Texans celebrated. The men looked squeamish about it, but they said they liked it. Maybe they were just being polite, but the containers were emptied quickly.

The women shared the sink to wash their fingers, while the men licked them clean. James was growing accustomed to such food.

"I look forward to eating this all the time when we're in Corpus," he said.

The men looked at him as if he abused their church.

"You don't eat real barbecue every day. It's a special-occasion thing. We do it for cookouts, picnics, and tailgate parties."

"What do you eat the rest of the time?"

"Regular food."

"Fish and chips, or bangers and mash?"

"Yeah, we do franks and mashed potatoes, sometimes fish. All kinds of fish. We even eat fried okra."

"OK. Great."

Rook patted the beginnings of his beer belly. "You don't go hungry in Texas. There are restaurants and fast-food places on every block. You just need to know how to pick 'em."

The Texans kept dropping vowels and adding consonants. James hoped he could learn their language.

• • • • •

The week after Emily left the hospital was a whirlwind. April took the kids to England so they could attend the wedding. What was planned as a small wedding quickly grew larger. Her doctor and a few of the nurses came, and several people from work attended, too, including Rebecca and the Howells.

At the reception, instead of rice or bird food, the company provided heart-shaped balloons, which dropped from the ceiling right after the cake was served, much to everyone's surprise and delight.

People planned to fly home the following day. James and Emily packed the things they wanted to bring. Most items would be shipped and would arrive in a few months.

When the family went to the airport, Julie lost track of things. She had both her kids to watch and didn't notice that Emily and James hadn't packed.

As she stood in line to board, Julie noticed Emily and James hanging back. "Why aren't you over here? We have to get on the plane."

"The doctor suggested I not fly yet," Emily called. "We're taking a ship."

"A ship? OK. See you. Keep in touch. Love you!"

They turned and waved.

"'Bye, Aunt Emily!" the kids called. "'Bye, Uncle James!"

Once the plane took off, the newly married couple were finally alone.

"Tomorrow we leave on our ship, but we don't have a place to stay for tonight," Emily said.

"Maybe we could board a day early. Let's ask."

They boarded later that evening with several bags, and Emily carried a large plastic bin.

"What's in the box?" James asked.

"My memories. I'm going to tell you the story of my life."

"Have I heard it before?"

"No. I've been saving it and you," she said, her finger pressed against his chest. "You can fill in any parts I forgot."

"OK. Then we'll make new memories, too."

"That's a lot of work. Maybe we'll need to stay on the boat longer."

"Cooped in this room with you, sounds interesting." He carried her through the door into their room, which was filled up by the bed. It wasn't like a hotel suite.

"I guess they think this is all we need," she commented.

"They're pros. Maybe they're right."

"We'll have to see."

He gently tossed her onto the bed. The doctors told them to be careful for a few weeks.

They didn't leave for dinner or a night walk. They spent the night in bed, talking. There were so many things Emily had to remember. Nestled in his arms, he gave his account of the day they became engaged.

"Do you remember when we were engaged?" he asked.

"At Stonehenge?"

He shook his head.

"The hotel suite?"

"We couldn't afford that unless you won a TV show." He laughed. "Which TV show was that?"

"*Let's Make a Deal.*"

"Is that really the one?"

"No, but you are."

"What kind of deal did you want?"

"I'll do the dealing."

They turned off the light and stopped talking.

· · · · ·

In the morning, they heard a knock at the door.

"Room service," someone said.

"Did you order room service?" she asked.

"No."

"See how much it is. If it looks good, we'll take it."

James pulled on his pants to answer the door. "I don't think we ordered this. How much will it be?" Eying the cart, he realized he was hungry.

"It's compliments of Mr. and Mrs. Howell. They said you'd probably miss breakfast, since your dear wife had an injury. We have a staff physician if you need one."

"Thank you. Can you thank the Howells for us? Emily's doing fine. I'm watching her carefully, but it's good to know there's medical care available. Thanks again." He reached into his pockets for a tip.

"Look in my purse," Emily said from the bathroom.

He found her bag and pulled out a bill. "Here you go. Thanks."

The waiter looked at him. "We aren't supposed to accept gratuities, but thank you."

After the door closed, Emily asked, "How much did you give him?"

"A five. Maybe it was it a fifty. He seemed happy to take it."

"I'll bet. I have to teach you our currency."

They sat at their little table and ate breakfast of eggs, bacon, toast, coffee, juice, croissants, and jellies. Everything tasted good.

"Ready to walk around?" he asked.

"Sure. Let's try out our sea legs."

Dressing, they went out to look around. There wasn't much to see. England was gone in the distance. The air was warm, and they felt saltwater against their faces.

Faded Sweetheart

"I wonder if this is good for my skin," Emily said.

"We'll find out."

"I want a bath. Once I get used to this, I'll be OK, but right now I feel yucky."

"Did you want to return to our room?'

"No. Let's find dinner and check the activity list. Maybe we should mingle a bit while we're here. Is there a jogging trail?"

"On a ship?"

"Where do they want us to do it?"

"I thought that was in the bedroom."

"You know what I'm talking about."

"Do you want to eat or do that?"

"Both, in that order."

"Let's eat fast."

She smiled. She ate slowly, feeling the waves in her stomach.

"What do you need?" he asked.

"Fewer waves."

"I don't know if the water can do that."

"Let's look at the box."

"OK. Should I choose something from it?"

"No. First, I need to explain what the box is."

"OK."

She looked inside the box and categorized what was in it. Her memory wasn't as good as she hoped. Seeing toys, she thought, *These must've been my baby toys, but I'm not sure.*

"They look like fun." James picked up the baby dolls and pretended they could walk. "Mum. Mum."

"I know my dolls didn't say that. I didn't have a mama, so I wonder if they said, 'Grandma.'"

They kept looking, but very little stirred her memories.

"I'm upset. I don't know why I had Rebecca ship this to me first. Were my memories that important?"

"My Emily." He held her face in his hands. "We can start

our own memories right now. As long as you don't get hit on the head, we won't forget."

He was right. Every day, while he showered, she went through the box to see if she remembered. She found report cards and read about two teachers who died at school. She saw some old-fashioned baby clothes.

• • • • •

Twelve days into the cruise, she found a picture in an envelope with a faded sweetheart. She and James were packing to leave the boat, which would dock in the morning.

She carelessly put the envelope in her carry-on bag and zipped it up. The plastic box she kept for so long would be left behind on the boat as trash. She and James would make new memories in their new home and new country, starting a new life.

• • • • •

When they arrived in Texas, they learned Julie had been injured and was bedridden until her back healed. Emily asked James to stop there first, so she could visit her sister. She still had the carry-on bag.

She almost broke Julie's leg when she jumped up to kiss her in Rook's recliner. The bag banged against Julie.

"Sorry," Emily said. "I forgot I was carrying this."

Being a very nosy sister, Julie unzipped the bag. Emily watched in despair, having no idea what was in the bag after packing so quickly.

"What does my little sister have in her bag?" Julie loved that game. She saw the usual things, like a paperback with a scrap of paper for a bookmark. "Rook, toss out these Vespa keys. Bad keys." She found candy wrappers. "Where's my chocolate?"

"I thought I left you some. Let me see."

Faded Sweetheart

"No. I'll find it." Suddenly, she stopped and looked at the couple. "Did you take your memory box home with you?"

"No." Emily shook her head. "I couldn't remember anything."

"It upset her," James added. "I told her we'd make our own memories."

All was quiet. Rook and Julie looked at each other, then at the couple who'd been at sea for two weeks. They looked tired. If Emily's memory hadn't returned, perhaps it was best she left the box. Somehow, Julie knew that Emily still had memories to recall.

She looked into the bag again and plucked out the envelope from the bottom of the bag. Emily, not knowing what Julie was looking for, walked closer to see.

"Do you know what this is?" Julie asked softly.

Emily looked at her. She didn't even remember dropping it into the bag. "How'd that get in there?"

"Emily and James, sit down. I'll tell you. Rook, order some pizza. This will be a long night. April, are you up there?"

"Yes!" She walked down the stairs, earbuds hanging off her shoulders.

"Call your uncles. We have memories to bring back."

Since they lived nearby, they arrived quickly. Even though Julie was recovering from a back injury, she was at her best, because she had something in her hands she found many years before. She smiled and began her story. The others contributed pieces or filled in the blanks. All hoped that telling the story would trigger Emily's memories.

James felt anxious and hoped Emily would start remembering. Finally, Julie took out the envelope and opened it to reveal a photograph of a young woman and man in uniform. The hand-drawn sweethearts on the envelope had faded, held captured in the drawer.

View other Black Rose Writing titles at www.blackrosewriting.com/books and use promo code PRINT to receive a 20% discount when purchasing.

BLACK ROSE writing™

CPSIA information can be obtained
at www.ICGtesting.com
Printed in the USA
FSOW01n1524030617
34696FS